My Husband Is On the Down Low…And I Know About It

A novel by

Janice Scott-Blanton

Library of Congress Control Number: 2005900672

ISBN: 0-9764688-0-8

The names have been changed to protect all characters. Incidental reference to public figures, products, and services are not intended to disparage any company's product or services.

Printed in the United States of America

JaRon Publishing Group, Inc.
P.O Box 371
Triangle, VA 22172
www.jaronpublishing.com
(703) 731-4828

ACKNOWLEDGMENTS

I have to give thanks to God for guiding my life's path in completing this novel. I must give thanks to Vielka Downer, Kim Black, Joyce L. White, Michelle Knolton, Cynthia Gray, Sam Bryant, and Katrina Scott for being my sounding boards. You gave awesome support; thank you for listening. Thanks to Marcus Williams, owner of Nubian Bookstore (Atlanta), Susie Ford of AfroBooks (Atlanta), and Gwen Richardson of Cushcity Bookstore (Houston), for providing an avenue for veteran and upcoming authors to gain exposure. I have to give a special thanks to my editor Harvey Stanbrough. Thank you for your patience. You took my manuscript and produced a novel that I am extremely proud. You didn't compromise my voice or style. Thank you! And last but not least, I'd like to thank my publications manager Lindell Scott, and manager Brian Dennis.

THE OLD CLICHÉ GOES, "IF ONLY I'D KNOWN THEN WHAT I KNOW NOW." That cliché has been a part of my life for some time now. It has been like a weight, a ton of bricks that have held me down for over 10 years. I can honestly say that if I'd known then what I know now, I would have never sacrificed my emotional stability, my time, and most of all, my heart. Several years passed, years plagued with deceptive secrets, anger, resentment, and lies. My heart ached on a daily basis, hiding the secrets that plagued my soul day in and day out, nibbling at my core.

There's another cliché: "Hindsight is 20/20." Since learning of his secret life, this cliché has been an element of my life as well. It has taught me to become more cognizant of others' behavior as well as a better judge of character. So many signs and clues stared me in the face, signs and clues that I never thought twice about because of the lifestyle we lived. I was so in love that I allowed my heart to blind me, over-shadowing my intuition. I was lost in our lifestyle because he allowed me to "eat my cake and have it too." He allowed me to be who I was without passing judgment.

Since the winter of 1988, James and I had been enjoying my bi-sexuality, my attraction to men and women. My attraction is not overwhelming or uncontrollable as if I just **have to** be with a woman and will do anything to satisfy a craving. It's not a craving. It's like being a social drinker. If I'm in that kind of environment, then the possibility exists that I might engage in the activities. I know that doesn't make it right, but that's just the way it is.

My bisexuality was no secret to him. It was clear during my early teens that I had an attraction to both men and women. One evening after showering, I began exploring my body. I soon discovered that I enjoyed my gentle touch. I liked the way my body looked, my curves. I never thought whether I was abnormal or anything like that. I just wondered how it could be that I was attracted to both men and women. We moved to a city in southern Germany where I started a new school. I was fascinated, in a rather special way, by a girl in my class. While my thoughts were not sexual, I often thought about whether I thought she was pretty. I had problems settling the issue in my mind, but I looked at her every so often and felt pleasure from doing so.

As time went on, I began to take a more active, although still very discreet, interest in other girls. In the locker room after physical education, I noticed that I was sexually attracted to several of the girls and later saw girls throughout the school that I was attracted to as well. I was also attracted to several boys in my school. I would look through the school yearbook to find their pictures to see what their names were. In addition, during my free time I would think about being physically close to them. Nevertheless, during this period of adolescence, I never really thought about what I was. All the things that took place in the emotional-sexual realm were admittedly real and concrete to me. I experienced real feelings for other girls and boys (infatuation, love, sexual attraction). However, at the same time on an intellectual level, I never confronted those feelings. So I continued to experience the feelings without worrying about them or trying to transform them in any way. They just *were*, and that was fine with me.

When I was fifteen, I became a Christian through baptism, accepting Jesus Christ as my Savior. That complicated matters quite a bit. According to my mother, I'd accepted Christ through baptism as a toddler, but I didn't remember it, so I asked if I could do it over. I felt satisfaction when I accepted Christ into my life and joined the church. I soon encountered attitudes among fellow Christians and in the Bible that were rather hostile towards homosexuality in any form. I adopted the negative attitude, and became quite a vocal homophobe. During my junior and senior years in high school, the other students knew me for being a devout fundamentalist Christian with a very strict view of morality.

Looking back, my feelings for boys were just as strong as my feelings for girls. I experienced feelings for both, but of course, all of this remained secret. How could I explain that I, someone who was *emotionally* bisexual, could attack homosexuality? My explanation is psychological in nature. That is, I believed I was homophobic not primarily to have people believe that I was straight — I never thought anybody doubted that anyway — but to keep myself in check. In a way, I was preaching to my inner self.

I gradually realized, on an intellectual level, what I was. Why did that take so long? I think because when I was growing up and hearing words like *gay* or *homosexual* or *dykes*, I thought of horrid, disgusting, immoral people. I used to have a picture in my mind of two boyish looking women or two men with mustaches, which I find very unattractive, kissing. I found it revolting. I thought, "I *can't* be one of them." Yet, in a way, I was.

I began to understand that the term homosexual didn't represent anything other than a *description* of which a person is attracted to emotionally and sexually. It didn't represent anything, in itself, regarding the behavior, looks or values of that person. When I realized that homosexual and bisexual people were like everyone else — that some are nice, some are rude, some are beautiful, some are unattractive, some are old, some are young, some are rich, some are poor, etc. — I had an easier time using the terms myself.

In a way, being bisexual is like being bi-racial (Black and White) in that some bi-racial people don't feel comfortable or even accepted by either ethnic group because their very existence challenges the concept of race. In addition, bisexuals have to struggle to reinvent their own identities to correspond to their experience in order to make sense and give meaning to their reality. At the time, while I knew what I was, nobody else knew. Moreover, it would take some more years before I told anyone, until I told James. For a long time, I remained convinced that I couldn't tell him because I feared that he would find it vexing. With the benefit of hindsight, I realized how easy it was to build up an unsubstantiated idea that being honest about whom you are could result in horrible reactions. You imagine that people will hate you too easily – when, in fact, they will love you no matter what.

For a long time I blamed myself for his actions because of my desires to be with a woman. I soon learned that my husband's actions were never a result of my desires to be with a woman, but a result of his own desires. No matter what I did, I couldn't disregard his desires. It should have been easy for me to understand why he wanted to have sex with other men, based on my own bisexuality, but I just couldn't. To me, it wasn't the same. I tried hard not to sound judgmental or be hypocritical, but the thought of two men together sexually was a thought I couldn't accept, couldn't envision, and couldn't understand. My husband's bi-sexual tendencies came to head eight years ago, or at least that's when I learned about them. I became a product of society in the respect that I grimaced at the thought of a homosexual act between two men. I'm sorry to say that I allowed myself to become a part of that way of thinking, society's way of being, if you will. I have since learned to accept people for who they are, regardless of their sexual orientation.

He would tell me that I was every man's dream, because I was bisexual. I understood that. I knew some men fantasized about being with two women. James had hit the jackpot.

Unfortunately, for me, my bisexuality became my enemy, my demise.

   ----**Alias**, Annette Hawkins----

Part 1

The Beginning of Her Journey

The Seduction

They fell in love in October 1984. He was everything she wanted in a man. He wanted to have children one day. He was intelligent and handsome, 6'1", and had a dark-brown complexion with a few dark spots on both cheeks. He had deep-set, dark-brown eyes that were mysterious, and he was sexy as hell. He'd chipped his front tooth on the left side while using a jackhammer, and he was very self-conscious about his appearance. He talked about having it fixed, which he eventually did. She was glad because she took care of her teeth and expected the same from the men she dated. He was romantic and hard working. Women wanted him.

In high school, they worked part time, he as a helper at a construction site and she as a clerk in a local department store. They had both been born in Decatur, Georgia. She'd lived there during her sophomore, junior and senior years because her father was in the military.

Her family moved back to Georgia after her father retired from the Army. He served 23 years. His travels took them to Germany, Louisiana, Texas and Georgia. Her mother didn't want to live in Atlanta, but she didn't want to live too far away either. Annette's family attended church most Sundays on the base.

Both James' parents passed away in the eighties. His father, a freight truck driver, died instantly when he lost control of the wheel while making a delivery to Beaumont, Texas. High blood pressure and diabetes plagued his mother for years. She was admitted into the hospital for complications from diabetes. She suffered a stroke and lost her battle with the illness. After the death of his mother, James became withdrawn, relying solely on himself. Aunt Mary, his mother's sister, took in his younger siblings. She also lived in Decatur. James was eighteen and had just graduated high school.

He'd always been a hard working young boy. He delivered newspapers for the neighborhood convenience store on Saturdays and Sunday morning before church. His mother and aunt made sure he and his siblings attended church every Sunday. That would sometimes include Baptist Training Union (BTU), which they would attend in the evenings after church.

Both Annette and James were the oldest children in their family. He had two sisters and she had a sister and a brother with whom she has maintained a great relationship. James and his siblings weren't as close as he'd hope they would be. The distance between them made it difficult. He and Annette saw each other all the time because they attended the same high school. He was a senior and she was a sophomore. He didn't date much in high school. In fact, he told her that she was the second woman he'd been with. After he finished high school, he worked full-time through the summer at the construction site until the fall. He attended Morehouse College in Atlanta, Georgia, where he earned a degree in Business Administration. He would sometimes talk about one day owning his own construction business. Annette attended Clarke Atlanta University after graduating high school. She earned a Master's degree in Social Work.

While in college, he and she developed a very close, intimate relationship. They would visit each other on both campuses, alternating the visits to be fair with each other. He had an old Buick Regal that he drove around Atlanta and back and forth from home, and would sometimes let her drive it or even keep it overnight if she had somewhere to go. They caught all the new movies at the theater. She even learned that James wasn't too fond of women who were moderately overweight.

One evening after dinner, they were sitting in front of her dorm watching people as they passed by and commenting on those of interest to them. An attractive young woman walked past them and Annette asked James whether he thought the woman was attractive. He said the woman had a pretty face, but that she wasn't his type. That left the door open for her to ask him about his type, and she did. He told her that she was his type. And that she was the right height and size and he explained by saying her weight was proportional to her height. Satisfied with his response, she changed the subject. James had quite a few male and female friends in college but he and Annette hung together mostly. He played basketball with friends some evenings.

He worked part-time at the construction site on days he didn't have class and on weekends. He often placed more demands on himself than others required.

He gave Annette small teddy bears and cards on every holiday and sometimes just because he was thinking about her. They went to dinner at Church's Chicken or McDonald's. It didn't matter that he didn't take her to the more upscale restaurants; as long as they were together, that was all that mattered. He did take her to dinner a few times at Red Lobster. Whenever he took her there, she thought he wanted to have sex because the first time they had eaten there, afterwards, he'd rented a hotel room. However, that wasn't always the case. In fact, it was just the opposite. She wanted to get a hotel room more often than he did.

One evening after class, she wanted to have sex so they got a room. They couldn't wait to take their clothes off. Annette sat in the car and waited while James went to get the room. Their passion was off the scales. When James returned to the car, he reached over, pulled her to him, and gave her a deep, passionate kiss. She felt his crotch to see whether he was hard. He was.

"Room 133," he said as he sat back to drive around the building. He parked, and they got out and went into the room, but they'd forgotten to ask each other whether they had condoms.

Breathing heavily and kissing him at the same time Annette asked, "Got any condoms, Baby?"

Still breathing heavily and giving her open-mouth kisses he said, "No, I don't. You don't have any?"

They stopped for a few seconds so they could figure out what to do. Their breathing deepened as their passion exploded. Clothes began to come off. Annette pulled James' shirt over his head and he pulled hers over her head. They were both wearing shorts because it was

85 degrees and humid that day. They hurriedly unbuttoned and unzipped their shorts, dropping them to the floor. James walked Annette back and she fell onto the bed with him lying on top of her. They were still wearing their underwear, but they were at the point of no return and decided to have sex without using a condom.

Afterwards, they lay looking at the ceiling, talking about what they had just done and the possibility of her getting pregnant. Annette assured him that she wouldn't get pregnant. She'd just had her period. Because of their love and trust in and for each other, they decided it was time to stop using condoms. Unprotected sex was not an issue for them. They'd used condoms only as a method of birth control. Since they decided to have sex without the condoms, she began using the pill. Despite all the reports in the news about the AIDS epidemic that was taking the country by storm, they loved and trusted each other, so the thought of contracting an STD wasn't a concern for them.

––––––––––––––––––––––––

It wasn't long before they found themselves in love and wanting to spend the rest of their lives together. They shared their deepest feelings, thoughts, and secrets. He told her that he'd thought about joining the military. They talked about their families. He shared with her his heartache over losing his mother and father and how envious he was of her because both her parents were still alive at the time. They had since passed away. Her father passed away in 1993 of congested heart failure and her mother died of breast cancer in 1998. Annette had concerns about having breast cancer. She'd lost her mother and an aunt to it. She performed a breast exam every month. She was determined not to let breast cancer get her. Once, she found a small bump under the skin on her right breast. An examination determined it to be a calcium deposit. She made sure she reminded her younger sister about doing a self-breast exam each month as well.

Her parents had always told her and her siblings, "Be honest with yourselves first; otherwise, you couldn't possibly be honest with other people." That was something she'd always tried to live by. However, for a long time she found it very difficult to follow her parents' golden rule because of the struggle she had within herself about her desire to be with a woman. Throughout high school and college, she was in a constant struggle with her desires. There were times she would see a girl that she found attractive, then go to her dorm room and masturbate thinking about her. She wanted to be in an honest heterosexual relationship with James, living up to society's standards on what a relationship is supposed to be, but at the same time, she wanted to satisfy her desire to feel the touch of a woman.

There was a time when she almost gave in to her desires in 1985. She'd gone to the library to do some research and study. This young woman sat across the table from her. She had a short crop-cut like Anita Baker wore years ago. The girl pulled out her books and began reading. Annette could feel someone looking at her, so she looked up and saw the girl gazing at her. They were the only two students at that particular table. The girl asked Annette what she was getting her degree in and she said, "Social Work." The young woman told Annette that she was still undecided. They continued to talk about their studies. The girl asked Annette whether she had a boyfriend. She told her she did. She also told her his name and that he was going into military. The young woman smiled and said, "Oh, that's nice." Annette smiled back. The young woman then decided that she would just be honest with Annette. Leaning across the table, the young woman whispered, "Look, I think you're very attractive. Yes, before you ask, I'm gay."

This caught Annette by surprise because she'd never had a woman be so straightforward. She gave her a dubious smile and said, "Thank you. You're quite attractive yourself."

The girl gave Annette her number and told her to call her if she wanted to hang out. Lying on the sofa one night feeling lonely, she picked up the young woman's number from her address book and held it in her hand. *No, this isn't right*, she thought. *I can't call her. I need to throw this away.* She got up and threw the number in the trashcan.

During the winter of James' senior year, the first semester of her junior year, in 1985, she shared her dark secret about her bisexuality with him. She'd enrolled in classes each summer so she could finish sooner because she'd set a goal to be finished with school, including graduate school, by the summer of 1987.

Annette had fallen deeply in love with James and

she wanted him to know everything there was to know about her. She also knew that he would be graduating the coming spring 1985, and she didn't want him to leave without knowing her dark secret, a secret that she'd never shared with anyone. He'd talked about possibly going into the military after graduating college. On a Thursday morning she called and invited him to dinner on Friday evening at their favorite place.

He picked her up at the dorm around 7p.m., and they drove to what had become their favorite eatery, Red Lobster. "Smoking or non-smoking?" the cheery host asked.

"None," she and James said in unison. They had to wait about twenty minutes before a table became available. Her heart was beating so fast she thought it was going to pop out of her chest. Her mind was racing: *What's he going to think of me? Will he think I'm some kind of freak or pervert? Will he tell me he doesn't want to see me anymore?* She didn't know what to think, nor did she realize how deep in thought she was until James nudged her and broke her trance. She faintly heard her name.

"Annette?" James whispered as he nudged her right shoulder again. She seemed catatonic, so mesmerized by her thoughts that she couldn't move or respond to his call. She remembered that day as if it was yesterday. "Are you okay Annette?" he asked, concerned.

"Yes, James, I'm okay. Just wondering how much longer we'll have to wait before we're seated." For a moment, she wished their wait time were even longer. She wasn't sure she was ready to expose herself to James, especially not knowing how he felt about homosexuals, lesbians or bi-sexuals for that matter. She wondered whether she was acting in haste.

She and James had already confessed their love for each other and that was good enough for her. So why was she so adamant about telling him about her bisexual thoughts? Well, she wanted to be very honest with him.

"James, party of two?" the host called.

"Right here," James said, raising his right hand and walking towards the host with her hand in his. The petite young woman escorted them to a table in the middle of the restaurant.

Annette tugged on James' hand to signal him to lean down so she could whisper in his ear. "See if we can get a booth so we can have more privacy."

He looked at her and smiled. Returning the smile, she told him to get his mind out the gutter. He smiled again, then asked the host for a booth. The host looked across the restaurant, saw a booth in the smoking section, and asked if they wanted to go ahead and take that available booth or wait for one to open up in the non-smoking section. They chose to take it.

Sitting in the booth, gazing into each other's eyes, lost in each other's soul, they were oblivious to the young petite caramel colored skin server who introduced herself to them. "Excuse me. Hello. Excuse me," she insisted.

James broke away from his stare. "Oh, we're so sorry. What did you say Miss?"

She smiled. "My name is Gina and I'll be your server. Can I get you something to drink?"

James ordered a beer for himself and lemonade for Annette, knowing lemonade was one of her favorite drinks. As the server walked away, they returned to each other's eyes. She told him that she'd wanted to come to the restaurant to talk because she didn't know how he would react to what she had to say. She knew James didn't like a lot of attention, so she knew he wouldn't get irate in a public place.

Just as she was about to pour out her soul's core, the server returned with their drinks and took their order. Annette ordered shrimp scampi and a salad. She said she was too nervous to eat a big meal. James created his own platter with fried shrimp, scallops, and a lobster tail. He told her he was famished and hadn't eaten since breakfast.

It was now or never for her to tell him about her secret passions. She cleared her throat. "James," she said with a serious look. Her gaze seemed to pierce his soul.

"Yes? What's with the grim face?" he said nervously.

"I have something to tell you. I don't know what your opinion of me will be after I've said what I have to say. I don't know what or how you'll view me. I don't even know if you'll want to see me again, but I have to say this."

"After you say what?" he said.

She hesitated a moment longer. "James, I have desires to be with women. I'm not saying that I want to be in a relationship with a woman or that I don't want to be with you."

He raised his right eyebrow, looking at her in disbelief as if she'd just told him she'd won the lottery. To avoid showing his approval or disapproval, he narrowed his eyes slightly, as he turned his head away. A moment later he looked at her and smiled. "Okay. And you —"

Her finger went to her lips. "Shush! Don't say anything James. Just listen. I hope this doesn't change anything between us. I know it might change some things, but I hope it doesn't change your heart, your love for me." She paused and took a deep breath. "I took a big risk telling you this. You're the first person I've ever told. I love and trust you, James, and after being in this relationship for almost two years, I felt I needed to be honest with you — be honest with myself." Her eyes welled up and the tears came.

He sat upright, his elbows on the table, and then his head dropped into his hands. He looked like he'd just lost his best friend. She didn't know what to think.

She looked at him, her eyes filled with tears. He raised his head and saw the tears as one flowed down her right cheek. She looked at him again, then looked down in shame. His stare was blank. With a sigh, he said, "Oh good. Here comes our food."

She raised her head and wiped her tears away just before the server made it to their table. He was rescued. She didn't think he was ready to comment on what she'd just said anyway. She didn't think he knew what to say or how to respond.

She sat there scared and confused as James sat across from her, looking into his plate and tapping the side of his plate with the fork. Feeling ashamed, she wanted to crawl under the table. *What have I done?* All she could think about was losing him.

He began eating. Still, he said nothing. She'd lost her appetite.

Embarrassed, she excused herself and went to the ladies' room. There was no one in there but her. She stood looking in the mirror. "What have I done? How could I have been so stupid?" The tears were streaming. "I knew I should've kept my mouth shut and not said anything. I kept it a secret for all these years — why did I have to let it out now? I *knew* it was a mistake! Damn! Shit!" She regained her composure, reached up and pulled a paper towel, then wet it and wiped under her eyes to remove the smeared mascara. She then walked into the stall to get some tissue to dry her eyes.

When she got back to the table, she took a quick glance at him. *He's looking at me. What's he thinking?* She couldn't look at him so she looked around the restaurant. As she approached the table, she sat down. He just stared at her with that same blank expression, and she felt even more ashamed. She looked at his plate and noticed he'd eaten most of his shrimp and scallops and was now working on the lobster tail. She had no idea that she'd been in the ladies' room *that* long.

He cleared his throat, then reached for his beer and took a drink. She still couldn't look at him. Instead, she focused on the water ring left from the glass of beer. She got lost in the circle, thinking repeatedly how much she regretted telling him her secret.

He looked into her eyes. "Have you ever been with a woman?" He looked down at his plate, then back at her, waiting for a response.

Not the least bit surprised by his question, she looked him in the eyes. "No, I haven't. These desires I have are just that. To be honest, I *have* fantasized about what it would be like to feel another woman's touch, but I've never experienced it, not in a sexual way."

"Do you *want* to be with another woman?"

She sat up and cleared her throat. "Well, if the situation arose and you and I were in agreement, then yes, I'd give it a try. This would be something that I'd want to share with you James."

He smiled. "I had no idea you had these kinds of

thoughts."

"I know you didn't. How could you have known? I didn't tell you. Let me tell you something that you may not realize. Unless you catch me in bed with a woman or I tell you, you'll never know. It's easy for two women to be together. We go shopping together. We do each other's hair. We hang out at the malls together. What I'm trying to say is that being together is normal for two women, so no one would suspect anything. Women have so many opportunities to do whatever they want. Always remember that. It's different for men because if two men hung out like that, it would make people suspicious of them. Now men do have their "boy's night out" where they go to each other's houses and play cards or whatever, and they may even hang out at a bar. But it's not too often that you'll see two men just openly hanging out with each other."

He shook his head. "Damn, I never thought about that." He grew quiet.

"What are you thinking James?

"I'm thinking about what you said. That's something else. So you could be sitting here lying to me saying you've never been with another woman, right?"

"Yes, that's right. However, I'm not lying to you. I wouldn't have told you if it weren't the truth. I could've kept it to myself and experienced it without you. But that isn't what I wanted."

"Okay, I believe that. It's hard to imagine that you have thoughts like that. As a man, I've fantasized about having two women, but I never thought I'd be in love with a woman who wanted to be touched by another woman. Damn!" He pushed his plate towards the center of the table, leaned back, stretching his legs to intertwine with hers under the table.

"Right now, at this very minute James, what do you think of me?" she said. He didn't answer right away. "Look James, I know that my possibly being bisexual seems inherently subversive and causes a blur with a lot of ambiguity. I know that it challenges the concepts of the traditional relationship and family structures and all that. Still, it's something I've thought about for a long time. The emotional stress I feel inside because of you not understanding, or worse, not accepting my attraction to women, is difficult for me to deal with."

"What do you mean what do I think of you? Hell, I'm in love with you. Remember? We talked about sharing the rest of our lives together. This has definitely caught me by surprise. I had no idea this is what you wanted to tell me. Hell, I thought you wanted to break up with me or something."

"Knowing what you know now, would you prefer that?"

He leaned forward, put his elbows on the table and looked in her eyes. Her heart palpitated. "No, that's not what I'd prefer. What I'd prefer is...." He paused, then leaned back against the seat.

Nervously she asked, "What? What would you prefer?"

"Just forget it, Annette."

"James, that isn't fair. You can't do that. We're communicating here. Don't do that."

He called out to the server. "Can we order dessert please?"

He ordered desser. As the server walked away, Annette began to probe again. She needed to know what he was about to say. "Please, tell me what you prefer. Please, Baby." He didn't reply. Relentlessly, she probed, desperately seeking a response. He insisted that she leave it alone. She could tell he was irritated with her. She stopped. After dessert, he paid the check and they left walking hand in hand.

As they approached the car, he reached to open the passenger door for her. After she secured her seat belt, he closed door. She turned to watch him as he walked around to the driver side. It seemed as if he were taking his time. He opened the door and got in, letting out a loud sigh. She turned to look at him. "Are you tired, Baby?"

He put the key in the ignition and started the engine. "No, not really. I'm just taking in this whole evening. You must admit, Annette, this isn't an easy thing for me to swallow. I know it wasn't easy for you to take the risk you took, not knowing how I'd react."

"No, it wasn't. It took everything I had to tell you that. I was so afraid of undressing my soul for the first time. But I wanted to be honest with you. I love you, James."

"I love you too, Baby."

They leaned towards each other and kissed. Their eyes closed, and the kiss was passionate. Finally, he slowly released her lips and pulled away, then turned on the headlights and drove out of the parking lot onto the street towards campus. The car was quiet. That moment of silence was as golden as it got. Her heart relaxed. *Does this mean that he's accepted what I revealed to him?* He still hadn't commented. She wondered how it would affect their relationship. *Is he okay, or is he looking for a way out of the relationship?* She was clueless as to which direction he would take. She hoped he would embrace her for who she was and join her in exploring her desires.

She turned to look at him. He looked worried, concerned. Abruptly he slowed the car and pulled off into a gas station parking lot. He put the car in park and left the engine running with the heat on because there was a chill in the air.

She glanced at him. "Is everything all right?"

"Everything's fine."

"So . . . why'd we stop in the parking lot of a gas station?"

He looked at her. "Well . . . I have something I need to tell you too. And I need to be focused and not driving when I tell you." He paused and took her hand. "First, thank you for being honest and trusting me enough to release your soul to me. I'd love to be a part of your experience whenever you decide to explore your desires to be with another woman." He paused again, looked down, and then looked back at her. "I've never been a part of anything like that, but if I was going to try it, I'd want you to be the person I experienced it with."

She burst into happy tears. He pulled her closer to him and put her head on his chest. "I love you, Annette." He paused, holding her. "Baby, that isn't all I have to say."

She raised her head from his chest to look into his eyes. His look was somber. She could tell he was reluctant to say what he was about to say. He let out several loud sighs before speaking. It was apparent that what he had to say was difficult, so she suggested that he take a deep breath. She took one as well.

"Now, what is it James?"

He looked at her. Her heart began to palpitate again. Frantic and afraid of what he was about to say, she panicked. "Oh no! Please don't break up with me! Please,

please, please! I love you so much James!"

He gently took her hands. "Stop crying, Baby. I'm not breaking up with you." He stroked her hair. "God, Annette, you're my whole world, my dream . . . . You're the kind of woman that any man would want to be with. I'll never let you go."

She dried her tears, cupped his face in her hands and kissed him. She turned her head to the side, perplexed. *He isn't breaking up with me, so what is it?*

He noticed her confused look and said, "Annette, what I have to say has nothing to do with you. Just trust me on this one." He cleared his throat. "I need to tell you about something that happened during my childhood. Many times my father or mother wasn't always around. That left me to take care of my younger sisters. When I was about eight years old, some of the kids in the neighborhood would gather in Mr. Walker's front yard. He'd sit on the front porch, smoking his hand-rolled cigarettes. I still remember the Prince Albert tobacco can sitting next to the old chair he would sit in, along with the bag of candy he used to give us.

Mr. Walker was about sixty years old. He had a scruffy, nappy gray and black beard. He always had on the same blue mechanic work pants and white tee shirt that had a couple of holes in it. He lived alone. His wife had died of a heart attack the year I turned nine. Everybody in the neighborhood knew him. He was the neighborhood candy man. All the kids went to his house to beg for candy. My mother used to tell my siblings and me not to go over to that dirty old man's house. I didn't listen to her all the time, but it was harmless. We played ball in his yard and he'd give us candy." He paused, taking a deep breath, then continued.

"One day after all the other kids had left, just I and one of my friends stayed. We continued to play in the yard until Mr. Walker called out my name. 'James, come here boy!' When I reached the porch, he had two pieces of candy in his hand. I remember it clear as day — a green Jolly Rancher and a Blow Pop. He asked me if I wanted one and I told him I did. He offered to give me both of them if I got my other friend and if we'd stand at the side of the house and watch him. We had no idea why he wanted us to watch him on the porch, but we did and he gave us both two pieces of candy.

We stood at the side of the house, eating the candy, watching Mr. Walker make one of his tobacco cigarettes. I had a grape Blow Pop and a green Jolly Rancher and my friend had a red Jolly Rancher and a grape Blow Pop. The sun had begun to set. We told Mr. Walker we had to go home, but he insisted that we stay a little while longer. He told us he'd walk us home if it got too dark. He gave us another Jolly Rancher and we stayed." Obviously nervous, James paused again.

"Well, he looked around, and then grabbed the front of his pants. I nudged my friend to tell him that Mr. Walker was getting ready to use the bathroom outdoors. We thought he was drunk, so we laughed. He undid the button, and then unzipped his pants. He reached down and pulled out what looked like a snake to us, at the time, because it was so big. He grabbed it and starting masturbating. I was scared and didn't know what to do. My friend ran. I couldn't move. I stood there with my mouth wide opened. Mr. Walker turned and looked at me and saw my friend running down the street to his house.

Then he told me to come to him. I didn't because I couldn't move. He stood up; his penis was sticking straight out, pointing at me as he walked to the edge of the porch to where I stood at the side of the house, trembling, afraid because I didn't know what he was getting ready to do. While stroking his penis, he asked me if I wanted to touch it. I shook my head 'no'. He told me it wouldn't hurt. He came down off the porch and walked towards me, saying if I touched it he'd give me another Blow Pop. I fought to avoid touching it, keeping my hands close to my stomach. He told me that it was okay and I didn't have to touch it right then if I didn't want to. He walked back to his chair and sat down, still masturbating. He told me to come over the next day and he would give me some more candy, but I couldn't let anyone know about our game. The next thing I know, this white stuff came shooting out. I ran home and never told anyone. This went on for almost six months until he passed away."

James let out a loud sigh of relief, and then ran his left hand over his face. "Whew! That was hard. That was a first." He laid his head back on the headrest, and turned to face Annette. His eyes were sad. "Now what?" he asked.

She just sat there, mouth partly opened. She tried hard not to show her amazement at his story. Her heart went out to him. She could see the sadness in his eyes. She took his hand and squeezed it tight, then told him how much she loved him and thanked him for sharing his story, for trusting her enough to let her into his intimate, fragile soul. He put the car in reverse and backed out, then drove off. She couldn't help wondering whether he'd had any physical contact with the man.

They were twenty minutes from her dorm riding down the seemingly endless road that led to campus. The car remained silent. Nothing else was said the remainder of the ride. With his had in hers, they drove in silence, both reflecting on the evening. It had been an evening they wouldn't soon forget. For the first time they'd bonded on a different level, one that would keep them together forever. Their secrets were their bond. That evening they discovered love.

—————————————————

Over the course of a month, Annette and James had grown even closer. They were spending evenings after school and most nights together in November and December. They spent Thanksgiving and Christmas day with her family in Decatur. At their first Thanksgiving dinner with her family, they all stood in a circle around the dining room table with heads bowed, hovering over the delicious meal her mother had prepared. A big turkey and ham adorned the middle of the table, surrounded by all the side dishes imaginable: collard and turnip greens, cornbread, macaroni and cheese, yams, giblet gravy, dressing or stuffing, cranberry sauce, rolls, and a bunch of pies and cakes. Before her father blessed the food, they all went around the table and each person gave thanks for their blessings. James stood across from Annette. When his turn came around, he gave thanks to God for bringing her into his life. Annette looked at him and a tear rolled down her face. She mumbled, "God, I love that man!" It was now her turn. She gave thanks to God for her beautiful family and for the *other* man in her life besides her father, James. They all smiled, acknowledging their acceptance of James. Her father blessed the food and they ate.

After dinner, she and James took a walk around

the neighborhood, hand in hand as lovers do. The weather was brisk and the air was damp. It had rained off and on most of the day. When they returned from their walk, everyone was sitting around talking about how good the food was. Her younger sister and brother, Cora and Dennis, were sitting next to each other on the sofa in the living room. Her cousins were scattered across the floor. All the grownups were in the den. It was great having James there with her family, she thought. It seemed he'd become a part of the family, and everyone treated him as if he was one of them. He seemed to have enjoyed being around her family as well. Initially, he was a little nervous because it was his first Thanksgiving dinner with her family, and he didn't know what they would think of him, but twenty minutes into being there, and he felt right at home.

After about an hour of talking with the family, she and James decided to take a drive and ended up in a hotel, making love. They had sex for what seemed like three hours. Around one o'clock in the morning he took her back home.

When she entered the house, it was quiet and dark. There was a light on from the stove. She quietly tiptoed in and went into her bedroom, closed the door and got into bed, thinking about what it would be like to be married to James. She wondered whether he planned to ask her to marry him. Would this be the year? She fell asleep.

Her questions were answered Christmas day when James came in bearing her gifts. She was disappointed when she saw the beautifully wrapped box he was carrying. She knew it couldn't be a ring because the box was too big. She'd given him a 14k gold cross on a serpentine chain. James was a very spiritual man. He didn't attend church every Sunday, but said his prayers on a daily basis.

In May of 1985, James was graduating in two weeks. In January, he'd moved into his own apartment in Marietta, not far from Atlanta. He and one of his fraternity brothers got an apartment together. He'd pledged Alpha Phi Alpha fraternity his junior year. In February, he took a job as a car salesman, something he knew nothing about but quickly learned so he could pay the bills. His roommate was in graduate school working on his MBA.

Annette was now in her first semester as a senior, well on her way to accomplishing her goal. Going to school year-round had paid off. She was in line to graduate during the winter semester of 1985 with a bachelor degree in Social Work. She'd applied for and been accepted into the Master of Social Work Program. Determined to have completed the program in eighteen months or less, she attended school like she had as an undergrad, year-round. She earned her MSW degree during the spring semester of 1987 and got a job as a social worker at the local hospital where she'd completed her internship

After becoming frustrated with his job as a car salesman in 1985, James sought out an Army recruiting station to learn more about the military. He told Annette he'd taken the entrance examination and was thinking hard about joining the Army. This was disappointing news for Annette because she'd hoped that he'd follow his dream and pursue his construction business. He told her the recruiter said he could go in as a Private First Class and later apply for Officer Candidate School. She wasn't pleased about the idea, but she understood that he needed do something about his financial situation.

His entrance exam score was high enough for him to get into military intelligence. He attended basic training in the September 1985, which lasted for nine weeks, and then attended AIT, advance individual training, which lasted two months, from November to December. He spent time training in Kentucky and Arizona, and being without James left Annette feeling lost and alone. They had spent most of their time together.

To get over her loneliness and longing for James, Annette got a membership at the local gym, where she worked out five days a week to keep herself occupied after work. She changed her eating habits, eating more baked chicken, fish and vegetables, and began reading fitness magazines. After about eight weeks of intense workouts, lifting weights, and running on the treadmill, she noticed a change in her muscle tone. Seeing the change in her body was enough for her to adopt working out as a way of life. She didn't particularly care for lifting weights or running on a treadmill, but after seeing the results she didn't want to stop. Working out had become a lifestyle change for her. She was now 5'7", weighed about 146 pounds, and looked good. She'd lost 12 pounds. Heads turned when she walked into the gym, and both men and women looked at her. All the attention made her feel even more self-assured and desirable.

After AIT, James visited her in Atlanta. She'd

moved into her own apartment, so he stayed with her the entire visit. He was on a two-week leave. They had sex every day he was there. They experimented with oral sex. They both were very open when it came to sex and trying new things. James had come a long way. There was a time when he was repulsed by the thought of "putting his head down there," as he once said. They visited an adult video store and purchased a tape to learn a few techniques. Annette didn't have a problem giving James oral sex; it was easy. All she had to do was pull it out and go to work. On the other hand, James needed to watch the tape again. He just wasn't hitting the right spot on her clitoris. She even opened it up so he could see it, but he was still having difficulty. He didn't have that rhythm technique. He would bring her to an intense sexual peak, change his rhythm, and she'd lose the feeling. She didn't have an orgasm the first try, but his tongue felt very good to her. In fact, she didn't have an oral orgasm until his last day in Atlanta.

Annette had difficulty reaching orgasm, and she'd seen her doctor about the problem. Her doctor found nothing wrong but told her she should experiment with adult toys. She did and had no problems reaching orgasm with her vibrator.

James received orders prior to coming to Atlanta. He was assigned to New York, and he applied for OCS in March of 1986. Six and a half months after applying for school, he received notification that his OCS application packet had been approved. He would report for training in January.

When he called Annette with the good news, she was so overwhelmed that she left work, taking the rest of the afternoon off. James had planned to come home for

Labor Day weekend to discuss their future. Annette tried hard to avoid jumping the gun and assuming James wanted to talk about getting married because she'd learned from before. Being disappointed wasn't a good feeling. But she couldn't help hoping from time to time that he would ask. He was going to be an officer, so she hoped now more than ever.

He came home the Thursday before Labor Day. That morning, as she read the *Atlanta-Journal Constitution*, Annette's phone rang.

"Hello?"

"Good morning, Baby," James said, his voice full of excitement. "How are you?"

"Hi Honey! I'm doing great. Where are you?"

"I'm at the airport."

"What time does your plan arrive so I'll know what time I need to pick you up?"

"Annette, there's no need to pick me up. As a matter of fact, I'm here to pick you up."

"You're kidding, right?"

"No, Baby. Remember when we spoke last night and I told you to pack your bags?

"Yes, and I did."

"Well, that's why I wanted you to pack them, so that all you had to do was picked them up and walk out the door when I called. So, here I am, I'm calling."

A smile spread across her face. "You are unbelievable!"

"Our flight leaves at 10:25a.m."

She had no idea he'd planned a trip. She called a taxicab and it arrived about ten minutes later. She didn't know where they were going, but after fighting to get through rush hour traffic, the cab arrived at the airport around 9:45 a.m.

She found James at the Delta Airlines terminal, patiently waiting for her. He was dressed in a pair of khaki shorts and a white, short-sleeve polo shirt, holding her ticket in the air. She still didn't know where he was taking her, and he wouldn't tell her.

Once they'd boarded the plane, the pilot announced that the flight was going to Washington, D.C. She screamed with joy, then clamped her hand over her mouth, still smiling, and looked at James. They had talked about one day visiting the nation's capitol about three years ago. She was blown away. There was no doubt in her mind that she would have a ring on her finger when they returned to Atlanta.

They arrived at Baltimore Washington International at 1:15 p.m., got a rental and drove into D.C. They arrived just in time to avoid rush hour and holiday travel traffic. The weather was great the entire trip, and although temperatures reached the upper 90's, they still enjoyed their visit.

James had made reservations at the Marriott, and they left the car with the valet. They didn't have many bags, but the bellhop took them up anyway. James gave him a $20 tip. The suite was spectacular. It was spacious with a separate bedroom, living room and kitchen area. Definitely the kind of place a man would propose in. They were partially unpacked when the urge to make love hit them. They decided to have dinner in the hotel restaurant afterward, and after dinner, they went up to their suite and made love again.

Early Friday morning about 2:30 a.m., James rolled over to spoon Annette, she felt his hard penis, and they made love again. They woke up at 9:20 a.m. and ordered room service. They were both famished. Annette went into the bathroom while James ordered breakfast. when they finished breakfast, they mad love again. It was as if they were on their honeymoon. Later they showered together, making love once again. James got out of the shower dripping wet and dried off in the bedroom, leaving Annette in the shower. She got out and pulled a plush towel from the rack, then reached into her cosmetics bag to get her birth control pills. They weren't there. "Oh my God!"

James didn't hear her because the door was closed. Frantically, she ran out, calling to him. She sat on the bed beside him, put her hand on his thigh and her head on his shoulder. The tears fell.

"What's wrong?"

"Baby, I don't have my pills!"

"What?"

"My birth control pills! I don't have them!"

"How did this happen?"

"What do you mean how did it happen? I thought I put them in my bag." Suddenly, she felt like James was insinuating that she'd purposely left her pills at home.

"It's okay. We'll get some condoms when we go out."

"Okay, let's do that. But what if it's too late?"

"What do you mean? Too late for what?"

"What if I get pregnant?"

"Hmm . . . . Well, if you do get pregnant I guess we'll have some decisions to make, don't you think?"

"What kind of decisions, James?"

"Look, let's not even talk about that. It's only one morning that you'll miss; the remainder of the trip we'll use condoms, so stop stressing yourself."

"I guess you're right." She couldn't believe how

naïve he was, thinking that she wouldn't get pregnant by missing just one day of taking her pill.

The remainder of their trip, Annette found herself consumed with thoughts of the possibility she was pregnant. *I remember taking my pill yesterday morning and putting the pack back on the sink near my cosmetics bag and then — oh damn!* She realized she hadn't put the pills back in her cosmetics bag. Hearing the phone ring and James telling her to come to the airport, she got sidetracked. Caught up in the excitement, she'd picked up her cosmetics bag and her other bag, then left. Annette knew they were not ready for children, especially with James going to school to become an officer. She tried to relax and enjoy the rest of the trip.

D.C. proved to live up to its name when it came to the sights and the nightlife. They'd once thought Atlanta was the place to be, but after visiting D.C. and seeing all the Black people there, they just had to come back one day. They didn't really need a car because the mass transit was great, so they left the rental parked during most of their stay. They visited the Pentagon using the metro. Annette was impressed with its size, like a little city with all the stores and restaurants. They wanted to avoid looking like tourists, so they didn't take too many pictures. They toured the White House, the Capitol, and the Smithsonian.

James reminded Annette that he would be going to Arizona for training in January. He coughed and put his hands together, squeezing them as though he was shaking hands with himself. He explained to her that it would be almost year before they could see each other again, and he stressed how mentally and physically challenging the training would be for him. He explained that it could cause a hardship on their relationship.

Although he assured her that nothing would come between them and the love they shared, she was still disappointed. She looked absently at him, wondering what she would do without him for such a long period. Her eyes filled with tears. Obviously, she was more upset than she realized. She had nothing to say.

James was required to commit three years to serving his country upon completion of his training. Perhaps the one good thing Annette saw from the military idea at the time was that his training would be in Georgia, about one and a half hours away. That gave her a little solace even though she knew she couldn't visit him. Just knowing he would be close was good enough for her. Her thoughts were interrupted by images of James being with someone else, but she wanted to continue enjoying the trip, so she kept her thoughts and feelings to herself. *Damn! All I can think about is him being away from me for so long, finding comfort with someone else, and forgetting about our love, forgetting about us. I have to stop thinking like this.*

She was beginning to realize that she was more insecure than she imagined. She had always examined and analyzed her thoughts and feelings, and she soon realized her insecure feelings were not about whether or not she trusted James; they were about accepting the reality of them being apart for an extended amount of time and him — or her, for that matter — finding comfort with someone else. Her insecure thoughts had gotten out of control. She found herself thinking about him leaving her for someone else so often that it almost cost her relationship with him. James became tired of her constant questions and accusations, asking him about whether he met anyone else.

Although James would constantly tell her their love was stronger than either of them could imagine, reassuring her had become a chore. However, she sometimes wondered about that because he still hadn't asked her to marry him after being in the relationship for almost five years.

Annette often believed marriage would solidify their love and provide the security she longed for in the relationship. She wanted so much for him to ask her to marry him that when she thought the time was right and he didn't, her feelings were hurt. Her hope and dreams were shattered. It was self-induced turmoil.

———————————————————

Monday evening, James returned to New York, and Annette boarded a plane back to Atlanta. Their trip was like a dream, except the end didn't happen the way she'd hoped it would. When she returned to work on Tuesday morning, her friend Jess asked whether James had popped the question.

Annette looked at her poignantly. "No, he didn't."

Jess and Annette had become close. She reminded Annette of herself, except that Jess was about two inches shorter and White. She had beautiful red hair that flowed down her shoulders. She worked out just as much as Annette and it showed. She was single and without children but engaged to be married. She and her love planned to marry in June of 1991 because she wanted to be a June bride. She told Annette she wanted Brian to finish med school. Jess was two years older than Annette. She was raised in Tuscaloosa, Alabama. She'd earned her MSW from the University of Alabama. She moved to Atlanta in 1989.

For months, Jess had known about Annette's desire to be with a woman. She'd told her about it after feeling her out to see what she thought about women who were bisexual. To Annette' surprise, Jess was as liberal as they come. Annette thought that unusual, especially since Jess had been raised in a household where her parents loathed gays and lesbians. Annette learned that Jess had had a few bisexual experiences in her college days and a year or so afterwards, when she graduated and moved to Atlanta. Jess considered herself a bisexual in remission, since it had been over three years since she'd been with a woman. She claimed that all her experiences had been alcohol induced, but also said she'd known what she was doing.

Annette never told James about Jess' bisexual tendencies or advances towards her. She didn't feel it was important enough to mention, since nothing happened.

Jess went to Annette's apartment around eight o'clock one Friday evening, just to chill and hang out. Annette was wearing a short black silk teddie because that's just what she wore most evenings, especially if it was hot. They were sitting on the sofa watching television. After an hour of watching TV, she remembered that she needed to sign and address her brother's birthday card so she could mail it on Saturday morning. She walked over to the kitchen table, leaving Jess sitting on the sofa. She began addressing the envelope. Jess walked over and stood behind the chair, looking over her shoulder. Annette didn't think too much of it and assumed she was just being nosy. Jess began massaging Annette's shoulders and it felt good. As she continued to massage her shoulders, Annette noticed Jess' hands were moving lower and lower down the front of her chest. She reached up with her right hand and gently grabbed Jess' right arm, then turned to look up at her.

"What are you doing Jess?" she asked.

"I'm sorry, Annette. I'm sorry. I didn't mean to offend you. I think you're sexy and . . . I wanted to touch you."

"It's okay. As I've told you before, I've had thoughts about it, but never tried it."

Jess didn't come on to her anymore. They watched TV until midnight, and she went home.

Wednesday evening before James was due to come home for Christmas, Jess, her fiancé Brian, and Annette were having dinner at Ruth Chris' Steakhouse when Annette became ill. Her stomach was cramping. She thought that maybe it was the medium rare steak. However, she'd never gotten sick before and that's the way she normally cooked her steaks. Jess and Brian offered to take her home but she insisted they stay and enjoy their dinner. She told them she'd be fine. James was due to fly in on Friday evening, on his way to begin his training. As she approached her car, she felt another sharp pain in her lower abdomen. She leaned on the car and grabbed her stomach. "Oh God! What's wrong with me?" She unlocked and opened the door then sat down. She thought of what she'd eaten that day, but realized she hadn't eaten anything unusual. "Oh no! I can't be! Lord no! I can't be! Please don't let me be pregnant! Not now, Lord!"

She started the car and drove to the nearest Wal-mart to get an over-the-counter pregnancy test. She didn't sleep at all that night. The next morning she peed on the stick and almost passed out when she saw the result. It was positive. She called in sick. Jess knew she'd gotten sick the night before, so she explained her circumstances to their supervisor. To be certain, she went to Wal-Mart and got another test kit. It was positive as well.

She didn't know how she was going to tell James about her pregnancy. He was on his way to training to become an officer. The last thing he needed was to be thinking about her being pregnant. She struggled with waiting until he finished training to tell him the news. She was afraid and prayed about it. She decided to tell him when he came home Friday evening.

James arrived at her apartment around 1:30 p.m. He used his key to let himself in. She'd taken off work at two o'clock so he didn't have to wait long before she got there. When she got home, he was sitting on the sofa watching CNN. He liked staying abreast of current events. She joined him on the sofa and they kissed each other, then made love right there on the sofa. She told James she wanted to turn around so he could take her from behind. He always hit her g-spot when she was in that position. After making love for an hour, they cuddled right there on the sofa, with her lying on top of him.

"James?"

"Yes, Baby?"

"I'm pregnant."

His eyes widened. "Are you serious?"

"Yes, Honey, I'm serious. Remember the D.C. trip?"

"Oh, I don't know what to say Annette. I'm going to

be a father?"

"Yes, you are James. You're going to be a dad. I haven't seen the doctor yet. I used two of those over the counter tests and they both came up positive. I didn't want to see the doctor until I told you about it. Besides, I just found out about it myself."

"I see," James said. "So, when are you going to see the doctor?"

"I've already called and made an appointment for next Tuesday."

"Well, you know I'm leaving on Sunday."

"Yes, I know. I'll let you know what the doctor says."

He pulled her closer and held her tight. He told her again how much he loved her and wanted to spend the rest of his life with her. She told him how much she'd struggled with deciding when she should tell him, before or after his training. James was glad she'd told him before he left for training. He assured her that they would make it work.

They decorated the apartment using a red and gold theme. The apartment wasn't extremely large — just less than 1700 square feet — so there wasn't a whole lot to decorate. It did have a nice floor plan. That's why she chose it. It had a huge living room and a separate dining area. She'd also fallen in love with the large, walk-in closet.

It has been three months since conception and by now, Annette's stomach was protruding. She'd not gained a whole lot of weight. In fact, James asked her if the doctors were sure she was pregnant. Annette had always had a flat stomach, so for her, seeing it slightly protruding was different. She thought about how her body would look when she was eight months and how it would look after the baby was born.

On Christmas Eve, she and James went to a dinner party that Jess and Brian were hosting. At the dinner party, James and Annette announced that they were having a baby. They asked Jess and Brian if they would be the godparents, and they accepted. The party was a delight. Jess lived in an upper middle class neighborhood in a very nice, 3000 square foot, two-level house. It had beautiful hardwood flooring and many windows. She didn't have a lot of furniture, but the pieces she did have were mostly antique. About seven o'clock on Christmas morning, James was up cooking breakfast. He cooked scrambled eggs, wheat toast, orange juice, grits and bacon. After breakfast, they got back into bed and made love. Afterwards they fell asleep and got up around 12:30 p.m. They were supposed to go over to her parents' house for dinner at four o'clock, so they got up and went into the living room to exchange gifts. Annette had bought James three pair of slacks, three sweaters and some Lagerfeld cologne. He'd bought her a beautiful, diamond-studded pendant with matching earrings. After exchanging gifts, they got dressed. Her mother didn't like people to be fashionably late. Annette got in the shower. When she got out, she put on her terry cloth robe and looked in the closet to find something to wear. She chose a brown pantsuit that she'd bought that had elastic in the side waistband, a cream-colored top and a pair of brown boots. James wore a pair of the slacks and a sweater that he'd gotten for Christmas.

Annette reached into her cosmetics bag to get her foundation and saw a little black velvet box.

She picked it up and opened it. Her jaw dropped. It

contained a beautiful marquis-cut diamond set in a white band. It had to be at least a carat. She ran out into the bedroom screaming, "James, I love you. I love you. I love you!"

Calmly he stood and smiled. "I take it you found the ring?"

"Yes, Honey, I did. I had no idea."

"Isn't that the way it's suppose to be? You're not supposed to expect it?"

"I guess you're right."

"Annette, I've been trying to tell you for the longest time that you mean the world to me. Moreover, given my situation before, not having the job and financial security I needed to take care of you the way you deserved to be taken care of, marriage wasn't an option. But now that I'm going to be an officer in the military, I want you to be my partner for life. I want to spoil you and give you everything you desire."

He had won her heart. She cried and held him as tight as she could. He pushed her back. "Be careful; you might hurt Junior." They looked at each other and smiled. He kissed her on the forehead and she laid her head on his chest for a few minutes before they got dressed and went to her parents' house to tell everyone the good news.

James' sisters no longer lived in Georgia; they both had moved to Houston, so James called them to share the news. Annette wanted to tell her family the good news about the baby and the engagement. As they approached the driveway, she noticed her mom's brother in law's pickup truck. Uncle Joe was always prompt or maybe even a little early when it was time to eat. Aunt Josie hadn't cooked dinner because her mother had invited them over. They went inside and the house smelled like Christmas should. The collard greens were distinct. The tree was beautiful at about six feet and covered with gold bulbs and colorful lights. There were gifts everywhere. Her mother always went to the extreme when she shopped for Christmas. Annette noticed Aunt Josie's delicious devil food's cake on the dessert table near the buffet counter. Her mother had put all of the cooked food on the dinner table, protecting it with aluminum foil and dish covers.

James and Annette decided to share their good news after dinner with hopes that everyone would be too full to move around and ask a lot of questions. Her parents cried. They were going to be grandparents. Her sister and brother were excited. Everyone congratulated them. The questions came from every direction: "When is the baby due? Have you set a date for the wedding? Do you want a big wedding?" They were both so overwhelmed from the questions and excitement that they took a short walk in the brisk night. When they returned, they went inside and said their goodbyes for the evening. When they returned to the apartment, they undressed and cuddled on the sofa to watch television before going to bed.

Part 2

Her Eyes Were Wide Shut

In March of 1987 Annette was six months into her pregnancy. It had been three months since she and James last saw each other. They'd spoken everyday on the phone whenever he wasn't busy. He finished the officer basic training and was on his way to Arizona. His training required him to be in Arizona for at least six months. It was there where he learned how to be an officer in military intelligence. Annette was lonely without him.

The baby was growing fast and she was now looking pregnant; her stomach was no longer just a small pouch. Her doctor gave her permission to continue her exercise routine, but recommended that she cut the number of days she exercised from five to three. Annette took pride in her body, especially after working so hard to get it to look the way it did. She'd had a nice shape to begin with, but when she saw how much better she looked after working out for several weeks, she wanted to look even better. At one time, she was more concerned about how her body would look after the pregnancy than with the pregnancy it self. She remembered James had told her before they started dating, that he didn't want a woman who carried more weight than her height allowed, so it was extremely important to her that she continued to exercise even during her pregnancy.

She had an ultrasound done and sent it to James. He was thrilled. He didn't want to know the sex of the baby and neither did Annette. They wanted it to be a surprise.

In February, James invited her to visit him in Arizona for a week in April. He had rented an apartment in Bisbee, Arizona, not far from where he was training.

Her flight arrived in Tucson on Sunday afternoon at 2:20 p.m., and it was hot. Luckily, she'd taken James' advice and wore something light, a yellow linen maternity sun dress with her hair pulled up in a ponytail. He was wearing a pair of cream-colored shorts, a burnt-orange shirt and a pair of rust-colored sandals.

Walking through the airport, Annette began to feel dizzy. The bevy of people walking towards her who had just gotten off a plane themselves appeared to be coming straight at her. She stopped in her tracks. The dry air almost astounded her. After about five seconds, she began to move forward as if she were walking in slow motion. From a distance, James could see her. He walked towards her, calling out her name. "Annette? Annette! Here I am." She saw him and her gait increased.

As they embraced each other, Annette gasped for air. "I need to sit down, James."

"Honey, are you all right?"

It was clear the heat had caught her off guard.

"Yes. I'm all right. The heat got to me. I need a drink of water."

As they walked towards baggage claim, James noticed a store ahead and stopped to get Annette something to drink.

After getting her bags, they left the airport to do a little sightseeing before going to Sierra Vista, Arizona. They stopped on Davis Monthan Air Force Base at the commissary to get something to drink because Annette was still feeling dehydrated. She'd never been in the desert. James had warned her about the lack of humidity.

The cacti were amazing. She got a chance to see sugauro cacti, the tall ones with arms, like she'd seen in an old John Wayne movie. Most of the homes didn't have grass; their yards were landscaped with small rocks. To her, it looked beautiful, but she still preferred grass. While driving through the mountains, they saw snakes that crossed the road as if they were pedestrians and some real scorpions. They weren't as big as they appeared on television.

On the way to Sierra Vista, their wedding day didn't come up. James did say that he wanted to get married as soon as he finished training. He wanted the baby to have his name. He was supposed to graduate in June or July. Annette shocked him when she told him that she wanted to wait until he went to his permanent assignment as an officer. He wasn't too thrilled with that idea, but had no other choice but to respect her decision. Besides, she didn't want him to think anymore than he probably had already thought that she'd tricked him. That thought still etched in her mind, so she wanted to wait a little while longer and prove to him that forgetting her pills wasn't a ploy to trick him but an honest mistake. She'd noticed his subtle message, putting the ring in her cosmetics bag where the pills should have been. She wasn't sure that was his intent, but that was the message she got from it.

They arrived in Sierra Vista after about an hour on the road, driving down what the locals called Fast Food Boulevard. The name of the street is actually Fry Boulevard, but the adopted name was appropriate because all they saw were fast food restaurants and a Wal-Mart. There wasn't a whole lot to the small town. It seemed to be a retirement town.

They arrived at James', it was a cream-colored southwestern style apartment complex with a flat roof. Many officers lived in that particular apartment complex, and most were in the same training James was in. They entered James' apartment, and Annette frowned. She couldn't believe what she was seeing. It was immaculate. He had a black and brown theme going. He had purchased a beautiful, two-toned chocolate and cream-colored plush leather sofa and a new oak dinette set. The top of the sofa was chocolate and the arms were cream colored. It was obvious he was doing okay. An off-white flokati rug covered most of the carpeted living room floor. Pictures of women lined the living room and bedroom walls. The color of the pictures accented his color theme.

"Hmm," she uttered softly as they walked through the apartment. She wondered whether she'd missed something. This just didn't seem like his style. She attributed it to him changing his taste. The place was immaculate. Not saying that James was a messy person, but it looked like an interior designer had decorated the place. He went into the blue bathroom in the hallway. She did what most women would have done, checked out the kitchen. It was there that she saw a small photograph of him posing in just a pair of navy blue biker shorts, sitting on the counter near the stove. He had an obvious hard-on and he wasn't wearing any underwear. In the picture, he stood in the doorway leaning on the door jam, posing with his left hip slightly pushed outward and his right arm resting on the doorframe. On the bottom of the picture was a strip of paper taped to the back that read *Looking for friends to hang out with for fun.*

A swinger's magazine lay next to the picture on the counter. Before the Internet, people used magazines to locate others for sex. Annette felt distressed. In college, she'd heard mention of swingers so she knew what they were, but that was the first time she'd ever seen that kind of magazine. It was interesting because when she'd heard about them in college, it seemed like a big orgy. She opened it and flipped through the pages, stopping on those who had completely exposed themselves. It was like watching a porno video. She was a bit shocked. She read *BiF4BiF, SBM4TV, MWC4Same*, and they went on and on. She had no clue what the codes meant. The only code that made sense to her was the obvious one BiF4BiF. She decided to ask James about them when he came into the kitchen. After all, she and James had the kind of relationship where they could communicate about anything. If she saw someone she thought was attractive, she could express that to James without fear of jealousy and he could do the same. So asking him about the magazine wasn't a big deal.

She asked him about the photo and the magazine. Shocked and caught off guard by her question, he made up a story, telling her that he was planning to submit the ad once the baby was born. He wanted them to find someone to give her that experience of being with another woman. He told her his classmates who lived in the building had given him the magazine to look through one afternoon. Because he cared enough for her to look into giving their relationship that experience, her love wouldn't allow her to think otherwise, and she believed him.

"James, what do the codes mean?"

"BiF4Bi —"

"No, I figured that one out. I'm talking about these." She pointed to *SBM4TV, MWC4Same, SWGM4Same,* and *SBM4GWM.*

"Well," pointing to them respectively, "This one is Single Black Male for Transvestite, and this one is Married White Couple for Same, meaning they're looking for another married white couple." He paused.

She looked up at him. "And what about this one?"

"That one is Single Black Male for Gay White Male."

Scratching her head, Annette asked, "How do you know so much about this?"

"It's not rocket science, Annette; they explain what the codes stand for in the front of the magazine," James said with a hint of sarcasm.

"Well, it's rocket science to me because I didn't know what it meant. I don't read those magazines."

"Okay, you have a point." James didn't want to make waves because he knew that Annette wouldn't have appreciated the fact that he'd lied to her, pretending not to know a whole lot about the magazine. She wouldn't have liked it if she'd known he purchased the magazine himself. *Damn! I can't believe I forgot and left that magazine out like that.* Changing the subject, James asked, "Is Junior doing okay in this desert heat?" He rubbed Annette' stomach, then kissed her on the lips. It was obvious that his diversion had worked.

"We don't know it's a Junior yet, James. It might be a girl. That's all you have in your family is girls," Annette said, laughing.

Annette didn't let it go; she wanted to look through the magazine just to see what it was. They sat on the plush leather sofa and looked through it together. She pointed out to him several women she found attractive. He also had her point out different men who she thought were attractive. Annette had this thing about big penises and James knew that, so he would have her chose the person with the biggest penis that she wouldn't mind having sex with. Abruptly James said, "Okay, enough of this." He took the magazine out of Annette's hand and tossed it on the coffee table. "Let's get something to eat. I thawed out some chicken. How do you and Junior want it, baked or fried?"

"I want it baked, and Junior wants it fried. So how are you going to handle that, big boy?"

"How about I fry a couple of pieces and bake the rest."

Laughing, Annette said, "That's one way to solve it."

"That's definitely my boy. He wants fried chicken. A chip off the old block," James said as he softly tapped Annette on the chin with his fist. Annette hits James on the back as he is walking into the kitchen. "Let's hope he's not like you in that respect. I don't want my baby eating all that fatty food, running up his blood pressure."

"Look at me," James said, doing a once over with his hands. "Don't I look good and healthy?"

"Hmm. Yes, you do look good. Make love to me right now," Annette said. "Looking at that magazine made me horny."

"Are you sure you can do this? Will it hurt the baby? You know I got a long reach."

She kissed him on the lips. "It ain't *that* long." She grabbed him by the arm and led him into the bedroom. James wanted to make love doggie-style because he was afraid he might hurt the baby if he were on top. After they both reached orgasm, James got up, put on his robe and went into the kitchen to cook dinner. Annette decided to lie in bed for a while. She reached over and picked up the International Male catalog on the nightstand. She thumbed through the pages, looking at the clothes, picking out what she thought would look good on James, rubbing her stomach and talking to the baby. "Are you okay, Baby? Daddy wasn't trying to hurt you. Mommie and daddy were horny. We needed some loving. Mommie hasn't had sex in over three months."

Unbeknownst to Annette, James stood in the door smiling as he watched her talk to their unborn child. Without disturbing her, he quietly turned and went back into the kitchen.

After dinner, they watched television because it was too hot to go outside, even though it was eight o'clock in the evening.

James had turned into quite the chef. When Annette woke the next morning, James had already left for class, but made breakfast for her before leaving, an omelet with green and red peppers, mushrooms, onions, and ham, toast, bacon and grits. It made Annette fall in love all over again.

Because he was in training, he couldn't leave. He called Annette on his ten o'clock break to see if she'd gotten up and had breakfast. He was unable to come back for lunch, so Annette decided to take a walk through the apartment complex to learn her way around area. She was outside for a short while before going back inside because of the heat. She wasn't acclimated to the dry humidity and high temperatures. She found it difficult to breathe in the desert air. It was 12:15 in the afternoon and 88 degrees. The temperature was supposed to reach 91 degrees.

Once inside the apartment, she plopped down on the sofa and turned on the television, surfing through the cable channels. Nothing caught her attention, so she decided to look through the swinger's magazine. She looked under the coffee table and got the magazine. As she flipped through the pages, she noticed those codes again. She walked into the kitchen to get the picture of James that she'd seen, but it wasn't on the counter. "I wonder what he did with the picture . . . ." She walked back into the living room just as the phone rang. *Should I answer it or not? If I answer it and it's a woman, I'm going to be mad as hell. What if it's James? Well, if it's him, he'll call right back.* She decided to let it ring and, sure enough, he called right back.

"Hello?" she said.

"Hey, Baby. How are you and Junior doing?"

"We're okay."

"I figured I'd better do the international code and call you right back. I knew you wouldn't answer the phone unless I called back. I see women know that sign just like men do," he said laughing.

She laughed. "Yes, we do."

"Did you enjoy your breakfast?"

"Yes, I did. It was delicious. Thank you. Junior appreciated it as well."

"You both are welcome. Are you up and about?"

"Yes. I went outside to walk around the complex, but the heat and humidity ran me back in. I don't see how you stand it."

Laughing, James said, "I told you didn't I? It takes about a week or so to get acclimated to these high temperatures and the lack of humidity, but you have to be out in it."

"Well, I'm not staying out here so I don't need to get acclimated. What time will you be in?"

"I get out of class at 4:30, so I should get home about 5:30 or so."

"I saw you have salmon in the fridge. Want me to cook it?"

"Sure. There's some rice in the cabinet, and that's also where you will find the other canned vegetables."

"Okay, Honey."

"Well, my break is over; I gotta get back in class."

"Oh, I almost forgot. Where is that picture of you that was on the kitchen counter? I can't seem to find it. I want to look at your hard dick...since you're not here. I'm still feeling a little horny."

"It's on the dresser in the bedroom. Just hold that feeling until I get home. I'll take care of it for you."

"You need to hurry home then."

"I will. Have a good afternoon, Annette."

"You do the same."

After hanging up the phone, she walked into the bedroom to get the picture. It wasn't there. She looked through all of the dresser drawers and even in the bathroom, but she couldn't find it. *That's strange; maybe he thought he put it on the dresser. I'll just ask him when he gets home this evening.* She went back into the living room and continued looking through the swinger's magazine. She thumbed through the pages, looking at the pictures.

When James walked through the front door, Annette was in the kitchen and didn't hear him come in. He walked into the kitchen and saw her taking a pan of salmon from the oven. He moved in behind her, grabbed her waist and began moving in a slow circular motion and said, "Is this what you've been waiting on, Woman?"

She flinched, turned and glanced at him out the corner of her eye. Laughing she said, "Boy, you'd better move before you make me drop this pan."

"Didn't you say earlier that you wanted this hard dick? Well, here it is."

Annette put the pan on the stove, turned around, and reached up to kiss him. He reached down, slightly bent over, and grabbed her buttocks.

"Hey, I can get use to this coming home to a hot meal everyday. Would you like to get married now?" he asked jokingly.

She laughed. "No. Why don't you take me in the bedroom and fuck me instead?"

"Oooh. I like it when you talk dirty to me, Baby," he said.

She smiled and turned off the stove, and they walked hand in hand into the bedroom.

Annette went into the bathroom to shower. As she

stood in the mirror looking at her stomach, reality set in. *I wonder if my stomach is ever gonna be flat again after the baby's born. And will I have those ugly stretch marks like some women get after giving birth? I wonder what James thinks. Does he think I'm getting too fat?*

While Annette was in the shower, James went into the kitchen to get ready for dinner. She came out of the bedroom wearing his silk paisley print robe. She tied the belt on top of her stomach.

He smiled. "Come on, sit down and eat, Baby." He kissed her on the forehead. "You look cute in my robe too."

"You're such a sweetheart, James."

They ate dinner then retired to the sofa. Annette was just about to ask James if he thought she'd gained a lot of weight, when she had to go to the bathroom. When she returned, he was watching television and the scene on the screen was of a female strip club in Las Vegas. She sat beside him on the sofa. He told her that he enjoyed dinner and was glad that she was able to take off work to come visit him.

Unexpectedly she asked, "Remember I told you that some of the ladies and I went to that strip club in Atlanta?"

"Yes. I remember you said there were a lot of overweight women in there."

"Yeah. Those women looked nothing like these women," she said, pointing to the television screen.

"What about it?"

"What do you think about the fact that a lot of overweight women were in that club?"

"I think an overweight woman would be hard-pressed to pull one of those men off the stage and get him to date her and be true to her and all that kind of stuff. I mentioned earlier, and you didn't 100% agree with me, that when a super-fit woman all but lives in the gym, chances are her significant other will be just as fitness conscious as she is. A man, on the other hand, will sometimes have an overweight girlfriend or wife at home who doesn't want any part of the gym."

"Right," she said.

"So I don't know, Annette. But then again, I still think we're talking about two different kinds of people here. If I'm in the gym because I'm into fitness as opposed to the man who dances at the club, those are two different kinds of men."

"I think you're right about the fact that if she's a fitness buff, chances are, he's one as well."

"I'd put my paycheck on it."

"So if he's a fitness buff, she won't necessarily be one?" Annette said with a raised eyebrow.

"Exactly. I've known some people like that personally and have seen it too many times for me to think something other than that."

"But why is that?"

"It's 'cause y'all are so vain."

"Say what?"

"C'mon, Annette, y'all are vain as shit!"

"Meaning women?"

"Yes!"

"Why the fuck would you say that?"

"Get the fuck outta here Annette. If you have six-pack abs and you're fit, you don't want a Pillsbury doughboy!"

"That's bullshit James. Like I said before, a woman will accept a man with a beer belly before a man will accept a woman with a big stomach unless she's pregnant!"

"I don't believe that."

Annette moved off the sofa and into the chair that sat across from the sofa. She wanted to see him when he spoke.

"And —," she started.

"Again, we're talking two different kinds of women. Any *normal* woman will accept a man like that, yeah, but I'm talking about the gym-rat woman. No way will a gym-rat woman accept a man with beer belly."

"Okay, you're right there . . . in most cases, but —"

"That's right," he said, interrupting.

"But a man who's a gym rat will accept an overweight woman? Is that because of him and his insecurities? You know, I can see that being . . . like...if he's a gym rat and he don't give a damn what his wife or girlfriend looks like . . . maybe it's because he *wants* her to be overweight so he knows she probably won't go anywhere. Could that be the result of an insecure man?"

"Okay, let's flip the script," he said in defense. "What about her having an overweight man? Maybe she's insecure because she thinks other women want her man."

"But that's what we're talking about here, James — the man who's a gym rat and he's got an overweight wife or girlfriend. And he's got her at home because —"

"Because he loves her."

"He loves her," she repeated. "Bullshit!"

He laughed. "Damn, Annette."

"Bullshit, James."

"Damn!" he said in a high pitch.

"It's not because he loves her, it's because he *might* love her, but sometimes a control factor is involved.

I don't know . . . the first time this really hit me was when I saw Lee Haney."

"Ah ha."

"Remember when he was Mr. Olympia several years in a row? It was obvious his wife wasn't a gym rat."

"Okay…"

"And I'm saying what the fuck! I thought he would have been married to my girl."

"But we don't know what's going on in their household, James. You know what I mean?"

"Okay. Of course that was the only time I saw them together. It's not that often they're in the public eye together when he's doing his promotions. That detracts from the picture of him being Mr. Universe."

Annette put her hands on her hips. "But that's his wife that he *loves* so much, right?"

Laughing, James said, "Yeah, but he has an image to uphold."

"That's such bullshit, James! Look at Arnold Schwarzzenger. His wife is always on his arm."

His eyes widened. "That's because she isn't overweight! She's a gym rat too."

"That's precisely my point! Lee Haney didn't want his wife with him in public. Is that what you're saying, James?"

"No! It's not him. He probably wants his wife there. Its the promoters and sponsors who don't want her in the picture. That's what I'm saying."

"Bullshit!"

"How can he promote fitness and health and go around telling people to buy their damn supplements when he's standing next to his overweight wife."

"You called her overweight. Why the fuck did you

call her overweight?"

He laughed.

"So how vain are *you*, James?'

"What do you mean?"

"When it comes to dating big women? That matters to you. You're a gym rat who likes to look good and fit."

"Okay…"

"So would you date a woman who's 200 pounds?"

He just looked at her.

"It's taking you too damn long to respond."

"I'm trying to find the politically correct words to use."

"There is no goddamn politically correct way to say 'no!'"

"Yes, there is."

"She'd have to have a lot of money," James said.

"You're trifling James. You didn't even mention love."

"And she'd have to cook damn good too!"

"You're shallower than I thought," she said, laughing.

"But you said date, not marry."

"Regardless."

"Okay, godammit. How did this shit get turned on me? You were talking about all the freaks in the strip clubs and now I'm defending myself. How in the hell did *that* shit happen? You outsmarted me again you damn Red Baron."

She laughed. "Say what?"

"You outsmarted me again."

Annette was always a step ahead of James in their conversations. She was very clever and skilled at eliciting information through manipulation, especially with James.

Abruptly, she stopped laughing. "Again, these are overweight women at the club, I'm talking 5'-5'8" tall and 20 to 50 pounds overweight."

"Okay. You said they were very attractive women, correct?"

"That's correct. They were dressed in their own unique way. Some wore the Flash Dance gear with the torn sweatshirt, off the shoulder thing and —"

He laughed. "Fuck that! They were flash-*back*ing."

"See, look at you. You *are* trifling. Obviously what they had on worked for them. And some were wearing those midriff-revealing tops and they shouldn't have been wearing them. But they all were attractive."

"What about the fit women who were there. What was going on in their head?"

"I can answer that question because I was one of them," she said, laughing.

"Damn! Excuse me!" he said. "I hear you tooting your own fucking horn in the background."

"To answer your question, I was sitting there watching the strippers and the women and how some of them were reacting to —"

"So, if she's there with her crew of girlfriends and she's fine and she's pretty, what do you think her situation is like at home, if she's married or living with someone? Is she thinking 'I'm going to put $90 in one of these men's thongs so I can be fucked,' or is she there just to watch as well?"

"That's a hypothetical question, but I would say it could've just been fantasy for her too."

"Why? Because she's got a couch potato at home?" he asked. "Chances are, she could pull one of those guys off the stage if she wanted too."

"Yeah, but I don't know if that's true either. And if she's there to pull, she can do that at a gym and —"

"And *that's* what I'm saying. So why was she even there?"

"It could've been for the fantasy of it or she could've just been there celebrating her girlfriend's birthday. It could've been a girl's night out."

He shook his head. "I just don't know about those sin dens."

Annette raised her eyebrows, amazed at what he'd just said. "What did you call them?"

"Sin dens."

"What makes it a sin den?"

"That's what people seem to be doing when they go in those places, sinning."

"They're sinning by watching strippers?"

"Yes. God didn't intend on that." The room became silent. James broke the silence laughing. "Guess you're thinking 'damn, I don't know where to go with this shit now.'"

"No, that isn't it."

"Don't fuck around, Annette. There's no need to justify it or try to deny it," he said, still laughing.

"I just never heard it called that. But what's the difference between that and watching a porno movie in your home?"

"What happens in the comfort of my own home is my own business."

"But you're watching that video...*watching* that video. The key word is watching."

"Nobody gets hurt," he said. "Those women in the sin den are out there giving away their rent and child support money."

"But what if she's not giving away *any* money?"

"Okay," he said.

"Didn't you have to spend money for the video you watched?" she asked.

He laughed and said, "No."

"Yes, you did too have to pay for it."

"After you've owned it for seven years, you've gotten your money's worth because you've watched it 3800 times by then."

She laughed. "That is *such* bullshit male logic, James. So are you saying those women aren't getting their money's worth if they take that visual home and masturbate, just as you do watching a porno movie?"

"I don't know. Did you go home and masturbate after you left the club?" he asked.

"No, I had no reason to. Besides, we're talking about those women who threw money on the stage. Now if they went home and masturbated, didn't they get their money's worth? Even if all they threw out there was a dollar?"

James became silent, searching for his next comment. "But they could've done that without giving up the dollar. Am I right?"

"They could have, yes, if that's what they did. But it's really interesting, you know," she said. "Why do people go to strip clubs and dish out money like that?"

"You're trying to find some deep, dark, philosophical reason, and the real reason could be they were just out trying to have some fun."

For the first time in their discussion, Annette agreed with James.

"That's right. Girls were out having fun, just like men go out and have fun," she said.

"Yeah, but it's different in the clubs," he said.

James didn't want to end their discussion with Annette having the last word. He continued to challenge her on most of her comments. However, Annette did agree that there was a difference in the male and female strip clubs.

"A man can't touch the female strippers, but the women can touch all over the men. I don't understand that," she said.

"That's because men are whores!"

"Finally, a man admits it!" she screamed and laughed.

"Well, I wasn't speaking for all man-kind and shit." He chuckled. "But why is it that as a male dancer, I can put on my thong and you can rub my dick, put a finger up my ass, and let me kiss and grind all over you, but if I did more than touch a female strippers ass while putting money in her thong, all hell would break loose?" he said.

"I have to agree with you there. It's different in that respect. But like you said, men are whores," she said, laughing.

"I would go so far as to say that women expect that to happen," he said.

"I don't know if that's true, James. Anyway, I'm tired of talking about this shit."

"Come on back over here and lay next to me," he said, moving back on the sofa to make room for her.

She walked towards him, but detoured to go to the bathroom. As she was walking back into the living room she said, "I never did find that picture I asked you about this morning."

James hoped he'd gotten off the hook with not having to explain to her where the picture was. He told her that he would have to look for it because he was certain it was still on the kitchen counter. He told her it must've been thrown away by accident. She decided to let it go.

_____

Annette flew home on Saturday morning. She wanted to have a day to get ready for work on Monday morning. After dinner on Thursday, they spent the evening listening to jazz, talking and having sex. They talked about the baby's due date of Sunday, June 10, 1987 and the possibility of James not being there for the birth. He wouldn't graduate from training until after that date. Annette had hoped the baby would be born on James' birthday, June 15, but the doctor had told her that she would be early, not late, if she didn't give birth on the anticipated date. Since James would finish school in June and go to his first permanent assignment shortly thereafter, they set the date to get married on Saturday, April 16, 1988. They wanted to get married before the baby's first birthday. James also told Annette that he might go to Tampa, Florida for his first duty assignment and would have to be there for three years. She was excited about that because she'd always wanted to go to Tampa. At the time, he didn't know whether that's where he would be going, but he was confident.

During their conversation, Annette noticed a strange look on James' face. Before she could ask him what he was thinking, he went into the kitchen to get a beer. "Will you bring me something to drink please?" she asked. He came back with a glass of ice water in one hand and a beer in the other. Annette had noticed during her visit that James had drunk more beers than she'd ever seen him drink over a four-day period. When she asked him about it, he just said that's what the men do out here, sit around and talk shit while drinking beer because there wasn't a lot else to do, but it wasn't anything to get alarmed over.

After four beers and a shot of Jack Daniels, James decided he wanted to confide in Annette. He wanted to talk about how some people go through life without a care in the world, but for some people, living life was struggle from the time they wake up in the morning until they lie down to sleep at night. In addition, for some of those people, sleep doesn't always come easy. By now, Annette wanted to know where he was going with his philosophical commentary. The last time he'd shared something with her, he'd left her speechless. She wasn't sure she was ready for another one of those days, at least not while carrying the baby. But because she loved James and wanted him to be able to talk to her, she told him to share whatever had him disturbed.

He began to question her love for him. For James, this was uncharacteristic. He had always been Mr. Confident and sometimes Mr. Arrogant.

"Annette, for a long time I've struggled with my demons. When I told you about my childhood a few years ago, I didn't tell you everything. I use to take walks at night trying to figure out what I could do to help my parents with the bills. Although they both worked, it still wasn't enough to pay all the bills and buy us things too. My mother didn't really know that I wasn't in the house on the nights I decided to go out for walks.

"When I was fifteen, I was out walking about 6:30 p.m. It was dark because of daylight savings time. I ran into Darryl, one of my friends. He's the one I told you about who was with me watching the old man. He had a troubled childhood as well. His parents neglected him, leaving him to find comfort and acceptance in the streets.

"Anyway, we walked and talked, sharing our dreams of going to college and getting out of the neighborhood and finding a good wife and having children. As we were walking down the street, we veered down the street where the corner store was. For some reason, that night the street seemed darker. Anyway, as we approached the store, he pointed to the back of the store and told me to come with him, that he wanted to show me something. Then, before I knew it, he'd pulled my shorts down and was giving me head." He paused, looking at the floor. "I'm sad to say that it felt good — it felt so good, I came on him. Then he told me to suck his dick, and I did, but not as long as he sucked mine. My dick got hard again and he wanted me to fuck him in the ass, and I did. At the time, neither one of us didn't know a whole lot about condoms, so we didn't have any."

By this point in his story, James and Annette had cried many tears. She got up to get some tissues. When she returned he continued.

"Like I said, I've struggled with my demons for years. I've been too embarrassed to talk to anyone about what I did. That's why I fell in love with you. You made it easy for me to talk to you."

Annette dried her tears, then asked, "That was the only time you and your friend did that?"

"Yes. That was it, and like I said, I've never told anyone else."

"James, maybe you should speak with a therapist to help you learn to cope with your issues."

"I can't do that, especially being an officer in the Army."

"But this happened when you were a child. They can't do anything to you for something that happened in your childhood. You need to see a therapist to learn how to work through the pain and suffering you've had to deal with."

He shook his head. "No. I can't do that. I can't take that chance. You don't understand, Annette; its embarrassing."

"You're right; I don't understand what you're going through. I do know what it feels like to have to hide things from people, though. I know what it feels like to struggle to keep from letting your secret out. I'm here for you, James. I love you."

"Thank you, Annette."

She felt sorry for James, but all she could do was to comfort him. They embraced each other and held on until they fell asleep. After an hour or so, she woke up with a sharp pain in her stomach. James panicked. When she sat up, the pain went away. The pain was a result of the way she'd been lying. James offered her some water on his way to the bathroom.

When he returned, she was lying down and silently crying. She told James that she'd had no idea that he was suffering so.

James looked worried, hoping she wasn't thinking differently about him. She assured him that she didn't. She told him that she couldn't blame him for something that happened to him as a child. She then asked him if he had anything else she needed to know about his childhood, and he told her no. She was relieved to hear that because she wasn't sure if she could handle another bombshell like that. He wasn't telling her things like his dog was run over when he was 4 years old; he was telling her things that could have a grave impact on their relationship and how she viewed him.

It had been three weeks since Annette's visit with James. She returned and prepared the extra bedroom for the baby. She and Jess went shopping for baby stuff. She purchased a crib, a car seat and a rocking chair for her to rock the baby in. Jess had given her a baby shower the same week she'd returned from Arizona. Her coworkers gave her many nice baby things at the shower, and she'd bought things she didn't have. At the baby shower, Annette announced the she and James had set a wedding date for Saturday, April 16, 1988. Everyone was thrilled about the news.

The baby had begun to take its toll on Annette. Sometimes it was difficult for her to get around because of her swollen ankles. A week before her due date she decided to take off work until after the baby was born. Jess called her everyday to make sure she was okay and didn't need anything. One day Annette was standing in front of the full-length mirror on the back of her bedroom door, wearing nothing but a pair of panties, looking at how big she'd gotten. *Oh God, what have I done to my body? I know this is your work and a blessing from you, God, but please give me my shape back after the baby is born. I want to wear thongs and fitted clothes that showed off my figure again.* She had resumed her workout since returning from Arizona, but not during the final week of her pregnancy.

On Monday, June 8, 1987, at 4:25 a.m., Annette gave birth to a seven-pound baby girl. On Sunday morning after breakfast around 10:15 a.m., she began feeling contractions while doing the dishes. She leaned over the sink until the pain subsided. After a few minutes, she called Jess, who came right over. When she got there, she found Annette unable to get up off the sofa because the contractions were too much for her to bear. Annette told Jess the contractions were coming faster and faster and that she should call James and Annette's parents to let them know she was on her way to the hospital.

Jess was unable to reach James but did get her parents. Annette pointed to the coat closet near the front door where she had a bag packed. Jess helped her off the sofa, grabbed the bag, and they walked carefully down a flight of stairs and into Jess' charcoal-grey BMW 525. Annette's parents met them at the hospital.

She was in labor for almost sixteen hours before finally giving birth. Jess was by her side the entire time. Jess had called into work to let them know that she was at the hospital with Annette, and she gave them all the good news about the baby. Annette's parents were proud; they were grandparents. They left the hospital an hour after the baby was born and told Annette they would return later in the afternoon. Jess finally reached James, and he was ecstatic. He called Annette and they talked for two hours. They decided together to name the baby Kynosha, a name they'd come up with while Annette was visiting him in Arizona. It was in honor of both their parents.

James graduated from training the following week and flew to Atlanta. When he arrived at Annette's apartment, he couldn't believe his eyes. "She's beautiful, just like her mother. She's perfect, just like you," he said as he stared into Annette's eyes. "Thank you so much for this precious jewel, Baby."

Annette smiled as a tear rolled down her right cheek. She was so happy to see James holding their child and showing her so much appreciation.

"No, thank you for giving me this child. And I thank God for giving me you, James," she said.

James received his first assignment as a second lieutenant. He went to Tampa just as he expected and served as a platoon leader. He had taken three weeks of leave before reporting to his new duty station. He asked Annette about moving their wedding date up by eight months so she could travel with him to Florida, and so that she and the baby could use the medical benefits. Annette was against the idea. She told James that her medical/health insurance provided what she and the baby needed for the time being. She said she didn't want to rush into marriage just because the baby was born.

James spent every day of his leave bonding with his baby daughter. There were times when Annette felt neglected because James was giving the baby more attention than her. However, it was short lived. She knew he was leaving in three weeks and that his daughter wouldn't be with him. Actually, she was glad he was occupying his time with their daughter. She didn't have to deal with the fact that he might want to have some kind of sexual contact. She wasn't ready for that, even if it was just performing oral sex on him.

After James left for Florida, Annette went back to work and her workout routine. She lost eight pounds and was on her way to losing another thirty by Labor Day. Labor Day weekend was the anniversary of Kynosha's conception, and they decided they would celebrate each year by buying something for their daughter.

It had been five months since they'd had sex, and James was more than ready. Annette, on the other hand, didn't feel comfortable enough with her body to have sex. During his visit over the Labor Day weekend, he never saw her naked. Even though Annette was just as horny, she didn't allow herself to engage in sexual intercourse. She did perform oral sex on him, but didn't want him to reciprocate. Although James wanted to please her and make her feel good, he didn't insist because it was what she preferred. They masturbated together, enjoying each other's caresses and kisses. She then asked him to let her watch him make himself come. He obliged.

Christmas 1987

Kynosha was six months old and on her way to Tampa with her mother to spend Christmas with her father. She was beginning to look like her father. According to Annette, she had her father's eyes, nose and cheekbones, but her skin tone, a caramel pecan brown. Annette was up and on the road by six o'clock in the morning on Wednesday, December 23. She'd packed her Honda Accord the night before. She was planning to be in Tampa for ten days. It was a long drive, but she didn't mind; she just wanted to be with James. It took her eight and a half hours to get there.

She made a stop in Tallahassee for about thirty minutes. She'd lost most of the weight with the exception of five pounds. She cut back on her caloric intake, eating baked and boiled chicken and baked fish in small portions and many vegetables. For two weeks, she disciplined herself to eat only 1300 calories a day, cutting out all sweets and bread, and it paid off tremendously for her. She was 150 pounds, able to wear some of her old clothes, and ready to show herself off to James. She didn't have any stretch marks to contend with.

They arrived at approximately 3:00 p.m. The weather was great. It was about 73 degrees and the sun was bright. James had his apartment decorated for Christmas and he stood at the door waiting for her arrival. He had a small tree with lots of presents. As she pulled into the parking lot, he went out to greet her and the baby. He was wearing a pair of Levi jeans and a wife-beater t-shirt with a pair of sneakers. Annette saw him walking towards the car and began salivating because she was so horny. He looked very good. His broad, muscular shoulders and sculpted arms were turning her on. It was obvious that he'd spent some time in the gym himself. He didn't have an ounce of fat on his body.

He approached the car and opened the driver's door, and she stepped out. The car engine was still running. They embraced and kissed very passionately, as if they could have dropped their clothes right there on the spot. Annette pulled her head back and told James the baby was in the car seat. He walked to the passenger side and opened the back car door, reached in and unfastened the seat and picked her up while talking to her. "Hey, Baby. Daddy missed you so much!" He kissed her on both cheeks, then walked back around on the driver's side where Annette stood watching him. *He's so good with her. She's so lucky to have him as a father.*

Annette walked to the back of the car, opened the trunk and pulled out her flowered print suitcase on wheels. She then reached into the back seat to get the baby's diaper bag. James took the suitcase from Annette and, still holding the baby, went into the apartment. Annette was once again impressed with the way he'd decorated his apartment, especially with the Christmas decorations. He told her that he didn't put all the lights on the tree because he wanted her to share in the trimmings. It was their first Christmas together as a family. He wanted it to be special and that meant saving some of the lights for her to put on and the star to top the tree. His spirit captivated Annette. She never realized until that day that the holidays meant so much to him. He had really gotten into the celebration.

He reached for her hand and led her on a tour of his three-bedroom apartment, and it was spectacular, she couldn't believe her eyes. It was decorated pretty much the same as his apartment in Arizona, with the exception of the pictures on the wall. Abstract black and white drawings covered most of the walls. The living room had a huge picture window and the view was of the parking lot, but it was nice. The master bedroom even had a little Christmas decoration. He surprised Annette and had one of the rooms decorated in beautiful pink ornaments for the baby. The full-sized bed was covered with pink and white linen. It was a bedroom fit for a princess, his little princess.

Annette looked around the room. "Think you went a little over board?"

He grinned. "Of course not. This is my little girl, my little princess, and she deserves nothing less than the best."

"Okay. I guess you're right. She is a little darling isn't she?"

During her stay, Annette didn't have to worry about doing anything. He even had the dinner menu and everything that it required. He did ask her if she would help him cook Christmas dinner and bake her famous sweet potato pies.

That evening James cooked dinner for Annette. They had grilled chicken breasts, a baked potato, salad and iced tea. Annette only ate half the potato. For dessert, James had bought a key lime pie from the bakery. They fed the baby as well. After dinner, James held Kynosha until she went to sleep then he put her in her bed. James went into the master bedroom then called out to Annette. "Annette, will you come here for a minute?" She was in the kitchen putting away the dishes and didn't hear him the first time he called. As she was walking back into the dining area, she heard him call out her name. "James, are you calling me?"

"Yes, I did. Will you come here for a minute please?"

"Okay, hold on a second."

She put away all the dishes and went into the bedroom. There she found James lying on the bed buck naked with a hard on. Her clothes dropped to the floor. She was *so* horny. She stood there naked, letting James admire her body, her hard work.

"Damn you look good, Woman!" he said as he lay there slowly massaging and caressing his hard on. "It's been a long time since I've seen you naked Annette. I can't believe how good you look baby. You don't look like you just had a baby six months ago. Damn you look good! Come here and sit on this."

Seductively she asked, "You like what you see, uh?"

Anxiously he said, "You damn right I do. You're fine as hell. You know that; I don't need to tell you."

She walked over to the bed and slipped down on top of James. They made passionate love, letting out screams and moans of ecstasy so loud they woke the baby. They stopped for a minute and she went back to sleep. They made love for the next hour and a half.

Later, when it was time for bed, Kynosha went to sleep and slept through the night. James and Annette made love until dawn. Kynosha was awake at 6:00am, and so were James and Annette. She'd gotten up a couple of times in the middle of the night to check on Kynosha and change her diaper.

On Christmas Eve, James invited a couple of friends over as part of their holiday celebration. He wanted them to meet Annette and their daughter. Their guests arrived at 7:20 p.m.; it was David and Linda, a White couple from Kentucky who was in the Army as well, and Pamela and Russ, a Black couple from San Diego who was in the Air Force. Russ and David were both lieutenants who were about to make captain in the coming months. James had taken care of the snacks, the drinks and the Christmas music.

Christmas Day, Annette got up and made breakfast, eggs, grits bacon, toast, orange juice and coffee. James' sense of smell woke him. He went into Kynosha's room, picked her up, and kissed her on the cheek. "Wake up, Baby. It's Christmas, my little angel. Merry Christmas to you." He walked into the kitchen with Kynosha; she was obviously still sleepy as she let out a big yawn and stretched. He walked over to Annette and kissed her on the cheek. "Merry Christmas, Baby."

"Merry Christmas, James. I love you." She kissed the baby on the cheek. "And I love you."

They had breakfast and finished cooking dinner. Annette had gotten up about 4:00 a.m. and put the small turkey in the oven. It was 9:15 a.m. and she'd prepared most of the food for the oven — the dressing, ham, and the macaroni and cheese. She made a sweet potato pie as well and the greens were partially cooked. Christmas was great. James had gotten all kind of toys for the baby to play with whenever she came to Tampa.

Two days later, Annette and James talked about their wedding plans. They decided the wedding colors would be light mauve and white, and held at their church back in Decatur. Annette wanted to have at least five bridesmaids. James had already invited David and Russ to be in their wedding and they'd accepted the invitation. David would be the best man. Annette's brother Dennis and her sister Cora would also be in the wedding. Jess would be the maid of honor.

After discussing their wedding plans, James started talking about Annette's bi-curiousness while she was looking through his International Male catalog that sat on the night stand. He asked her if she was still interested in having that kind of experience. She told him that she still wanted to try it one day, but had not thought about it in a while. He was glad to hear that. He had made New Year's Eve plans for them to go to a party at one of the local nightclubs that Russ and Pamela had invited them to. She was thrilled that James had put so much effort into making her visit a pleasant one. It was more of a vacation for her than a visit. He'd even made baby-sitting arrangements. David and Linda were going to keep Kynosha on New Year's Eve night because they weren't going anywhere. They were keeping her until noon on New Year's Day.

James took Annette shopping to buy a dress for her to wear on New Year's Eve because she hadn't brought anything to wear. They bought a short little sequined dress that showed lots of leg. Annette had great, shapely legs that looked fabulous in a pair of pumps. James thought so anyway. She picked out a pair of black patent leather pumps and a pair of sparkling, chandelier costume earrings by Monet.

On New Year's Eve, Annette and James spent the day at the apartment with Kynosha, playing with some of her toys. Most of the gifts under the tree were for the baby. James had bought Annette a diamond tennis bracelet and she'd bought him clothes because she liked seeing him dressed in slacks and he didn't buy too many when he shopped.

Later they took Kynosha to Linda and David's house and came back to the house to get dressed. They were walking out the door at 10:15 p.m., on their way to Russ and Pamela's house because they were driving to the club. When they turned into the driveway, Russ came out to move his car so James wouldn't block him in. They went into the house. James was looking sexy in his black tuxedo with a cummerbund.

Russ looked at Annette. "Girl, you look like a million bucks! How did you hook up with him?" They all laughed.

Pamela smiled. "Yes Annette, you do look quite scrumptious."

Annette thanked them. "Well, you all look good enough to eat to me."

"Let's have a drink before we head out," Russ said. "I want to make a toast." He went into the kitchen and got a bottle of Asti Spumante and four champagne glasses. He popped the cork and poured the glasses half-full, then held his glass high in the air. "I'd like to make a toast to the beginning of a lasting friendship." They all chimed in, "To a lasting friendship."

After making the toast, they left for the club. When they got there, Annette noticed all the nice cars in the parking lot; it was obviously a place for the affluent. There were Jaguars, BMW's, and Mercedes Benz. Then a limo pulled up to the front door as they were walking through the parking lot. "I wonder who's getting out of that," she said.

Pamela nudged her. "It could be any celebrity or professional athlete. That's mostly what hangs out here."

Russ said, "That's why we like coming here; you don't have to worry about a lot of riff raff. You have to be invited."

James grinned at him. "Russ, I'm not going to ask you how you got an invitation; I'm just gonna go with the flow."

Russ laughed. "Good, that's best."

They went in and Annette couldn't believe her eyes. The place was immaculate. It had four levels, cages with beautiful women in them everywhere you turned, mirrored walls throughout and the people were all beautiful. Most of the men were tall and muscular. The women were scantily clad in glitzy dresses. Annette almost felt over dressed.

After a few drinks, they danced the night away. After the midnight toast the tone and mood of the club changed and the dancing was slower and sexier. There was more closeness and women began dancing with women. James looked around the club, he and Russ enjoying what they were seeing.

James looked at Annette. "Hey, why don't you and Pamela get on the dance floor?"

"What? Are you serious?"

"Russ encouraged her. Yeah, go ahead. A woman dancing with women is normal in this club. Nobody is going to look at you strange."

Pamela smiled. "Okay, I'm feeling good right now." She reached for Annette's hand. "Come on, Annette; let's go." Annette gave in and accompanied her to the dance floor. They came off the floor an hour later.

While on the dance floor Annette and Pamela got a

little more familiar with each other. They were all ready for a scene change. At 1:30 a.m. the crowd was thinning. Russ and Pamela had a hotel room reservation at the Hilton because they didn't want to drive all the way home. Even though James and Annette were riding with them, they were courteous enough to ask if they wanted to stay with them at the hotel until they all sobered up. James and Annette agreed to stay.

At the hotel suite, there was a bottle of champagne and strawberries waiting. It also had two beds in the bedroom. Before they knew it, Pamela shared with them that she and Russ had talked about them earlier and what it would be like to party with them.

Annette said, "Well, now you know. You just did. We had a great time dancing, Pamela. I know I did anyway."

Pamela laughed. "No, I'm talking about swinging. Russ and I are swingers. I like being with both women and men. Russ likes having sex with other women, and I don't have a problem with it because we're secure in our marriage."

James and Annette looked at each other and smiled. They were speechless. Russ said, "I hope we didn't offend you. We just thought we would share that with you if we were going to be friends. We just thought you should know."

"We're glad you told us," James said. "This is a great way to start the New Year."

"Since we're sharing information, I've had thoughts of being with another woman," Annette said.

Pamela stood, reached for Annette's hand and escorted her into the bedroom to speak with her in private. She began seducing her, pulling Annette close and whispering to her that her legs turned her on. Annette was scared but excited at the same time because she was about to experience something that she'd thought about for a very long time. Pamela laid Annette back on the bed, and slid her dress above her waist. She slowly moved her hands up to Annette's breast, and began massaging and caressing them. Her touch was emotionally satisfying for Annette because she appreciated the gentle warmth of feminine affection. Annette's hands trembled and her body shivered.

Pamela's hands felt like velvet gloves, just as Annette had imagined a woman's touch would feel. That night cemented her newfound status as a bisexual woman. Overcome with emotion, her body began to respond. James and Russ heard moans coming from the bedroom and went to check them out. They found Pamela and Annette enmeshed. Annette had wrapped her legs around Pamela's head and shoulders as she squirmed from the touch of her lips, her mouth, and her tongue. James and Russ stood at the door, their mouths and eyes wide. James watched as Pamela made Annette's body jolt as though she'd been touched with a live wire. Annette had three orgasms.

Annette discovered that the fantasy of sharing her husband with another woman produced a disturbingly powerful thrill. They made passionate love as they watched Russ and Pamela make love while watching them. In the missionary position, passionately kissing, James whispered in her ear, "Did you enjoy the way she licked you?"

Barely able to speak, Annette whispered, "Yes, I did."

Looking over on the other bed at Russ and

Pamela, James whispered in Annette's ear as he penetrated her harder and deeper, but very slowly, "Look at them. Does that look good to you?" Annette turned to look over at Russ and Pamela. She squeezed her legs even tighter around James' waist and said, "Yes . . . Yes it does."

"Does Russ look good to you?" James said, still thrusting gently into her.

"Yes."

"Do you like his body?"

"Yes."

Annette turned her head to the other side, looking away from Russ and Pamela. She was trying to position her head to a more comfortable position. James reached up and turned her head back so she could look at Russ and Pamela, then asked, "You like his big dick?"

"Yes I do."

"You want his big dick in you? You want him to fuck you?"

"If you want me to fuck him, I will."

"Do you want to fuck him?"

Thinking that it was what he wanted she said, "Yes."

After she answered him, James looked at Russ, who was looking at him and Annette, and signaled him to switch partners. Russ whispered to Pamela that James wanted to switch and they did. James got up from the bed. Then Russ got up and walked over to the bed where Annette was laying. James told Annette that he wanted to watch her and Russ, so he sat on the bed with Pamela and they watched. Pamela reached into her purse and gave Russ a Trojan Magnum condom then excused herself to the bathroom to wash up, in anticipation that

James might give her oral pleasure. Russ gave it [the condom] to Annette to put on for him. Nervously fumbling, she managed to tear the pack open and slide it onto Russ' hard penis.

Pamela returned from the bathroom, reached over and began to slowly massage and fondle James' penis as they both watched the couple on the other bed. Russ pulled Annette to the foot of the bed on the edge and inserted his penis. She let out a loud moan. He began to penetrate her slowly, inserting more and more of his large penis as he thrust deeper and deeper. Pamela began to coach Annette through what seemed like a hard task for her. "Just relax, Honey," Pamela encouraged. "He's got a big penis but he's very gentle with it. He won't hurt you — just relax." Annette relaxed and Russ slid all the way in, then grabbed her waist and moved her back and forth on his penis. By now, Pamela was giving James oral pleasure as they continued to watch Annette and Russ. Annette had gotten more relaxed, raised her legs higher, and opened them wider to take more of what Russ had to give her.

He went deep in one thrust and she screamed out as they exploded in ecstasy. Russ, almost in slow motion, fell on top of Annette with his arms stretched out over her head. In the meantime, Pamela was still going at it, trying to make James come. Not even Annette had been able to accomplish that. James helped her, stroking his penis with Pamela still suckling it, until he came. Then he went into the bathroom to clean up. When he returned, he sat on the bed and saw that Pamela was still hot and ready.

She wanted Annette to taste her. Annette tried to explain to her that she'd never done it before, but Pamela insisted. She told her that she would show her what to do.

Pamela coached her on the art of cunnilingus as a surefire way to please a woman. That gave Annette enough self-confidence and stimulation to complete intercourse to her satisfaction as well. She got up off the bed and move to where Pamela was lying. James moved to the lounge chair across from the bed and Russ sat on the other bed, as they watched Annette experience once again, her first time. Annette was still wearing her party dress. It was above her breasts. James told her to take it off, and she did.

Annette began rubbing Pamela's thighs and breasts just as Pamela had done to her. Pamela responded with a moan. Annette moved her body up, pressing gently onto Pamela as she sexily crawled up to her breasts. She kissed both breasts, then worked her way back down her stomach, kissing her with moist pecks. She was actually stalling, trying to avoid going down on Pamela. But when she reached her pelvic area, she had no other choice but to try it. *Okay, let me go ahead and do this. It might be the only chance I'll have. She told me that she'd teach me, so if I don't do it right she'll let me know. I'll just do to her what she did to me.*

Pamela was in for a big surprise. Annette performed oral sex on her as if she was a pro. She even added a few things. She used her tongue more than Pamela did. Pamela had an intense, explosive orgasm. After she came, she pushed Annette's head away. "I don't believe this was your first time Annette."

"I promise you, it's my first. I just did what you did. When you were doing me, I paid close attention to the movement of your tongue, your mouth."

Grinning, Russ said, "You sure looked like you knew what you were doing to me, Annette."

"It doesn't take that much, especially if you're in tune with what's making your partner moan and react to your touch. It's not rocket science, boys." After two hours of sexual frolicking, they were all sexually satisfied, still tipsy and ready for some sleep.

Morning came and they left the hotel, got some breakfast, then went home to Russ and Pamela's house. Annette and James got into their car and drove off. They never discussed anything that had happened the night before. They stopped to pick up Kynosha a little early and went home.

It had been a month since Annette and Kynosha's visit to Tampa. Driving back, all Annette could think about was how Pamela had made her come so many times and that she'd not come once with James while having oral sex. This bothered her quite a bit because she came so quickly, almost spontaneously. It also bothered James. He asked her on Saturday morning after New Year's Day, if she enjoyed what Pamela had done to her. In an attempt to spare hurting his feelings, she told him that she had lied about coming three times. James told her he didn't believe that she'd come three times anyway because she'd never come like that with him.

Annette told Jess about their New Year's Eve soiree and she couldn't believe that Annette had finally satisfied her curiosity. Jess told her she didn't have to go all the way to Tampa to do that; she could have had sex with a woman in Atlanta because they had the same type of clubs. Of course, Annette told her that wasn't her reason for going to Tampa and that it had all just happened. Everybody was in the mood and it just happened. Annette also said that if she had it to do all over again, she would do it in a heartbeat. She'd never come like that before and the feeling was unforgettable.

1988

Two weeks before Annette's wedding, she put the final touches on her dinner menu. She was back to her normal size 8, weighing 146 pounds. She'd worked very hard to reach her desired weight before getting married. She and Jess picked up her dress from the boutique so she could try it on. Annette wanted to make sure she had a little room to spare just in case she gained a pound or two before the wedding. Before she made it completely out of the dressing room, Jess shouted, "Oh my God, Annette! You are so beautiful. You're going to be a beautiful bride! Your dress fits perfect!"

Annette walked over to the mirror and was overcome with emotion. "I can't believe it. I'm getting married!" She wiped the tears and spun around to get a complete look at the dress. She said, "I do look beautiful, don't I?"

The wedding was beautiful, the church decorated with pink and white roses. The five bridesmaids wore mauve gowns and held pink roses. The maid of honor wore a mauve and cream gown that came off the shoulders. The groomsmen wore white tuxedos and shoes, with mauve cummerbunds and pocket squares. The flower girl wore a cream-colored dress, and the ring bearer wore a white tuxedo. When Annette came down the aisle, everyone stood to welcome her. James didn't take his eyes off her as she walked in to "You Are So Beautiful."

After the wedding, they left for their honeymoon in the Bahamas. Kynosha stayed with her grandparents.

In his final week of leave, James helped Annette pack her things to move to Tampa and took her and Kynosha to a base in Atlanta to get their military identification card. Annette resigned from her position as a social worker one week before her wedding and already had interviews lined up in Tampa. Within one week of being there, she went on three interviews. It didn't take her long to find a job. She accepted a job as a social worker in the psychiatric department at the base hospital. They found a very good baby sitter for Kynosha, who was now two weeks shy of her first birthday.

On Saturday, June 11, 1988, they gave Kynosha her first birthday party. Her birthday was on Wednesday but they couldn't take off work. They invited a couple of the children from the baby sitter.

Two years after James had moved to Tampa, he

made first lieutenant. Annette grew accustomed to living in Florida and the military lifestyle. She liked her job as well. She was a dutiful, perfect officer wife. She went to all the social gatherings sponsored by the officer's wives group, baked brownies and cookies for the bake sales their group sponsored, and smiled and mingled at all the formal parties and ceremonies that James was required to attend. She even flirted a few times with the colonel, thinking it might help get James promoted to captain. She enrolled Kynosha in a latchkey kind of program for toddlers. But she would soon get tired of being the perfect wife. She went to the beach most weekends. Kynosha loved the water. Annette made many new friends, but maintained her close friendship with Jess, who came to visit her several times over the summer.

She expressed her frustration to James about being the perfect "officer wife." To make her feel better, he arranged for a sitter, then took her out to dinner.

After they had sex, James asked Annette about getting into the swinging lifestyle. He told her that he'd done some research and thought it was worth a shot. They could at least explore it to see if it were something they would be interested in. Annette was surprised because they hadn't spoken about that since New Year's Eve with Russ and Pamela. The conversation brought back memories that she'd put on the back burner. She agreed to try the swinging lifestyle.

She asked, "Honey, whatever happened to that photo you took when you were in Arizona? I never did find it."

"I have no idea. That's been over two and a half years ago Annette. Why are you asking about *that*?"

"Since we were talking about swinging, I just

thought about it."

"Oh, okay. I don't know where it is."

"All right." She remained bothered by the missing photo, but managed to keep her concern hidden from James. "So how do we approach this swinging thing, James?"

"Let's get a couple of magazines and look through them.

"Okay. Why don't we do that now? We'll pick them up before we get Kynosha," Annette said, excitement in her tone.

They went into an adult video store and began browsing, looking at the different dildos, vibrators, penis rings, anal plugs, underwear, and all the other weird things that hung from the walls. The swinger magazines were kept behind the counter so you had to ask for them. James sent Annette to the counter to get the magazines because he was embarrassed. He waited for her near the dildos. When she returned, he pulled a huge dildo from the wall and showed it to her. He put it down where his penis was, pointed it at Annette and told her to bend over. They both laughed.

When she looked down, she noticed he had a bulge in his pants. She touched it to be certain. He was hard as a brick. He asked her if she wanted to sit on it, as he rubbed it against her butt. She got horny from looking at the dildos, vibrators and his hard dick rubbing on her. They went to the counter and asked the sales clerk if they had an empty room, but they didn't. It was dark when they left the store, so they had sex in the parking lot with her bent over on the hood of his Acura Legend.

When they returned home, Annette put Kynosha to bed. She and James got into bed after taking a shower.

James picked up the magazine lying on the dresser and brought it to bed. As they were looking through it, they saw a picture of a very attractive Black woman who lived in their area. Her ad read *SBF looking for couple or BiF for fun, movies, and going to the beach. Will call if interested.*

Annette called the number and left a message for her ad code with the ad message center. The woman called back the next day and they met for drinks at a bar. James and Annette found Wanda very attractive and sexy. They wanted to take her home, but she wasn't ready for that. She was 5'7", light brown and had a short crop cut with a Jheri Curl. She was an Air Force captain and had been in the area for three years. She told them that she'd just gotten out of a relationship four months ago, with a married woman who was a major in the Army. They had been seeing each other for the past year and a half. She told them it went bad when the woman's husband, who was also a major in the Army, found photographs in a shoe box in her closet of the two of them having sex. He threatened to expose her and have her put out of the military if she didn't break it off, so she did.

Annette and James had become fond of Wanda. They spent a lot of time together at the movies, and the beach. Wanda liked them a lot as well, especially Kynosha, and Kynosha liked Aunt Wanda. They built a relationship that would last for a very long time.

Annette and Wanda spent a lot of time together, more so than the three of them did, but James didn't mind. One afternoon James came home for lunch and found Annette and Wanda on their lunch break, having sex. Wanda had brought over her strap-on dildo and was fucking Annette just as hard and good as a man would.

James stood in the door watching as he masturbated. He didn't say anything. When Annette came, James walked over to the bed and finished her off with oral pleasure. Wanda got dressed. She didn't allow a man to touch or penetrate her. She hadn't been with a man in 20 years. She was a full-blown lesbian and comfortable with who she was. They got dressed and Annette made sandwiches for lunch.

1990

James received orders for Atlanta and Wanda transferred to Wrightstown, New Jersey four months prior. Annette contacted her old job and they re-hired her. Annette was thrilled that she was going home.

Kynosha turned three on June 8, 1990, and talk of a possible war in Iraq had already begun. The military immediately implemented a Stop Loss policy, prohibiting all reassignments, retirements and discharges. Troops deployed to Iraq for the beginning of Desert Shield. Soldiers could leave the military on a case-by-case basis. James informed Annette that he might have to go to Iraq. She was scared. The thought of him going anywhere to fight in a war was something she'd never imagined. As far as she was concerned, James went into the Army for the financial and medical rewards so he could take care of his family. Fighting a war was an after-thought. However, it had become a reality and Annette had difficulty dealing with it. She and Kynosha took a 2-day vacation and went home to Decatur. Upon her return, James told her that he wouldn't deploy but would have to work long hours to support the unit. That meant early mornings and late nights. Annette had no problem with that. As long as he came home at night she didn't care what time he came in.

Desert Storm began in January of 1991. Some nights James didn't come home until 11:00 p.m., and had to get up the next day at 4:00 a.m. It was taking its toll on him. He and Wanda worked seven days a week. Wanda called Kynosha and Annette all the time to make sure they were doing okay. Friday was family night, but since the war had begun, Fridays were just Annette and Kynosha. She was three years old and her dad wasn't spending any time with her.

Annette even spent their wedding anniversary and Kynosha's third and fourth birthdays without James. When he went to work, she was asleep and when he came home, she was asleep. Annette could see the sadness in her daughter's eyes because she missed her daddy. James called and talked to her everyday before dinner, but that wasn't enough, nor was it enough for Annette. Annette wanted him home.

The war lasted 100 days, through the second week of May. Then Desert Shield went on for the next 4-6 months. James came home more frequently after the war was over, but he still missed Kynosha's fourth birthday because troops were returning from Iraq.

As a token of his love and appreciation for enduring the long, lonely nights without him, James took Annette and Kynosha to Washington, D.C. for the Labor Day weekend. Their reservations were at the same hotel, the

Marriott in the heart of the city. To Annette's surprise, Wanda was there waiting at the suite. James had invited her to join them. Annette was so happy. She'd missed Wanda and so had Kynosha. Moreover, Wanda had missed them. James spent time with Kynosha, giving Annette and Wanda time together. Wanda became Annette's weekend play toy. They went to the movies, dinner and shopping. It didn't matter where the military took them in their travels; they stayed in touch and visited one another.

James and Annette returned to Atlanta rejuvenated. They'd grown closer on their trip. They decided to explore the world of swinging once again. Annette wasn't sure how she would handle seeing James with another woman, but thought it was only fair to the relationship that he get the opportunity to play around too. They were now accessing the Internet to find partners. A plethora of websites had people looking for people for sex. They also visited chatrooms. They met an attractive Caucasian couple for drinks at a local hotel in Perimeter/Dunwiddie area. After getting to know each other, they learned the man was bisexual, and that turned Annette off because she wanted a straight man. They hadn't mentioned that on their profile. The man wanted James, but he sat quietly and let Annette do all the talking. They told the couple nicely they were not interested, then left the hotel. That night, however, James wanted to explore their sexual activities a little more. While giving Annette oral pleasure, he inserted a finger in her ass. She immediately tightened her muscles and said, "No. What are you doing, Baby? I'm not ready for that."

"I'm only putting in one finger," he said.

She resisted and told him to remove it, and that

spoiled the mood for the moment. He continued to give her oral pleasure. She began thinking about her first time with Pamela and how she'd made her feel. She came. When he finished she turned around in the 69 position with her body off to the side of his face because her clitoris was sensitive and she didn't want him to touch it. She began giving him oral pleasure. He told her to 'lick his balls.'

It was difficult for her to do it the way he wanted her to because of the position she was in, so she turned around and went down on him. He whispered, "Put your tongue in my ass." She pretended that she didn't hear him. He said it again, "Oh Baby, that feels good. Put your wet tongue in my ass."

She ignored him again, but she put her index finger in her mouth to wet it, then inserted the tip. He moaned, but told her to take it out because it was uncomfortable. He said he'd have to train his ass for her to put her fingers in it. She got up and sat on his hard penis and rode it until he came. Annette thought it strange that James wanted her to put her tongue in his ass, but she remembered what it felt like to her when he did it, so she guessed he wanted that same sensation.

James and Annette began working out at the gym together. They met most evenings at 6:00 p.m. One evening after their workout, Annette told James about a man she'd seen at the gym who looked good to her. She told him that he looked like he was packing, meaning he looked like he had a big dick. He told her to describe him. He wanted to know what he was wearing to see if he'd seen the same man, but he hadn't. That same evening after putting Kynosha to bed, they made love in the missionary position. It was James' favorite position because it allowed closeness when they talked dirty during sex.

James asked her again about the man at the gym. "Did you like what you saw at the gym today, since you said he was packing?"

'Yes, I did. He looked very good to me."

"Why didn't you say something to him?"

"Like what? He was wearing a wedding band."

"Oh. But you liked what you saw though, right?"

"Yes," she said.

His moans were louder. He penetrated her deeper and harder, and suddenly shouted, "Oh shit! I'm coming." He flopped on her and they fell asleep and woke up around 11:15 p.m. to the telephone. It was Wanda calling to see how they were doing because they hadn't spoken in three days. While Annette was on the phone with Wanda, James began giving her oral pleasure. Wanda heard her moaning and told her she'd talk to her later.

They got up the next morning and took Kynosha to visit her grandparents in Decatur. She stayed with them on alternating weekends. When Annette and James returned to Atlanta, they picked up lunch and made a stop at the adult toy store. James wanted her to pick out a new strap on dildo for her to play with whenever Wanda came to visit. They went into the store and James asked, "Did you like my tongue and fingertip in your ass?"

She turned to face him. "Your tongue felt good, but I'll have to practice loosening it up before you do the finger again."

They walked over to the wall to look at the myriad of 'butt plugs.' James said with a chuckle, "Here you go." He handed her a small and large butt plug. "Here's something that will train your ass to take this dick."

She laughed. "What is this?" She looked more closely. "A plug for your butt? What am I supposed to do with this?"

"According to the back, it helps you learn to relax your ass muscles."

"I never said I wanted to have anal sex, did I?"

"No, but you never said you didn't either." They both laughed.

"You're right. I didn't. We can try it and if I don't like the plug, or if it doesn't work, then you're shit out of luck, James."

They moved to the dildos and Annette picked out a brown leather harnessed dildo that cost about $82. She was reluctant to pay that much but thought the fun she would have with it would be worth the money. They bought the strap-on dildo, two butt plugs, and a bottle of massage lotion. When they got home, they tore open the packages and sanitized the dildos and butt plugs, then put them away.

For Columbus Day, they received an invitation to dinner at the colonel's house. They had to be there by 8:00 p.m. They were celebrating Columbus Day on Saturday. Annette never understood why James and all the other officers couldn't be five minutes late going to the colonel's house. James would fuss at her and accuse her of purposely making him late, even when it was his fault.

Annette didn't like going to social events at the colonel's house because some of the wives were snooty and stuck up, but she went to support James. She didn't like being around all the sucking up all the junior officers and their wives were doing. And she loved Kynosha, but she got tired of hearing the other officers' wives talk about their kids all the time. That included James. He was doing it because everybody else was doing it. She knew he didn't care to participate in those social events. He did it because it was the right thing to do. He knew that if he was going to make colonel, he needed to hobnob and get to know the other officers.

When they left the colonel's house, they wanted to go party. Kynosha was at her grandparents' house, so they went home to change clothes. Annette wore a black dress that accentuated her curves. They went dancing at one of the well-known clubs in the city. They decided they'd role-play with her sitting at the bar as though she was alone. He would sit at a table and watch her. They role played this scene quite a bit when they went out dancing. James got a beer, then sat and watched the men approach Annette. He saw her flirt with over twelve men, and turn away over twenty. She had at least three drinks waiting for her and she turned down several others.

Then she met a rambunctious man named Phillip, who radiated an electric, masculine energy that galvanized her very being. Their acquaintance swiftly developed into a passionate arousal like she'd never felt before. They danced around their intense attraction for each other, both trying hard not to expose their sexual fascination. She didn't let either him or James know that her strong, spontaneous responses to his well-defined physique were an ineradicable part of her consciousness. She excused herself, walked over to James' table, and told him how much the guy had turned her on. He encouraged her to seduce him to see if he would go home with her, and she did. They played this game at least once a week. Sometimes Annette wasn't in the mood, but would go along just to make James happy because it was what he wanted to do. When she was certain the man would go home with her, she got his number to call him later.

When they got home, she made a rum and Coke, then jumped in the shower to freshen up to get rid of the cigarette smoke scent. She was wearing a pair of see-through silk pink lounging pajamas, with a pair of white thong panties. Under James' direction, she called the man from the club and invited him over. He accepted the invitation and came over. Unbeknownst to him, James would be hiding in the bedroom closet watching. Annette was a bit of an exhibitionist and voyeur.

James orchestrated every scene. In order for him to do that without being seen, he told her to bring the man into the bedroom and let him fuck her from behind, in the doggie-style position. He didn't want Annette to use a condom when the man came. He told her to let him come inside her. He wanted her to give him a side view from where he was in the closet. He wanted to see everything, and that included her facial expressions. Many times, James encouraged Annette to go to the club and 'make some dicks hard.' Whenever she returned home from her night out on the town, they had sex. He liked asking her if she'd made any dicks hard and whether they were big and whether they felt good to her.

During sex, it seemed the only way he would have an explosive orgasm was to bring someone else into the bedroom. Whether it was physically or mentally, there was always someone else there. If they were not he came in less than ten minutes, and otherwise he would go for at least forty-five minutes before reaching an orgasm.

There was a knock at the door and Annette yelled out "Who is it?"

A deep voice replied, "It's Phillip, the man from the

club."

Putting the final touches on her make up then spraying on a little perfume, she yelled, "I'll be right there."

As the young man stood patiently waiting for her to open the door, she got final instructions from James on what to do next. She answered the door and, to her surprise, Phillip was very handsome. He looked a lot different than he did under the club lights. He stood 6'5"; his skin tone was a dark chocolate. His teeth looked like he wore veneers. They were white and even. He had a receding hairline with a close cut, almost bald. He wore a big diamond stud in his left ear and was dressed to the nines.

They went over and sat on the sofa, and Annette offered him something to drink. He asked if she had Jack Daniel Black, and she did. She made him a Jack and Coke. After about thirty minutes of conversation, Annette got to the point. "You know why I wanted you to come over here, don't you?"

"Yes, I think so, but you can tell me if you would like. I don't want to seem too audacious."

"Oh, you're not," she said in a seductive tone. "I think you're extremely handsome, Phillip, and when I see something I want, I go after it. Thanks for playing along."

"You're welcome. It's my pleasure."

"Yes, it will be and mine as well."

Phillip was a criminal law attorney. Annette didn't care if he was married or not. She wanted him just for the sex. She reached for Phillip's hand and escorted him into the bedroom. She sat on the bed, then summoned Phillip to come to her and they began to kiss, but she didn't kiss him on his mouth. She and James had agreed that kissing was too intimate. Soon the clothes started coming off.

Phillip stood up to unbutton his belt buckle, then pants.

She slowly unzipped his pants as she looked up at him. "Are you sure you want me to do this?"

He was breathing hard. "Oh yes, Baby. I want you to."

She glanced at the closet and could see James stroking his dick as he watched her play. Phillip's pants dropped to the floor. His penis was ready. Annette commenced giving him oral pleasure as she glanced at James. Afterward, Phillip pushed her back and gave her oral pleasure. She moved her hips in a circular motion until she screamed, "Oh shit!" She murmured, "I want you to fuck me from behind." He flipped her over onto her stomach and she reached for the night stand to get a condom. She put it on and guided him into her. With Phillip banging her, she watched James as he masturbated in the closet. Phillip's moans got louder. She told him to take off the condom because she wanted to feel him.

He withdrew and took off the condom, then put it back in and three minutes later he screamed, "I'm coming!" She reached back to pull it out. He came in her and on her as she tried to pull it out. She showed him the bathroom in the hallway. Annette turned to look at James. She whispered, "Did you come yet?"

James nodded.

Phillip returned to the bedroom and got dressed, and Annette escorted him to the door, naked, and then went into the bathroom to clean up. When she returned to the bedroom, James was lying on the bed and told her to come and sit on his face and let him taste her. When she did, he got hard and wanted to fuck her. After he was inside her, he asked her if she'd enjoyed fucking Phillip and she told him she'd enjoyed it a lot. He said, "He had an average size dick, not as big as you're use to. Did it fill you up?"

She smiled. "It got the job done."

The next morning James brought Annette breakfast in bed as his way of showing his appreciation for her playing along with his game. After breakfast, they got dressed and went to pick up Kynosha from Decatur. They spent the day in Decatur and had dinner at her mother's house.

When they returned home that evening, Annette was watching the local news. The phone rang and it was Jess. She told Annette that she was unhappy with Brian since he'd finished med school. Jess and Brian had been married in June in a beautiful, fairy tale wedding. Annette was Jess' maid of honor. Now Jess wondered whether she'd made a mistake by marrying Brian. She expressed to Annette that they were having problems before they'd gotten married and that the problems seemed to have escalated. Annette and Jess set a date for dinner on Monday after work so they could talk.

After Annette got off the phone with Jess, she sat on the sofa thinking about Wanda and Pamela. She compared their techniques for making her come and chose Pamela as the standard. James walked into the living room where Annette was and turned on the television to watch the news. James turned to MSNBC and they were discussing Presidential Candidate Bill Clinton and his stance on gays in the military — the "don't ask, don't tell" policy that allowed homosexuals to serve in the military if they kept their sexual orientation secret and refrained from homosexual conduct. The military prohibits asking questions about the sexual orientation of a service member. There are restrictions placed on commanders who attempt to investigate any service member that might be homosexual.

Annette decided to engage James in conversation to see what his views were about homosexual acts and gays in the military, because for all practical purposes, it seemed that it was rampant among women. "James, we have a playmate who's an active lesbian and she's also an officer in the Air Force. I've met numerous females who are serving in the military who are bisexual. How does the military carry out this 'don't ask, don't tell' policy? Actually, what is it? Where did it come from and what does it mean?"

"During Clinton's campaign, the issue came up. I believe he said it wasn't a terrible idea because homosexuals are Americans just like everyone else serving this country. Once he was elected president, he chose Colin Powell as the head of the Joint Chiefs of Staff. General Powell was the one who actually wrote the policy. Then Congress approved it."

Annette said, "I remember in an earlier conversation we had about this issue, you were distinguishing between homosexual acts and what a person can be put out of the military for?"

"Oh, okay. You can be homosexual, if you are in the military," he said.

"Okay," Annette said.

"However, you cannot perform homosexual *acts* while you're in the military."

"So, you cannot be a *practicing* homosexual?"

"Right," he replied. "You can go to gay clubs, you can buy gay magazines. You can march in gay pride parades. You can do everything that you want to do as an individual citizen, except practice homosexual acts. Hypothetically speaking, if you go into my room in the barracks and look under my mattress and find a stack of gay pride magazines, that isn't enough to put me out of the Army. And if you see me on the local news at a gay pride parade, that's not enough to put me out of the Army. I can go in the commander's office and say 'Sir, I'm a homosexual,' and even that's not enough to put me out of the Army. You have to actually be doing homosexual stuff to be put out of the military."

With a confused look, Annette asked, "That isn't homosexual stuff"?

"No. Actual homosexual acts — sexual intercourse, fellatio, and sodomy — are considered homosexual acts."

"According to the military?"

"Yes."

"Okay."

"There's a big distinction, because if you get put out of the Army for homosexuality, it's called a Chapter 15. And if you get out on a Chapter 15, you'll get full benefits and an honorable discharge as well."

"Hmmm."

"And with that being said, a lot of people, when this thing first came out, were saying 'I'll just say I'm gay and I can get out in the morning and still get all my benefits. Then I can get married next week if I want to.'"

"So people could just do that? Go in and say they were gay just to get out of the military?"

"That's what they used to do when it first hit, before all this 'don't ask, don't tell' first started."

"So the purpose of the 'don't ask, don't tell' policy sounds like it's still the same thing. If you're found out, then you can still get put out," she said.

"Yes, but there's not a witch hunt trying to find you out. Your own sexual orientation and your own sexual practice is nobody's business but yours. That's why I cannot ask another soldier if he or she is homosexual, and they aren't suppose to tell me."

"So your supervisors or superiors can't ask you about your sexual orientation?"

He sat up on the sofa and said, "I tell you what Annette, if I as a platoon leader asked a soldier if he or she is gay, all hell would break loose."

Surprised, she said, "Really?"

"Yes. All hell would break loose."

"Why is that?"

"Because again, back to 'don't ask' — trying to protect their own individual rights; protect their freedom; trying to protect their privacy. It's none of my business at all. If Joe comes to work and does his job everyday, what his sexual orientation is, is not my business."

"So if a senior enlisted person or officer asks a soldier 'Are you gay?' that's against policy?"

"Yes. That's the 'don't ask' portion of it. Back in the day, one of the questions they had to ask you was 'Are you a homosexual?'"

"Right, right," she acknowledged.

"Recruiters can't ask you that either now."

"So 'don't ask, don't tell.' I understand the 'don't ask' part, but the 'don't tell' part means don't voluntarily reveal that information?"

"Yes. You're not supposed to flaunt your homosexuality or sexual orientation. Again, just because you go to a gay club doesn't say you're gay. You could've ended up in a gay club for a lot of different reasons."

"I see."

"And we will get annual training on it each year. It's called the *Homosexual Policy*."

"You mean the whole military?"

"Yes," he replied.

"Not just officers and senior enlisted?"

"No. That's military across the board, enlisted and officers. It goes from the lowest rank to the highest. One of the regulations, 350-1, covers what the mandatory training is, and the Homosexual Policy is one of them."

"When will it be implemented?"

"When the 'don't ask, don't tell' policy is approved. We have what's called *chain teaching*. The officers are trained from their higher ups. Like three stars would have to be trained by four stars. In addition, two stars would have to be trained by three stars and it goes all the way down the chain. It will go throughout the ranks. Moreover, of course, it will only be as strong as that leader's implementation. Some might say, 'Yeah, that's what the regulation might say, but don't let me catch your ass.' But if someone told on him that he made that kind of comment, he would be in trouble. The Army takes this very seriously."

"What about the other branches?"

"I don't know how seriously they take it. However, I swear to God, if I'm sitting in my office right now, and the first sergeant or some lieutenant walked into my office and said, 'I think Johnson is gay,' I wouldn't touch it. In addition, I would advise the first sergeant and the lieutenant not to touch it. I would call the judge advocate general, the JAG, and explain what transpired and ask for legal guidance. The soldier could be sucking as many dicks as he wants to, but if I approached it the wrong way or found out the wrong way, then my ass is out. Again, the

Army is very serious about this."

"Now, is the military just as hard on the women as they are on the men?"

"No, not really. I've seen women put out of the military and have heard of some being put out, but not like men have been. There's no doubt in my mind, if leaders know Bob and Jim are in the barracks doing something, eventually they're going to get caught or found out some way. But if Sally and Jane are doing the same thing, you'll damn near have to hit the commander in the face to make him do something about it."

"What if a soldier is carrying herself like a man?"

"You mean butchie?"

"Yes, with the short cut and —"

"I've known my share of soldiers like that, both junior and senior, and I don't know if this is a compensation issue or not, but those that I have known like that, are damn good soldiers. You know what I mean?"

"Yes."

"It could be I'm compensating. Like if the shit hit the fan, I need to be a good soldier but at the same time, I can't be fucking with Johnson because I need her ass in the motor pool.'"

"But wouldn't their physical appearance make people look at them? They say sometimes you can look at a man and tell he's gay if his gestures are over exaggerated. So if a woman is trying to look like a man, wouldn't it make you look more closely at that particular woman? You know what I mean?"

"Back in Arizona there were at least four women who looked just like boys and there was no doubt that they were stereotypical lesbians. But I couldn't say anything to them. There are some homophobes who might want to go after those kinds of soldiers, but they're asking for trouble if they do."

"I see. I wonder what Wanda thinks about this policy. She's a full-fledged lesbian serving her country. Maybe one day I'll ask her."

"You should, just to see her side since she's in the Air Force."

"Well, I'm going take a shower. Would you like to join me?"

"No, I'm gonna tuck Kynosha in for the night."

"Okay, Baby." Annette exited the living room. By the time James came into the room, she was already asleep.

Christmas 1991

Three weeks before Christmas, on one of the coldest days of the winter, Annette was out with Jess, shopping for presents. James had stayed home to start the tree decorations. He and Kynosha, who was now four going on sixteen, had almost finished the tree by the time Annette returned home. She left the bags in the car, not wanting James or Kynosha to see the gifts she'd bought for them. Kynosha would always grab the bags whenever

Annette or James walked in the house. James and Kynosha were relaxing on the sofa watching cartoons. James got up and handed Annette the star to top the tree. This had become a tradition for their family.

Just as they had for Thanksgiving, Annette and James were staying home for Christmas and New Year's Eve. They decided to visit Annette's parents the day after Christmas. For them, this was the year to get use to spending the holidays at their home with family and friends. For as long as Annette could remember, she'd spent the holidays at her parents' house. Breaking the tradition had her a little dismal on Christmas day, but she quickly got over it when she opened the gift James had gotten her. He'd bought her a collection of perfumes — Opium, Giorgio, Nina Ricci, Halston, Oscar De La Renta, Poison, and Passions. He knew she loved perfumes and remembered seeing her one day when they were in the mall, spraying on several testers she liked.

On Christmas afternoon, Jess and Brian came over for dinner. Wanda flew in on Christmas Eve to spend Christmas and New Year's Eve with Annette and James. Christmas was great. Kynosha played with her toys all day. She was in bed by 9:00 p.m. Jess and Brian left about 1:00 a.m. Wanda fell asleep on the sofa and James and Annette went to bed. They were all tired from a very long day.

James woke up around 4:30 a.m. to running water in the shower; Annette and Wanda were bathing each other. Annette thought James would get upset, but he didn't. He went back to bed. When he finally got out of bed later that morning, he told her that he didn't have a problem with what she'd done because he knew she'd not been with a woman since Labor Day. They all had breakfast then went to her parents' house for leftovers.

New Year's Eve was quiet. Annette and James spent the evening ringing in the New Year with Wanda and Kynosha. Kynosha fell asleep two hours before midnight, but the adults were awake until 5:00 a.m. They brought the New Year in having sex. Annette got a chance to use the strap on dildo she'd bought. She used it on Wanda and Wanda used it on her as James watched. He had begun to feel left out because they were having so much fun without him. He tried several times to intervene, but Annette made him sit back and watch.

Eventually he got tired of watching and left the room. They didn't notice he was gone until they finished. Annette looked in the bedroom and found him lying on the bed masturbating. His penis glistened with baby oil. She asked him to come back into the living room, but he decided to masturbate until he came. Annette walked over and sat on the bed to assist him, and saw that the anal butt plug they'd bought for her to practice with sitting on the night stand on top of the International Male catalog he'd received in the mail. When she questioned him about it, he told her that he was hoping she'd come in and let him put it in her to begin her training. Feeling guilty for not letting him join them, she let him insert it. It was uncomfortable at first, but after putting more baby oil on it and relaxing more, she was able to take it all in. Seeing the plug in Annette's butt was a big turn on for him. As he stroked her with the plug, he masturbated himself until he came, within a matter of minutes. Wanda had gone to bed.

By noon on New Year's Day, James was exhausted because he'd not gotten any sleep. Wanda's flight was leaving at 5:15 p.m., and Annette decided to take her to the airport since James was asleep. She took Kynosha with her so she could say goodbye as well. On the way, they made plans for Annette to come to New Jersey when the weather changed. Wanda wanted to take her to Atlantic City, a place that Annette had talked about seeing one day.

When they arrived back home, James was lying in bed. Annette walked in and she saw him with the butt plug once again. She asked him about it and he told her that he was training his ass for her. He told her that he wanted her to fuck him like she'd fucked Wanda.

Annette was astonished, speechless. She walked out of the room, gave Kynosha some of her toys to play with to keep her occupied, then went back into the bedroom and confronted James on his fantasy. She asked him if he'd ever been with a man, besides the incidents he'd told her about when he was a child, and he told her he'd not. He told her that if he was going to experience it, he wanted it to be with her. He wanted her to do it.

She loved James enough to try many things with him, but she wasn't sure whether she could honor that particular request. For the first time, she understood why some men might feel intimidation when their woman wanted to use a vibrator or dildo. Then she thought about it. "Well, I guess I would feel better knowing that I'm the one whose giving you that kind of thrill as opposed to another man doing it. What the hell, we can try it. But if I don't like it, James, I'm going to stop."

"That's fine. It's just that when you insert your finger it feels damn good, and I want to know what it feels like to have one in me. That's all." Annette asked if he were bisexual and he vehemently denied that he was.

She believed him, especially since he wanted *her* to be the one to give him that experience.

Then again, she wondered whether he would like it enough to want to experience the real thing. She didn't know what to do. She wanted to honor his fantasy in hopes that it would keep him from going outside of their marriage, but she wondered if he would enjoy it enough to stray. It was a double-edged sword. *This is a helluva way to start the year. Last year I experienced my first homosexual encounter and this year, my husband wants me to fuck him in the ass with a plastic dildo. Damn! What's a girl to do?*

Wrapped in confusion, she had no one she could tell. This was extremely frustrating for her because she took pride in being able to talk about any and every thing. However, this time she was too embarrassed to tell even her closest friend, Jess. She was afraid that Jess might think that James was bisexual or gay. Annette believed that James couldn't possibly be gay because he loved women. But she hoped he wasn't bisexual either, having a desire to be with men. She put her thoughts in the back of her mind and went on with her life as usual.

Annette became withdrawn. Jess noticed that she didn't call her as much as she used to. In addition, at work, she had lunch by herself. When Jess questioned Annette, she insisted nothing was wrong, and said she just needed some time to put things in perspective. Jess gave her the space and time she needed. Two weeks later, she was back to her old self. She was talking more and they had lunch together like they used to do.

Over that two-week period, Annette found herself struggling with her husband's odd request. She began to act out, even calling on Phillip, the man she'd met at the club. They hadn't spoken since that night, but when she called, he remembered her. She made plans to meet with him after work. They met for dinner at a local restaurant. She told James that she would be working late and he needed to pick up Kynosha from the sitter.

At the time, she didn't realize that having an affair with Phillip would compound her current issues. She didn't care. All she knew was that she wanted to have sex with Phillip. After dinner, they went to his home. He escorted her into the bedroom and undressed her, whispering in her ear, "This time you can let yourself go without worrying about your man watching us from the closet. He's not here."

She didn't say anything. She was shocked and embarrassed. She had no idea Phillip had seen James hiding in the closet. The sex was better than it was the first time. She let go and allowed her sexual prowess to unfold. She screamed several times in ecstasy. Later, she went home as if nothing had happened. She was relieved that James was tired and didn't want to have sex. As they lay in bed, she thought about how good the sex was with Phillip. *I guess it's true what they say about sex being better when you're sneaking it. It has a kind of euphoria that's like none other I've experienced.* She vowed never to contact Phillip again.

On the third Saturday in April, Annette hosted a cookout for the women, a girls' evening out. James and Kynosha had gone to Decatur for the weekend. She invited Tonya, whom she'd met at the gym, and Patrice and Jess. She and Tonya had become close over the last four months and worked out together every once in awhile. Tonya was a sergeant first class in the Army. She'd told Annette early in their friendship that she thought she was bisexual. She disclosed that to her because she felt that Annette would understand her. Patrice, an attractive blonde-haired woman, was the wife of an Army captain. She and Annette clicked right off the bat. She was also a closeted bicurious bi-sexual. They'd met at an officer's wife support group meeting. What was supposed to be an evening of playing board games and conversation ended up being an evening of girl sex.

As they sat in the living room drinking wine and talking about men and children, a conversation ensued about religion, bisexuality, and homosexuality. Annette described religion as a belief in God and a system of worship. She explained that when she was growing up, homosexuals were seen as outcasts and were not accepted by religion and the church.

Jess said, "I think the homosexual acts described in the Bible are very different from what we know it to be today."

Patrice said, "I despise people who say that the only way to live is the heterosexual way. Says who? If people knew what went on behind the closed doors of a lot of people in this country, even their neighbors, they might have a different opinion."

"She's right," Tonya said. "Just look at us — look at me. I consider myself bisexual. I serve my country, I'm a born again Christian and I go to church most Sundays. I drink occasionally and I don't smoke. I've voted every year since I turned eighteen. I believe God loves me regardless of what my sexual orientation is. I've been blessed knowing I couldn't have come from anywhere else but Him."

Annette said, "I don't see why the physical sexual act has to be the decisive factor to determine whether or not someone is moral."

"I agree, Annette," Jess said. "When two people express affection and gain pleasure from doing so, that doesn't make it sinful just because it's homosexual. The same criterion should apply whether the relationship is heterosexual or homosexual. With commitment, openness to responsibility and genuine love, God isn't shut out. God can enter any relationship where there is a measure of selfless love."

Tonya spoke up. "Well, all I can say is, any passage in the Bible can be challenged, including those that condemn homosexual acts. On that note, I'm tired of talking about this. It's depressing me."

The conversation about religion ended and Patrice offered to give Annette a shoulder and neck massage. Tonya blurted out, "Have either of you ever had thoughts about being with another woman?"

Patrice, Jess and Annette looked at Tonya. Then Jess looked at Annette. Patrice stopped the massage and looked down at Annette. Annette said, "What are y'all looking at me for?"

"Answer the question," Jess said.

"Hell, why do I have to answer it? Why don't you answer it?" Annette said.

Tonya stood up and went into the kitchen to pour more wine in her glass, then returned to the living room. "I guess all of you must have thoughts about it since none of you want to answer the question. I know I'm not the only one."

Patrice turned to look at Tonya. "I've had thoughts about it, but I've never been in a situation where it could happen."

After Patrice's disclosure, Jess decided to put Patrice and Tonya at ease. She said, "Well ladies, I have to admit that I've been with women before. I'm no longer bi-curious. I consider myself a bisexual in remission because it's been so long since I've been with a woman."

Annette's eyes widened. "Do tell Jess. What kind of experiences have you had?"

Jess looked at her. "None of your business!"

Based on Tonya and Patrice's facial expression, they'd noticed the subliminal messages that were radiating between Annette and Jess.

"Okay, there's obviously something going on and one of you isn't telling the truth. Who's lying? It's you Annette. I've seen you look at other women at the gym," Tonya said.

"Excuse me!" Annette said.

"You heard me. I've seen you look at other women," Tonya said.

Patrice and Jess sat watching as Tonya and Annette went back and forth. Annette eventually told Tonya that she'd been with a woman.

Patrice was surprised, but glad. She looked at Annette. "How do you approach a woman? I have no idea how to do that. Guess that's why I've never acted on my curiosity."

Jess answered the question. "In a way it's just like approaching a man. If you see a man you're attracted to, how do you know if he's remotely interested in you?"

Tonya said, "My experiences have been with eye

contact. If I see a man I liked and we made extended eye contact, then I'll eventually approach him."

"Oh, I couldn't approach a man!" Jess said.

"I couldn't approach one either," Patrice said.

Tonya stretched out on the floor. "I don't have a problem approaching men; it's approaching women I have problems with. I'm not looking to approach a woman; I just want to know how to do it, just in case. I hope to one day satisfy my curiosity."

Annette said, "It's pretty much the same way when approaching women. Sometimes you connect with a man, and sometimes you don't. I've never approached a woman, but I've made eye contact with a lot of them. A few have approached me because our eyes connected. And it's interesting; each time I was approached, they were right on target because I did find them attractive. Although none of the connections went anywhere, we exchanged numbers for future reference."

Annette looked at Patrice, who sat quietly, taking in everything. She returned the look and Annette asked, "Patrice, are you interested in satisfying your bi-curiousness?"

The question took Patrice back. She hadn't expected it to go so far. Reluctant to answer the question, she said, "Ah...I'm not sure. There is no set time for me to try it, but I would imagine that one day I will. I just don't know when."

Jess looked at Patrice. "Well Patrice, I need to let you know that I find you quite attractive."

"Thank you; I think you're attractive too," Patrice said.

It was obvious that Patrice wasn't used to telling another woman, face to face, that she was attractive.

Annette looked at her and asked, "Are you okay, Patrice? Are you nervous, or uncomfortable?"

"No, I'm all right. I'm enjoying this conversation," Patrice said. "I'm almost thirty and I'm looking forward to trying new things."

Jess looked at Patrice seductively and invited her to go out on the patio. Jess refilled her and Patrice's glass and went outside. Annette and Tonya stayed inside, talking. Annette stood and walked towards the patio. She saw Jess stroking Patrice's hair. She called Tonya over, and Tonya began touching Annette on her shoulders. Annette quickly gave in and found herself kissing Tonya and exchanging caresses. They lay on the carpeted floor in each other's arms. Annette's foot accidentally hit the glass door, and Jess turned around. She and Patrice came to join in. Annette went into her bedroom to get a blanket. She gave Tonya her first bisexual experience and Jess came out of remission and gave Patrice her first.

After an hour and a half of sexual female pleasure, they lay on the floor, trying to understand where their bisexuality came from. The conversation made Annette do some soul searching.

Jess and Patrice left around 3:00 a.m. and Tonya stayed overnight.

The next day, Annette sat in the living room thinking about the conversation. She went into the bedroom to write in her journal.

Last night we had our first female sex party. It was a lot of fun, never expected it to be so much fun without men. Tonya was scared to give me oral pleasure, so I did her. That made me a little upset, but I got over it and enjoyed her anyway. The next time I'm going to make her eat this pussy.

I believe there are many women who are either bisexual or bicurious. I wouldn't be surprised if most women have had thoughts of being with another woman. I wonder if my childhood had anything to do with my attraction to women. It was nothing for me to play with other little girls, touching them when we were growing up. We combed each other's hair and played with each other's dolls. We kissed each other and nobody said anything. We didn't know what we were doing when we kissed, but we tried it. I also kissed little boys.

I had this older childhood friend when I was in sixth grade who I played with almost everyday. She came over one day, we were in the bathroom, and we touched each other's small breasts. Maybe that has something to do with my attraction to women. I also remember a time in seventh grade when I was at my physical education teacher's house with some of my other friends. She'd invited us to come over for hot dogs. She treated me different from the other girls. She even bought me a necklace to replace the one my boyfriend gave me. It wasn't a real necklace, but it was special because my boyfriend had given it to me. Most of the girls called me the 'teacher's pet', especially when she called me into her guest bedroom to show me her daughter's picture. We sat on the bed and she laid me back and kissed me on the lips. I didn't move or try to run. She told me the kiss was for being a good student.

I never thought about those events until now. I wonder if I forgot about them purposely because in my mind, I knew it was wrong. Wow! What an epiphany! I can't believe that I just thought about that. Now that I think about it, I'm certain that's where my bisexual tendencies came from. I was exposed to bisexuality early on but didn't understand that's what it was. I thought it was 'girl's play.' Hummm...very interesting. I think I just diagnosed my behavior. I don't know if I want to share that with James. Oh my God! Does this mean James is bisexual as well? He had a couple of homosexual experiences growing up. Naw, he couldn't be. I know he likes me playing around his ass, but I can't say that's enough to call him bisexual. He loves women too much.

I don't believe I blocked that from my mind for all these years. I guess it's true that we remember what we want to remember. But I don't understand why I hid it and never told anyone. I'm flabbergasted. I don't remember if they told me not to tell anyone. Maybe they did, and that's why I forgot about it. Damn. This is amazing. I'm a social worker and I have my own deep-rooted issues. I have to tell James about this. There is no need to hide it; I didn't do anything wrong. He shared his secrets with me, so I think it's fair that I share this with him. But this isn't a secret — hell, I just didn't remember it. I honestly forgot about it.

Just as she finished journaling, James drove up with Kynosha. She jumped up, ran into the office and put the journal back in its secret location. She pushed her hair out of her face, pulled her shirt down and stood at the door. She peeped into the powder room and took a quick glance in the mirror to make sure she looked all right. She opened the door and Kynosha gave her a big hug as James leaned over to kiss Annette. Kynosha was jumping around, and wanted to tell her mother about her weekend. James unpacked Kynosha's bags in her bedroom, while she told Annette about her weekend. Afterwards, he went into the kitchen, opened the fridge and grabbed a beer. He walked back into the living groom, flopped on the sofa, popped open the beer and took a long sip.

"Ahhhh…I've been waiting all weekend for this," he said.

"Was your weekend that long baby?"

"It seemed like it was." he pointed at Kynosha as he turned up his beer. "Your parents really love her."

"Yes, they're crazy about her. She's their first granD.C.hild. I don't know when Cora is gonna have children. And Dennis, he's another story," she said.

James turned up the Heineken can and emptied it. Annette turned to look at him. "Hey, after we put Kynosha to bed, I need to talk to you about something."

"What is it? Is everything all right?"

"Yes, everything's fine, I just need to tell you about something," she said. "Why don't you run Kynosha a bath and I'll get you another beer""

"Okay."

James walked Kynosha into the bathroom, and Annette went into the kitchen to get a beer. She poured herself a glass of red wine as well.

Before James returned, Annette finished her first glass of wine. She asked him to pour her another glass before he sat down, then said, "Guess what?"

"Baby, don't make me guess, just tell me."

"You know I had friends come over yesterday, right?"

"Yes," he said.

"Well, a conversation came up about bisexuality."

Laughing and clearing his throat at the same time because beer went down the wrong pipe, he said, "Who brought it up, you?"

Annette hit him on the shoulder. "No, I didn't. I think Patrice brought it up. What made you think I brought it up anyway?"

"I know how much you enjoy women," he said.

"That's true. I enjoy them when I'm in a position to enjoy them. Anyway, I think I may have figured out why I like women."

"Girl, what are you talking about? We know why you like women. You like 'em because Pamela turned you out. That's why!" he said.

Annette looked at James seriously. "I'm trying to share some intimate shit with you and you're playing around. Just fuck it. Maybe I'll tell you when you're not in such a playful mood."

He grabbed her arm as she attempted to walk away. "Damn baby, I'm sorry. I didn't realize it was that serious."

Annette hesitated, then told him about her epiphany. He was shocked and couldn't believe they'd had similar childhoods. He told her that he didn't think things happened like that to military children. She assured him that it could happen to anybody and that no class of people is exempt from child molestation. She told him that she was glad his childhood experiences hadn't had the same affect on him, making him a bisexual.

James stood and went into the kitchen to get another beer and refill her glass.

Her gaze followed him to the kitchen. "You didn't comment about what I said. What do you think, isn't that amazing?"

Avoiding eye contact with her, he opened the fridge and reached in for a beer. "I think it's great. At least now you can understand it better."

"James, I can hardly hear you," she said.

He yelled out, "I said at least now you know where your tendencies come from."

"I think you might be right. I feel different right now. I feel relaxed. Maybe subconsciously, it was weighing me down," she said.

He came back into the living room. "How could it weigh on your subconscious if you forgot about it?"

She agreed with him to end the conversation, then told him she was getting in the shower and then bed.

Now that Annette understood herself more, she was more comfortable with being herself. She decided to tell Jess about the revelation from lapsed memory. Jess disclosed to her that she had a similar incident happen to her, but she was the aggressor in her episode. She told Annette that she'd made out with a girl who was in fifth grade when she was in seventh. Annette dealt with her bisexuality more openly around her circle of friends. She'd not revealed it to her co-workers and had no plans to do so.

James received orders to Watertown, New York and had to report in January 1993. That is where he'd first applied for OCS. They transferred after the holidays. He was informed that he would be promoted to captain in the fall.

Annette threw a big party to celebrate his promotion to captain. She and Kynosha took him to dinner at Red Lobster on Friday evening. When they got home, Annette took the cake out of the refrigerator that she and Kynosha had baked and they had dessert. On Saturday morning James took Kynosha to breakfast at McDonald's and then to the sitter so Annette could get things ready for the party.

For the adult party on Saturday, she invited several of his colleagues and fellow officers as well as some of his enlisted friends. She invited some of her friends as well, including Wanda. In addition, as a surprise, she invited Russ, Pamela, David, and Linda, all of whom were still living in Tampa. James was pleasantly surprised when he saw them come through the door. He hadn't seen them since New Year's, 1991. Everyone had a great time. Russ, Pamela, David and Linda flew back to Tampa on Sunday afternoon.

Annette and James decided to stay home for Labor Day to get ready for their move to New York. They spent Saturday at Six Flags with Kynosha for her conception anniversary. When they returned home, James cooked a couple of steaks on the grill. It was a quiet day without friends. Jess and Brian had invited them over for dinner on Sunday, but they declined the invitation because they wanted to spend time together as a family. Now that Kynosha was old enough to understand, they took her to the Coca Cola Museum on Monday afternoon. She enjoyed her tour. She got a chance to buy a lot of Coke memorabilia, even though she couldn't appreciate what she'd bought at the time.

The leaves had changed and fallen to the ground. Annette was so consumed with her demons that she didn't notice the season had changed. She was struggling with whether she should tell James about Phillip. The affair was tearing her apart. She also struggled with a decision to tell her parents about her bisexuality. Her father was in the hospital and she thought that it was time to let them know before something happened. Before disclosing the information she felt compelled to learn everything she could so she could explain to her parents why she'd turned out the way she had. She began to research bisexuality on the computer.

At one point in her life she'd felt confused and lost because of her attraction to be sensual with and engage in a sexual relationship with either men or women. She knew that many people were attracted, both emotionally and sexually, to people of the same sex, but to her that was homosexuality. She also knew that some people were only attracted to people of the opposite sex. She conducted research and found the Kinsey Report, which included the Kinsey Scale of zero to six that was developed by Dr. Alfred Kinsey and his associates in the late 40's and early 50's. She printed the report and studied it to learn where she stood. She thought maybe it would show her that she was just experimenting or going through a phase of exploration.

According to the Kinsey scale, heterosexuals are at zero on the scale and homosexuals and lesbians are at the other end of the scale at six. Everyone between one and five are bisexual. Those who fall at one or two on the scale have heterosexual desires. However, they have some attraction and experiences with partners of the same sex. People who are three on the scale are equally attracted to both men and women. People at four and five on the scale will choose same-sex partners, but are not completely gay or lesbian. They have heterosexual tendencies.

She got a rating of two. She liked the strength and feel of a man's body. It made her feel safe, especially being in James' arms. But on occasion, she liked the softness, scent and beauty of a woman.

Annette decided against telling her parents about her bisexuality, especially since her father had just had a heart attack in June. She knew that her telling him about her tendencies would probably kill him. They were Southern Baptist Christians. She remembered growing up how her parents had talked bad against homosexuals. She couldn't imagine hearing her mother calling her names, and saying bad things about her because she liked having sex with women. She knew her parents loved her, but she couldn't risk losing their respect for her. She remembered her mother's words about being honest with people in order to free your soul, but at a time when she needed to be honest with her parents, she couldn't.

They arrived in Watertown, New York only to turn around and come back home in March. Annette's father had a fatal heart attack. She was devastated. It took her months to get over the grief. At his funeral, she stood at his casket sobbing because of the secret she'd kept from him. She apologized to him for not telling him, for not following their family creed. The guilt she felt forced her to tell her mother and siblings. Her biggest fear was rejection, losing her family's love and acceptance, but to her surprise, they accepted her for who she was — a daughter and big sister. Knowing her sexual orientation had no bearing on their love for her made all the difference in the world. Her mother told her she understood her sexual orientation, and that it wasn't who she was, but a part of who she was. Again, she felt guilty, believing that her father would have accepted her as well.

Since Annette hadn't found a job yet, she decided to stay home for a couple of weeks after the funeral, while James returned to New York. She took advantage of the time with her mother by explaining her bisexual tendencies. It was obvious to her that her mother had changed over the years in the way she viewed homosexuality. The situation wasn't as bad or life changing as she thought it would be. Her brother still had some issues about being around men who were homosexual, but had no problem with her. Her sister confided in her, telling her that she'd fantasized about being with a woman, and thought it was a normal thing for most women. Annette felt even more confident and comfortable with her disclosure to her family. She also wondered if it were something that was hereditary since her sister had homoerotic fantasies as well.

Sitting on the sofa at Jess' house sipping on a glass of Merlot, Annette and Jess talked about their views on bisexuality. Their views differed in the respect that Jess believed it was hereditary and Annette believed it was learned behavior based on one's social environment.

Annette and Jess had never been sexually intimate. Even the night at Annette's apartment before leaving for New York, they hadn't touched each other. Jess thought it would ruin the friendship. It was like an unspoken rule between them. No matter how horny they were when they were together, crossing the friendship boundary wasn't an option.

When Annette returned to Watertown, James told her how much he loved her and that one of the reasons he'd fallen in love with her was because she overlooked his physical flaws, like his chipped tooth and dark spots on his face, and she talked to him. He felt special. He told her for a long time he didn't really like Black girls and only wanted to talk to White girls because they didn't seem to mind his chipped tooth and dark spots. It was another bonding moment for them.

Finding a job was difficult because the base was small and the people who were in those jobs had been in them for a long time. Annette talked it over with James and became a stay at home mom, for the first year and a half, after which she got a job working with social services. It wasn't what she wanted, but it got her out of the house. She was still grieving the death of her father. She lacked the motivation and enthusiasm she used to have.

They spent three years in Watertown. Kynosha started first grade in September 1994 at the age of six. They drove her to school and picked her up, just as proud parents always do on their child's first day of school. When they picked her up from school, she was very excited that she'd made new friends. It was obvious to them that Kynosha liked going to school. The teacher had given her papers to give to her parents, and she couldn't wait to get home to get them out of her book bag. Annette and James were proud of Kynosha because she liked reading. One of her favorite books was the *Velveteen Rabbit* by Margery Williams. Annette had read it to her almost every day since she was born.

There was very little to do in Watertown. Although James and Annette had made a few friends, they were more comfortable by themselves. James became quite the ladies' man and with that came an obsession with his looks. He began reading *Men's Fitness* magazine, and his workouts became too strenuous for Annette so she opted out and began working out on her on.

During those three years, they explored many of their sexual fantasies. They watched porno movies, using them as tools to learn how to please each other. She finally gave in, tried anal sex, and liked it. They had anal sex at least once a week, and sometimes James wanted it more often.

Towards the end of 1994, they encountered a problem with having anal sex. He became upset when she wasn't in the mood. Once a week was enough for her and if he was nice, she would reward him with a night of anal sex. But it had gotten to a point when that wasn't good enough for him. She felt responsible for him wanting to have anal sex more frequently because she did it whenever he wanted it. There were times when he got very testy with her and wouldn't talk to her for the rest of the night. That made her give in. The last thing she wanted was for him to be upset with her because she didn't like arguing, knowing Kynosha was in the house. Anal sex for Annette turned into work. She found herself feeling pressured and stressed when he wanted to have anal sex. One day the pressure got so bad that she took

Kynosha and they flew to Decatur just to get away.

One day they sat down to talk about their problem and were able to come to a compromise. James apologized for being greedy. He told Annette that he enjoyed her and felt so special that he got carried away and was truly sorry for the way he'd acted. Annette apologized to him for using sex as a weapon. After talking and negotiating, their sex life was once again, on track.

On their way to the mall to see *The Pelican Brief*, starring Denzel Washington and Julia Roberts, they went into the bookstore. E. Lynn Harris' *Just As I Am* was on the shelf. Annette picked it up and read a couple of pages, then purchased it. When she got home, she read the book in one night. After she was finished, she got in bed.

Walking through the neighborhood hand-in-hand with Kynosha the next day, she unexpectedly whispered and asked James if he still wanted her to use her strap-on dildo on him. Shocked by her question, he stopped and looked at her. He whispered, "Can we talk about this when we get home?"

Smiling, she replied, "Okay."

That night after dinner, they talked about how they would approach what was about to take their sexual repertoire to a level they'd never imagined. James told her he'd been training for the day when she would use her strap-on on him. He told her that he'd used the butt plugs. Annette was surprised; she hadn't realized that his desire was so strong. She believed giving that to him would rekindle what they had lost. She would no longer have to feel pressured by his wanting to have anal sex with her; she could now do him.

Three weeks had passed since that conversation and things were great, even though they had not yet experienced her using the dildo on him. The anticipation made James more relaxed and at ease. He was no longer pressuring her to have anal sex. She gave it to him willingly. James also read *Just As I'm*.

James threw Annette a small birthday party on October 7, 1995. Wanda came and stayed the weekend, and they had a great time. James had invited a few people, one of whom he'd become good friends with, Lt. Thomas Bonner, whom he'd met at the gym. Annette seemed to have clicked with Thomas, who was White, and Jenny, a gorgeous Latino woman from Los Angeles. She was visiting Thomas for a couple of months. She was about 5'10, size six and looked like a model. She was a professional erotic dancer.

Thomas was a ladies' man as well. He looked like a young Rock Hudson. He had good muscle tone and nice thighs. They had been dating for two and a half years. Annette had once told him that she would fuck him if they weren't friends. They became close friends and vowed to stay in touch, even when they changed duty stations.

Thomas and Jenny turned out to be closer to Annette instead of James. She spoke with them on the phone and invited them over most of the time. Whenever Jenny was in town, they always came over to visit. Sometimes James would go out with them without Annette, and of course, she didn't mind. During one of their visits, the four of them went out to dinner. Annette felt something strange, almost distanced from Jenny. She looked over at James and saw him glance at Jenny out the corner of his eye. Jenny smiled and continued to eat.

Something just didn't feel right to Annette; Jenny had a different look in her eyes. She flirted with James as she played the stereotypical woman, asking him questions about himself and listening as though she were fascinated with his responses. She maintained eye contact and smiled, universal flirtation signs. It seemed like a game, a careful charade of deception and role-playing, volleying back and forth and sending ambiguous signals. For a moment Annette felt like she was in the middle of *The Crying Game*, a movie that exposed homosexual and mainstream audiences to an attractive fantasy of alternative sexuality.

On the way home, she told James she'd had a strange feeling at dinner and that Jenny had seemed distant. James told her she was probably just tired because it was late. She overlooked her suspicion and intuition and they went to bed. Jenny was going back to LA and wanted to hang out with Annette and James before she left. They went to dinner the day before her flight.

Two weeks later on Friday evening, James and Annette watched one of the movies they had bought when they were in Atlanta. They purchased several normal movies as well as porno movies when they were in Atlanta, and they hadn't watched any of them. After putting Kynosha to bed, they showered and got in bed. James reached in the drawer on the night stand and pulled out the video tapes for Annette. She chose a porno movie. Watching the movie, she reached down and felt her crotch. Looking at the women in the video touching, kissing and rubbing each other turned her on. She told James and he reached over to fondle her breasts as she masturbated. They had a very healthy sex life and enjoyed each other tremendously. Their kisses were always passionate and deep. The sex lasted for hours, and they knew how to get each other going again after they reached orgasm.

Annette masturbated to orgasm with James watching her and the movie as he stroked his penis. When she finished, he wanted to have sex. She rolled on top of James to sit on his penis. He wanted her to turn her back to him so she could watch the movie. To her surprise, James had seen the movie before, and pretty much knew the scenes. He began talking to her about what she was seeing and had her describe what she was looking at. When she told him that she was watching two women in a sixty-nine position with a man in a doggie-style position with one of the women, she felt his penis throb. "You like that, uh?"

"Yeah, that sounds good. What are the women doing?" he asked.

"They've turned around and one is on her back; the other is eating her."

He moved his hips, grinding harder, and asked, "What is the man doing now? Is he fucking the woman doggie-style?"

On the verge of orgasm, she replied, "Yes," then moaned louder and came. He asked her if the man had a big dick. Exasperated, she held her head up to look at the television. "Yes." She'd become frustrated with James asking her about the man's dick in the movie. He continued to bring other people into the bedroom. She'd complained to him about that before and for a while, he'd stopped.

He told her to get on her knees. Not only was it her favorite position, it was his favorite as well. He reached for the remote control and turned the television off. He vaginally penetrated her and Annette responded, pushing back onto him. He leaned down and asked if she wanted it in her ass. She told him if he wanted to. He took his penis out of her vagina and went into the bathroom to get some baby oil. When he returned Annette was on her back. They had never tried anal sex in that position, so he was confused and thought she didn't want to do it.

He said, "Everything all right?"

"Yes. Everything is fine," she said. Annette had reached into her toy drawer and pulled out the butt plug and strap-on dildo. It was dark in the room and James didn't see it on the bed. The only light was from a candle sitting on the dresser. She told him to get in bed and he did, still holding the baby oil. She told him to lie down, then sat on top of him and, holding the strap-on in her hand, whispered. "I'm going to fuck you tonight." She felt his penis pulse with anticipation.

As he lay on his back, she masturbated him and lubricated his anus, then inserted the tip of the butt plug. He flinched, tightening his muscles. As he relaxed, she slowly inserted more. Before she knew it, the entire plug was inserted. It was coned shaped and about three and half inches long. She began thrusting it in and out of him. "How does it feel?"

Moaning, he replied, "It feels okay. Slow it down."

"Oh, I'm sorry. I've never done this before, so I don't know how slow or fast I should be going," she said.

"It's okay, Baby. It does feel good. It feels different from when I used it myself."

"Does it hurt? Is it uncomfortable?"

"No, it's okay."

"Are you ready for me to fuck you?"

"No, I'm not ready yet. It's been a few days since I trained it. Just keep doing what you're doing."

Annette continued to stroke him with the butt plug. She was careful to wipe the plug off each time she took it out and reinserted it. She poured more baby oil in her hands and lubricated the plug some more. After about fifteen minutes, James said, "Okay, I'm ready."

Annette got on her knees to put on the strap-on harness as James lay watching. She asked him if he wanted to lay on his stomach or back, and he chose his back. She lubed the dildo on the harness and James' anus, then inserted the tip. He flinched. She moved back and forth very slowly. Before she knew it, she'd inserted half the dildo.

He asked, "How much is in?"

"About half of it," she replied. "Does it feel okay?"

"It feels very big."

"Well, you know it's not that big," she said.

"Well, when you're not used to anything being in your ass, anything inserted will feel big. The banana and the cucumbers were small, but they felt huge," he said.

Thrusting in and out, she said, "You're right. I know your dick felt huge when you fucked me in my ass."

James was only able to take half of the dildo. He reached and began stroking his penis. Annette saw that he was stroking it faster. She knew he was about to come, so she increased her speed and he came, screaming "Oh shit! I'm coming!" She slowly removed the dildo. After he came, he lowered his legs. Annette fell on top of him and asked him how he felt and he told her that it was an amazing feeling.

He turned on his side to face her. "You'd better not tell anybody about this!"

She laughed and said, "Trust me, I won't."

They spent Christmas in Manhattan. Annette

wanted to shop and they wanted Kynosha to have something to tell her friends when she went back to school after the holidays. They stood in the middle of the World Trade Center in awe of their height. Kynosha was amazed that she couldn't see the top of the buildings, where they ended, from the ground. They also saw the Statue of Liberty. They took many pictures. They loved going to the museums.

For the first time, they spent New Year's Eve at home with Kynosha awake. Annette made her take a nap so she would be awake at midnight. The three of them watched the ball drop in Times Square; afterwards Kynosha went to bed. Annette and James watched the celebration a little while longer, and then made love.

For the next three months, James' bisexual tendencies consumed her. She'd never been with a man who wanted her to use a dildo on him. Moreover, she never thought she would marry one. She understood once again what James felt when she'd told him that she had bisexual tendencies. She thought it was just a phase. He'd said he wanted to try it because her finger and tongue felt good. She didn't want to bring it up again for fear of starting an argument. Surely, he would have told her that he wanted to try having sex with a man if that's what he was thinking and feeling. Hell, he'd let her use a strap-on on him, so she knew he would have told her if that's what he wanted. She tried desperately to understand his reasons. *Could James be suppressing his bisexual tendencies? I guess for me to understand or comprehend it, it must be made visible to me.*

With Kynosha going into second grade, James received orders for Killeen, Texas. Kynosha was disappointed when they told her they were leaving, but was glad she got to stay until school was out. James didn't have to report until June 1996. Annette bought her a small address book so she could get her friends' address and write them when she went to Texas. James looked forward to going to Texas because he would be closer to his siblings who lived in Houston.

Two days before the movers came to pack their household goods, Annette walked in on James in the bathroom. He was wiping his face with a towel. She walked over and kissed him then said with a curious look, "What have you been doing? You smell like — you've been in here masturbating, haven't you?"

Embarrassed he said, "Yes. I was horny. You haven't given me any in two days so I needed to do something."

_____

Fall/Winter 1996

They settled into their new home in Killeen, Texas. A month before moving, they took a week of leave and flew to Texas to find a place to live. Kynosha spent her birthday and part of the summer at her grandmother's house in Decatur. Annette and James took a vacation and went to Las Vegas for July 4. Kynosha had started fourth grade. James made contact with his sisters in Houston, and they talked everyday and visited each other at least once a month. Kynosha, now nine years old, got a chance to spend time with her other aunts on her father's side.

Annette found a job working at the hospital. James hoped he would make major, and be selected to attend the Command and General Staff College (CGSC), a ten-month leadership course that's required before being selected for lieutenant colonel. They talked about having another baby. This conversation came at a welcome luncheon with other officer wives where someone had asked them if they had plans to have another child. They talked about it but it was short-lived. Annette said she didn't want to go through labor again, but it turned out that she was more concerned with gaining weight. Some of the other wives talked about how the second child always brought on weight gain that was harder to get rid of. Besides, James didn't want to have another child. They agreed Kynosha was enough.

Wanda called Annette from Guam. She told her that she'd gotten promoted to major and would be there for a year, and then she would transfer to the Pentagon. Thomas had extended for another year in Watertown, but assured them that he would stop through and visit for the holidays on his way to see Jenny. David had been promoted to major and attended CGSC. He and Linda had transferred to Washington, D.C.. Russ got promoted to major, and he and Pamela were stationed in Montgomery, Alabama. Annette sent all of them an email with their new address information and an invitation to visit them for Christmas at their new home in Texas. Wanda replied and told her that she wasn't sure if she would come home for Christmas, but would let her know. Annette enjoyed hosting dinners and social gatherings for their friends, but hated going to the officer wive's support group meetings. She didn't particularly care to have meetings at her house either.

James was known as "that fine Black captain." The women out there had given him that name, and he loved it. He and Annette were working out together again and heads turned when they walked into the gym. They were an attractive couple and people would tell them that all the time. One evening when she was coming out of the locker room, Annette noticed a young woman standing close to James as he waited for her near the free weights. She walked up and said to the woman, "Pardon me, but he's with me." The young woman walked away. She found herself on many occasions having to reclaim her man from other women. She told James that he could have any of the women that approached him, as long as she was there and involved. He told her the next time a woman hit on him, he would let her know what she'd said. They laughed and began their workout. Annette and Jess talked most evenings. One evening after the gym, Annette called Jess to tell her about the women who had been flirting with James.

"Can you believe it? These bitches out here are after my husband. We just got out here and they are all over him. Black, White, Hispanic, all of 'em. Can you believe that shit?"

"You know James is fine, Annette. What do you expect?"

"I know he's fine, but that doesn't give them a right to disrespect me. Does it?"

"No, it doesn't. Did they know he was with you? Was he wearing his wedding band?"

"I don't know if they knew he was with me, but they knew when I walked up that he was with me. Yes, he was wearing his band. He never takes it off."

"Well, I don't know. Just don't be out there kicking nobody's ass over James, girl!" She laughed.

Laughing, Annette said, "You know I will, Jess."

"Yeah, I've known you for a long time. How's the weather out there in Killeen?"

"Oh, it's nice. It's not hot at all right now. The nights are a little cool, but overall, the weather is nice."

"Let me get off this phone. Brian is on his way home and I need to cook. I'll talk to you tomorrow."

"By the way, how is Brian?"

"He's good, but sometimes he works my nerves. I'll tell you about it tomorrow."

"No. You can't just hang up like that and leave me hanging. What's going on? Is everything all right with you two?"

"Everything's all right; we're just having some issues about intimacy and who wants it more and what we should keep private and what we shouldn't, that's all."

"That sounds like an interesting conversation, but serious Jess."

"In a way it's serious because I don't think Brian has a right to know everything that goes on with me. And if I want to tell him something that's personal, I'll do it on my on time, not his," Jess said.

Annette could hear irritation and frustration in her voice. "Okay, Honey. Have a good night and we'll talk tomorrow."

"Okay, you do the same. 'Bye."

"'Bye."

Soon as Annette hung up the phone, James questioned her about her jealousy and the conversation she'd had with Jess.

"Did I detect a little jealousy from you in your conversation with Jess?" he said.

Slapping him on the shoulder for eavesdropping, she said, "You were listening to my conversation, uh? That was wrong. And no, I wasn't jealous. I just didn't like them disrespecting me."

"What? You were standing right there; they probably didn't know you and I were together, Annette."

"Where's Kynosha? Did she do her homework?"

"Yes. She's up in her room doing it right now. It's Friday, and she only had a few words to look up. She's already eaten. I gave her leftovers when I got home."

Jokingly Annette said, "You're a good husband and father when you wanna be."

It was obvious Jess had struck a cord with Annette about the privacy issue. She and James had problems a few years ago with intimacy and who should share what with the other. She loathed James whenever he listened to her phone conversation. They both kept journals. A few years ago, she'd caught James reading her journal. She told him that she felt violated and wondered if she could trust him, but he apologized and she forgave him.

"Do those women ever ask if you're with someone?"

"No. You don't give 'em a chance."

"Oh, so you're blaming me?"

"No. I'm just saying, you came charging in —"

"Hey, I was protecting my own and if I was wrong for doing that, oh well!" She stood with her hand on her hip, then turned to walk into the kitchen.

Laughing James said, "I hear ya, Baby; that's right, protect this dick."

She turned and looked at him. "Boy, please! You didn't have any business listening to our conversation anyway."

He asked her to bring him another beer from the fridge.

Handing James the beer, she said, "Do I look like a server to you?"

"No, but I saw this nice little number at the mall the other day that I could buy you and you can pretend to be one," he said, laughing as he reached for the beer.

"You're sick!" She said, as she sat next to him on the sofa to eat her salad. She didn't bring James the salad she'd made for him because he wanted her to bring a beer instead. Not that she kept track, but Annette noticed that James was drinking a little more than usual. The last time she said anything about his drinking was when he was in Arizona in 1987. Sometimes he drank four to six beers in one night. He didn't gain any weight because he ran everyday. His body was like his job, so he wouldn't allow it to get out of shape.

"James, do you know we still haven't unpacked all our stuff?" she said, with a mouth full of salad.

"Girl, didn't your momma teach not to talk with your mouth full?' he asked jokingly.

Laughing with her mouth full, she said, "Fuck you,

James."

"You're so trifling, Annette."

"You married me; I must not be too trifling."

Laughing he said, "You got some good pussy; that makes it easy for me to overlook it."

"And don't you forget it either," she said with a smirk.

"I'm glad Kynosha is upstairs so she can't hear how nasty her momma is," he said.

"You're just as nasty, and you know you like my nastiness."

"You're right again, Girl. About those boxes, maybe we can go through them tomorrow, it's Saturday and I don't have any plans to do anything," he said.

"Okay, nor do I. James, I'm feeling a little horny. Are you in the mood?"

"Of course I am. Would you like to watch a movie when we put Kynosha to bed?"

"Sure."

At 11:00 p.m., Annette and James were in bed. James turned on the television to watch the movie. While he was doing that, Annette was massaging and caressing his semi-hard penis. She commenced giving him oral pleasure. He fumbled with the remote, trying to put it on the nightstand. He watched the movie as Annette watched him enjoying her. She mumbled, "This head is so fat! You're really turned on aren't you? Damn! I want to feel this hard dick in me. Wanna put it in me, Baby?"

Moaning he said, "Yes, Baby; bring me that ass."

Annette turned over on her back so James could penetrate her in the missionary position. He whispered, "Is this what you wanted? You want it deeper? Spread your legs so I can give you the whole thing." Annette spread her legs as wide as she could and James thrust deep inside her.

She moaned, then clamped her legs around his waist. "This dick seems bigger than normal. I can't take it, Baby. Damn, it feel so good! I'm coming James!"

James, not ready to come yet, wanted to fuck her from behind so he told her to get on her knees. She turned over to get on her knees, facing the television so they could watch the movie. James took his time penetrating her. She reached back to massage his balls and he moaned. Looking at the television James asked Annette if she liked the woman with the big breasts and she told him she did. Then he asked her if she would eat her pussy, and she told him she would. Annette could feel James get harder as he penetrated her deeper. In a soft voice, he leaned down and whispered, "Can I have that ass, Baby?"

Without hesitation, she said, "Yes."

James kept a bottle of baby oil in the nightstand. He covered himself then her with the oil and slowly put the head in. Annette took it in with no problem. She'd gotten use to having anal sex. Once he was deep inside her, she lowered her shoulders, digging her face into the pillow to keep the noise down. As James began to moan louder, she coaxed him to orgasm. He grabbed her waist, began thrusting faster, and moaned, "I'm coming, Baby." He pulled out and came onto her back. She raised her head and looked into the television screen. The movie was still on. She saw two beautiful women who had nice breasts; one was White and the other Black. Annette thought the Black woman had on a strap-on dildo, so she told James to look at them. Then she looked a little closer. "Oh snap! That's a man! Oh, shit! That's a man too! Both of them are men! Damn! I thought they were women. I don't believe it! Their tits look just like a real woman's! Hell, they're better than mine!"

James agreed with her saying, "Yeah, they do look like women. Hell, I'd fuck 'em. They're pretty as shit too."

"They're not women James; they're men with breasts — transvestites. I didn't know that transvestites did it with other transvestites."

"There's some of everything out there. Whatever your fetish, it's out there," James said.

Two hours later, they fell asleep, waking up the next morning at 10:15 a.m. Kynosha had already eaten cereal and was watching cartoons.

Later that afternoon Annette was unpacking the boxes. James had decided to hangout and play basketball with some of his officer buddies. While unpacking a box marked *office supplies*, she came across James' journal. For thirty minutes, she struggled with whether she should read it. She remembered when he read hers and how it made her feel, even though she didn't have anything in it to hide. She thought he might walk in on her, so she called his cell phone to see what time he'd be home. He told her that he and the fellas were gonna have a beer after they finished playing ball, and that was all she needed to hear.

Kynosha was next door playing with the neighbors' daughter. Annette sat on the sofa, beating her forehead with the journal. She threw it down on the coffee table, then picked it up again. She went through that for at least another ten minutes before finally opening the pages. When she opened it, she put it close to her chest and said a prayer as her eyes filled with tears:

Lord, I know what I'm about to do is wrong. I know this Lord, but I pray that you please forgive me for my sins. I know I shouldn't be doing this; it's a violation of his privacy. Lord, just please forgive me.

She pulled the journal from her chest and began to read from the middle:

Sometimes when Annette and I are talking, I don't always know how to express myself. I don't like it when we trade off, who's more important and need's intimacy. Sometimes we get into some serious arguments, trying to control how the other one responds. I know that sometimes I can be cold, trying to be 'the man' by resisting her clingy female attempts to manipulate and get information out of me. There are times when I don't want to talk to her, but I do because I know she needs to talk.

Annette closed the journal, saving the place with her thumb, dumb-founded by what she'd read. She couldn't believe that James had such thoughts. She began to feel angered and wanted to know what else he'd had to say about her, so she continued to read, this time out of spite.

Just as often, it happens the other way around and of course, I see her as a bitchy Black woman with an attitude who won't respond to me. Then I become the one who's genuinely in need of a response. It's funny how that works sometimes.

Sometimes I wonder if Annette has ever slept with anyone other than the folks we play with. There are times when she wants to keep some things to herself. I know she needs her privacy as much as do I, but we agreed that we wouldn't question each other about what went on in our session with the chaplain a few years ago. Although I did ask her what they talked about, I knew it would detract from the usefulness of talking to him. We also keep our journals private so we can have a place to think aloud without worrying about the other person.

Annette was again feeling guilty, but she just couldn't put it down. She closed it, saving her spot with a thumb, and just sat on the sofa. James' private thoughts were getting more interesting to her. She went through guilt, sadness, and anger all in a matter of seconds. She had to know more. She couldn't just close it without knowing what James had been thinking. She took a deep breath and continued to read:

Whenever I hear people, especially women, talk about having their privacy, I find myself wondering what their motives are for wanting to keep things from the ones they love. I wondered why a spouse feels a need to hide a part of their life from the other. Why have I? I can understand why hiding things from your loved one could cause them to be anxious. Maybe that's why Annette bugs me so much when she's feeling suspicious of me. She will bug me until I tell her. I know I'll bug her too, not because I want to know everything there is to know about her, but more because I want to know why she would have a need to hide something from me. Identifying what we'll keep private has worked really well for us so far because it gives us our freedom and it eliminates any kind of fear or conflict.

Once again, she put the book on her lap. "This is exactly what I was trying to explain to Jess when she was telling me about her and Brian. That's odd, what does this mean? I was just talking to her about this and here I'm reading it in his journal. That's some spooky shit." Tapping into her memory bank she went back to the affair she'd had with Phillip and the weekend James and Kynosha went to Decatur, she'd had the girls over, and they'd had a sex party. "Oh God! If he got hold of my journal now, he would find out about them. I have to find it and get rid of it. He can never find out!" Guilt was tearing her apart as she continued to read.

I'm glad I have my journal to talk to because there is no way I could talk to Annette or any of my friends. Everything should be ideal, but it isn't with me personally. Sometimes I feel like my life is turned upside down and the only person who could remotely understand is Thomas. He is the only male friend I have that I can talk to about anything. We talk about 'man' things and sometimes sexuality. He knows how much I love Annette. He calls me the luckiest man alive that I have a woman who will allow me to sleep with anyone I choose, as long as she's a part of it... Hmm, isn't that something.

One day Thomas and I were talking about women, men and sex and he told me about one of his adventures. He went into a large bookstore looking for porno magazines. He said he didn't want to go into the adult stores because he didn't want to be seen, so he chose a more public place. He saw there were numerous magazines for both men and women, so he got one of each. They had plastic wraps with just the titles showing. He had me laughing when he told me that he spent an hour in that store trying to build up the nerve to go to the register. He said all he could think about was someone shouting over the speaker for everyone in the store to hear, 'I need a price check on aisle three' for whatever the name of the magazine was. I would be so embarrassed if that ever happened to me! That's why I don't buy those magazines. Annette and I go to the adult store together. When I was in Arizona, I went once to buy a swingers magazine, but haven't gone back since. I was afraid someone would see me back then. I understood exactly what Thomas was talking about. He told me he finally got the nerve to get in line to make the purchase. He was faced with whether he should go to a female clerk or the male clerk. He said he went with the shorter line and as faith would have it, it was the female clerk. He said the clerk asked him if he wanted a bag and he told her, 'hell yes', then he left the store before someone saw him.

I feel scared and confused that everyone can 'see' what I'm thinking. I don't know how Annette would react and I'm too afraid that she'll take it away from me. I'm afraid to talk about it aloud because it's embarrassing. It would force me to see how poignant it is. Since my first adult experience, back in Watertown, I've run the gamut of feelings and emotions. They return when I least expect them. I've had feelings of profound depression, self-hate, and have even an occasional suicidal thought. I wouldn't do that anyway. Nothing is worth that. I've always had *self-doubt, I'm glad Annette has never seen it. Sometimes I'm good at hiding my emotions and sometimes I'm not. For the most part, depending on whom I'm around, that determines my self-esteem and confidence level. But when I'm alone and with Annette, my self-esteem is at its lowest.*

Annette cried out, "Oh my God!" She knew James had spoken a few times about being depressed but never knew he'd contemplated suicide. She continued to read, flipping through the pages.

I thought one day I would be revolted and disgusted by it all, and quickly return to being normal. I thought, maybe it was a phase because I was getting older; after all, I'm a married man. Growing up I'd never been the ladies man. That didn't come until I was much older. Although I've always been shy, I know a lot of people and people seem to like me. I'm very shy around women; except Annette. She allows me to be me. That's why it hurts so badly. I feel like I'm cheating her out of a part of who I am. Sometimes when I'm around other women, I find myself over-compensating by talking and laughing loud, trying hard to hide my shyness. I've spent most of my life working and never learned the art of making real friends. I'm not conceited; it's just that I've been busy with more important things in my life. Sometimes I feel like I've missed many things in my life.

Sometimes my mind changes with my emotions. I'm married to a wonderful woman and have a daughter whom I love with all my heart. I love my wife more today than the day we were married. And I'm not willing to tear my family apart for this. It's just not right.

Reluctantly, Annette put the journal back in the box and taped it up before she read something that would force her to confront James and jeopardize the trust he had in her. She opened another box that had CD's, VHS movies and old cassettes tapes in it. She saw several porno movies that she didn't realize they had. James had apparently purchased some of the movies on his own. Some of the movies were of all women and she remembered buying some of them. There were she-male movies that she knew James had to have bought. She'd never purchased any with him. In addition, there were a few straight hetero movies with women playing with women in them. When he got home, she told him that she'd begun to unpack the other boxes. She asked him about the she-male movies, and he told her they belonged to Thomas and that he'd recommended them. He told her that he'd not watched them until the one they watched Friday night. Annette had no other choice but to be okay with his explanation because she'd just violated his trust by reading his journal.

After dinner, they watched television and went to bed. She tossed and turned all night. At one point in the night, she thought about getting up to read more of the journal. However, she didn't want to risk James finding out.

Annette awoke the next morning, feeling a need to go to church. She invited James to come with her. On their way to church, James noticed a distance in Annette and asked her if something was bothering her. He told her that he'd felt her tossing and turning throughout the night. She lied and told him everything was fine, then changed the focus off onto Kynosha. She turned around and asked her what she wanted for Christmas. To avoid talking too or even looking at James, she engaged in conversation with Kynosha until the reached the church parking lot. Sitting in church, thoughts of what she'd done were weighing heavily on her soul; however, she couldn't help but wonder what else he had to say. She closed her eyes, oblivious to the choir singing and began to pray:

Lord, please take these thoughts from me; I don't want to violate the trust that James has in me any more than I already have. Help me Lord. Amen.

That short prayer lasted for what seemed like thirty minutes for Annette. When she opened her eyes, they choir was sitting down and the announcements were being read.

James nudged her. "Welcome back."

She smiled, put her hand on his knee, and listened to the woman reading the announcements.

James' journal became an obsession to her. She struggled with not reading it. Each day brought about anxiety and guilt that she hid from James. Some evenings she avoided talking to him when it required her looking at him face to face. Sometimes she ate dinner before he got home just to avoid looking at him. Two weeks later, she couldn't take it anymore. She had to know what else he'd written. She wanted to know what kind of encounters he was referring too. She pulled the journal out one evening when James was working late. She'd folded the corner of one page to hold the place where she'd left off, just enough so it would go unnoticed. She struggled again, with whether or not she should read it. For the sake of her own feelings, she finally decided to put his journal away and write about her struggles in her own journal.

> *I've prayed and asked God to give me strength to put James' journal away and out of my head. It's so hard. Damn, I never should've read it because now it has me going through mental gymnastics. I know I'm wrong, but I can't help myself. I want to know more. I've already broken the rule and invaded his privacy. The damage is done. How much more damage can I do? If I read it and found out that he's been seeing someone else, what would I do? That's what I have to ask myself. I couldn't go to him and tell him that I read his journal and found out. Nor can I question him about whether he's seeing anyone. He hasn't given me any indications that he is. Hell, our lifestyle allows us to sleep with whomever we want, so there is no need to cheat. But I did violate that and cheated with Phillip and he didn't know about it. So I really couldn't get mad at him if he did have an affair, because I'm just as guilty.*

After writing in her journal, Annette called Jess.

"Hello?" Jess said.

"Hey Girl, how are you doing?"

"I'm okay, Annette. How are you doing?"

"Look, I'm not doing too good right now."

"What's going on?"

"You have to promise that you will never tell anyone what I'm about to tell you."

"You know me better than that. What's going on?"

"I read James' journal."

"You did what! How could you do that, Annette?"

"I didn't mean to. I —"

"What the hell you do mean you 'didn't mean to?'" If

you opened it, you meant too. That was wrong and you know it!"

"Dammit, I know I was wrong Jess. I didn't call you for you to yell at me. I needed a friend Jess."

"Well, if you called me to tell you that what you did was okay, then I'll talk to you later."

"No, Jess. Wait a minute. I'm sorry. Look, I know what you're saying is right. I hate myself for what I've done, but I can't turn back."

"What do you mean, 'you can't turn back? Are you crying? What have you done?"

"Jess, he wrote about some encounters he's having."

"What kind of encounters?"

"I don't know. He said he didn't want to talk with me about them because he was afraid that I would take them away from him."

Jess was silent. "Are you there, Jess?"

"Yes, I'm here. I'm listening."

"But that isn't the problem Jess. I want to read more to find out what these encounters are. I need to know if he is having an affair with some other woman."

"What if he is? Then what are you going to do, Annette? You can't confront him; he'll know that you've been reading his journal."

"Don't you think I know that?"

"When did you read his journal, and how did you find it?"

"Two or three weeks ago. I was unpacking our boxes and came across it. I couldn't help but read it."

"Annette, I know you better than that. Do you have suspicions about James having an affair?"

"Of course I don't. But reading his journal...I don't

know."

"Annette, I know this may be hard to hear, but you need to leave it alone before you ruin your marriage."

"You're right. That's why we have the journals anyway, so we can have a safe place to think. Thanks, Jess."

"You're welcome, Dear. I'll talk to you later."

Annette hung up the phone, then sat on the side of the bed crying. She couldn't believe she'd allowed her desire to read James' journal to overwhelm her the way it had. But even writing in her journal didn't help ease the desire at all. She was determined to read what James had written.

————————————————

For the first time since their mother had passed in 1985, James and his sisters celebrated Thanksgiving together. His two sisters, Erica, the youngest of the three, and Daphne, the middle child, came to their home. Neither had children, nor were they married. It was an emotional celebration. They cried as James blessed the food. After dinner, they sat for hours catching up on conversation they all longed for, but never initiated. They apologized for not calling more. They also apologized to Annette for not getting to know her the way they should have. Annette apologized as well. Erica told James that she left Decatur because she couldn't stand being in the neighborhood since their mother and father were no longer there. It had too many memories that had become hard to bear. Daphne left for the same reason.

Erica and Daphne stayed in Killeen until Sunday. They spent most of their time reminiscing about their childhood. James asked Erica about his childhood friend, Darryl. Erica and Darryl were the same age and had gone to high school together. She told him Darryl was gay, that his family didn't want anything to do with him, and that he'd committed suicide by shooting himself in the head just before Christmas in 1995. James wasn't surprise that Darryl was gay, but he was shocked that he'd committed suicide. When Annette asked James who Darryl was, he reminded her that he was the childhood friend he'd told her about, and she remembered.

_____

Two weeks before Christmas, Annette and James put up decorations. In keeping with their tradition, Annette was responsible for placing the star atop the tree. Kynosha added a few bulbs she made at school. They decorated the outside with lights and turned the front door into a large, wrapped present.

Thomas called to let James know that he and Jenny had agreed to spend Christmas with them and New Year's Eve in L.A. Annette was excited because everyone they'd invited had made plans to come to their home for the holidays. Annette was a great cook. She planned a southern style menu that included turkey, ham, collard greens, macaroni and cheese, dressing with giblet gravy, cranberry sauce, rolls, apple pie, peach cobbler, potato pies, and a coconut cake. She didn't make the best greens, so she had to call her mother to ask her what she needed to put in them to tone down the strong taste.

While James sat at the kitchen table going over the guest list, Annette was cutting her collard greens so she could freeze them for Christmas. She decided to prepare most of the food two days before Christmas so she wouldn't have a lot to do when her guests arrived on Christmas Eve. She wanted to sit and enjoy their company, especially Wanda, if she was coming. Annette had spoken with her several times but Wanda had never confirmed.

They all arrived on Christmas Eve, everyone except Wanda. Annette was disappointed, and so was Kynosha because she'd told Kynosha that her aunt Wanda would be there. James made reservations at a local hotel for Russ and Pamela. David and Linda stayed at their house. Thomas had made his own reservations because he wasn't sure what day he and Jenny would arrive. Russ and Pamela unloaded the rental car, taking out the gifts to put them under the tree. Although Kynosha was the only child there, she was excited about having all the people at her house because they all brought gifts and toys for her. She didn't know them, but she got to know them quickly.

After putting Kynosha to bed, they went into the family room to socialize and have cocktails. At around 3:00 a.m., Russ, Pamela, Thomas and Jenny went to the hotel, and Annette, Linda, David and James went to bed. Before going to sleep, Annette put the turkey in the oven and turned it on low. The phone rang at 7:45 a.m.; it was Annette's mother calling to wish them a Merry Christmas.

Incoherent, Annette answered and told her they had friends in town and had just gone to bed and she would call her when she got up. Three hours later the doorbell rang, and Annette thought it was the phone, so she answered it. It was obvious that she not only went to bed late, but she'd had a little bit too much to drink as well. She didn't hear anyone on the line so she hung the phone. The doorbell rang again. Kynosha answered the door with Linda standing in the background watching her. She screamed with joy; it was her aunt Wanda. She'd surprised them by showing up on Christmas day. She asked for Annette and Linda told her they were still in bed. Wanda and Linda smelled something burning and went into the kitchen. The turkey in the oven had dried out and almost burned. Wanda asked where Annette's bedroom was and went to knock on the door.

"Yeah, who is it?" Annette asked. Without responding, Wanda opened the door. Annette was on her knees with James penetrating her from behind.

"Guess I should've said it was me, uh? But it looks like I have perfect timing."

They were both happy to see her. Annette told her to come in and shut the door.

"When did you get here?" Annette asked.

"I got in late last night. I wanted to surprise you," she said. "Oh, by the way, your turkey is burned."

"Oh shit!" Annette jumped up, put on her robe and ran into the kitchen, James still on his knees. Linda had taken the turkey out and put it on the stove. Annette looked at it. "Damn! I can't believe I let this damn turkey burn!"

"It's not that burned Annette," Linda said, trying to make her feel better.

"Yes it is. It's too dry to eat. Guess I had a little too much to drink last night."

"I think we all did," Linda said.

James and Wanda were still in the bedroom. Wanda asked James who Linda was and if she was a player in the game. He told her she and her husband David were friends and they didn't play like that. Wanda told him Linda was cute and he told her to stay away from her.

Laughing, Wanda said, "I am. If you say they don't play, then I won't play with them."

"We do have two other couples here you can play with. You've met Russ and Pamela, but I'm not sure you've met Thomas and Jenny," James said.

"I think I did. Were they in Watertown with you?"

"Yes. You did meet them. Oh, okay. They're at the hotel and will be over later. Let me get up and put some clothes on." He got up and Wanda went into the kitchen to comfort Annette.

Christmas dinner was good. Although partially burned, they enjoyed the turkey anyway. There were no leftovers, except for desserts. Thomas and Jenny flew out two days after Christmas, going to LA. Russ, Pamela, Linda, David, and Wanda stayed for three days, leaving on Sunday morning. James and Annette promised Daphne and Erica they would let Kynosha come visit them Thursday, the day after Christmas, and stay until after the New Year. Kynosha was looking forward to going to stay with her aunts.

James got up early and took Kynosha to Houston. Annette called his cell phone to let him know they'd started the party without him. When he returned home late that afternoon, he walked in on Wanda, Annette, Linda and Pamela having girl sex. Jenny, Thomas, Russ and David were sitting around the room on the sofa and floor watching.

"Well damn, why are y'all sitting over there watching? Join in," James said.

"We didn't even hear you come in, Man," Russ said.

"I guess not. Y'all got your eyes glued to what they're doing down there on the floor," James said.

Annette invited Jenny to join; however, she chose to watch instead. Jenny did allow David and Russ to fondle her breasts while she kissed Thomas, but she didn't let them near her crotch to penetrate her with their fingers. She told them she wasn't into that.

James leaned over to David and whispered, "You didn't tell me you guys were into this."

"You didn't ask. We didn't know y'all were into the lifestyle, Man," David said. "James, you'd be surprised at the number of people I know who are in the lifestyle. Remember that major we met at the gym in Tampa?"

"Yes, I remember him. He had a nice wife."

"We've been with them several times, Man."

"This is a small world," James said. "I see now that Linda is no amateur."

The women gave the men a two-hour show before calling it quits. Afterwards, they got with the partners and called it a night. Thomas, Jenny, Russ and Pamela went to their hotel. David and Linda stayed another night with

Annette and James.

_____

Two days before New Year's Day, Annette decided to write in her journal.

Christmas was fantastic. I got a chance to see my good friends, especially Wanda. I missed her touch. I missed her mouth and more. She pleases me orally is better than anything I've ever had. She's even better than James. I hate to admit that but it's true. It's something about the way she's able to find the right spot on my clitoris and apply the right amount of pressure that drives me crazy. Over the past four or five years, I've cemented myself as a full-fledged bisexual. Although my family knows of my bisexuality, I'm still 'in the closet' with some of my friends and co-workers. My sexual orientation really is nobody's business but my own, so if they never know, that's fine with me. My family knows and that's all that matters.

It's funny because, sometimes there are days that I feel straight and some days I feel bi. Now, I notice both men and women.

I don't want to take this guilt into the New Year, so I'm making the choice to write it here and leave it. I'm making a promise to myself, with God as my witness, that after I read James' journal this time, I'll not read it again. If temptation crosses the threshold of my psychi, I'll fight the urge with all that I have. I love my husband and don't want

to lose him. I don't want to jeopardize his love and trust...
    Ah...Love, what is it anyway? What does love mean to me? Hmmmm, it's the feeling of deep affection that I have for James. It tempts me emotionally for seeking devotion and regard. The outside appearance as well as internal [similarities] tempt me, make me wish. When the qualities are pleasant, I respect them and that generally leads to my devotion. This is what I have with James, and I don't want to lose it. James is my love...

    She lost focus while writing in her journal. She couldn't take it anymore; his journal was eating at her core. "I can't take this anymore. I want to know what he's talking about."
    She went into the bedroom they turned into an office, opened a box and took out James' journal. James wasn't home and Kynosha was in her room playing with the neighbors' daughter. She opened the journal to where she left off, sat down in the computer chair, and began to read.

    Actually, in retrospect, I don't believe this has any thing to do with privacy at all. I think it's more of an issue of whether I'm okay with what's happening in our relationship. I don't know if I like Annette's homoerotic activities. I sometimes feel imprisoned and jealous. It seems she enjoys it more when a woman is pleasing her. I've noticed how she reacts, how her body responds to Wanda's touch. It's nothing like the way she responds to me. For a while now, I've been concerned about Annette and whether or not she'd prefer to be with women. Sometimes when we talk about her bisexuality, I can hear apprehension in her voice. I think she knows that I have these insecure thoughts, but I'll never tell her. If I told her about my insecurities, I'm afraid she might use it against me.

Annette closed the journal, holding her spot with a thumb. She put the journal in her lap and leaned back in the swivel chair. She'd had no idea James was feeling insecure about her bisexuality and how she responded to women. She was numb. Annette's curiosity had put her in a situation where the only way out was for her to be honest with James and tell him that she'd read his journal, but that wasn't a risk she was willing to take. She opened the journal and read more.

I'm in my most intimate and committed relationship with a woman I love with all my heart. She is the mother of my child. She is my best friend. But how could I cause her so much pain, pain that she has yet to feel? I sometimes want something that seems antithetical to our loving marriage, our family life. She's caught in the middle because she loves me so much and I've made numerous promises to her. That makes it very difficult for me to be at peace with this situation.

Sometimes I find myself going into a depression. I'm glad I have a wife who's a social worker because she has been able to help me identify the signs of depression and how to pull myself out before I go to deep. I know I'm hurting her, whether she knows or not. It's nobody's fault, not hers or mine. Who can I blame for wanting something that I know will cause her pain? I don't know if I'll be able to understand how she might feel. It's obviously a violation of the basic concept of marriage as she knows it. I try so hard to give her love and understanding. I love her so much and especially enjoy the love we make and the sex that we have with our friends. I'm so angry at myself for the pain I have caused her.

Oh God, my life is so complex. I never knew there would be circumstances in which I would have to judge myself for things I've done. I'm a religious person too, so I believe I'll be condemned to the fiery depths of Hell for what I've done. I know I don't attend church like I used too, but I still believe in God. I try to tell myself that God knows my heart. He is the Creator of us all, so I don't think he will condemn me to eternal damnation for what's in my heart. Still, I don't know, and it does concern me. I go out of my way to help other people. Hell, I serve in the US Army, helping to protect millions of people; that counts for something, I'm sure. Maybe I won't go to Hell after all.

I feel very strongly about honesty in our marriage. I don't know that if I was honest with her, that our marriage could survive. I can't imagine living without her and Kynosha. I know I'm wrong for making decisions for her. I know I should give her a chance to decide what she wants for herself. Keeping her married to me, if it isn't what she wants, is wrong. I know that I'm being very selfish for lying to her. But sometimes it seems rational to do so. I want so much to grow old with her, but I know that if she found out, she wouldn't want to stay married to me. I know her very well, and I know that she wouldn't stand for it. So I lie to her, keeping her married to me against her will, unbeknownst to her. In altruistic terms, this way, I can preserve my family and relieve her of pain.

But the question still remains for me, why should I be the one making that choice for her instead of letting her make it? Why not let her decide if she wants to stay married to me? What if I was in her shoes? Would I want to know the truth about what was going on? Of course I would. Sometimes I feel that there are moral reasons to lie. I can even stretch my imagination and say that there are reasons to lie pervasively to someone you love about something that you know matters a great deal to them. However, I have to be honest with myself; I know that it's pure selfishness on my part for not being honest. This helps me keep my marriage and my secrets and I don't want to lose either one. Therefore, I can't be honest with her because she might make a choice that I don't want her to make. Hence, I continue to control her decisions.

Annette became teary-eyed, and then the tears fell. She didn't need to read anymore. Her suspicion was right. When she read his journal the first time, she thought he was having an affair even though there was no admission of guilt or evidence of it. In her heart, she believed he was seeing someone outside of their recreational swinging with their circle of friends. She needed to make a choice. She realized that each time she opened and read his journal, she was forced to make a decision on whether or not to tell him, jeopardizing his trust. Now, she was in too deep and her 'womanness' wouldn't allow her to just leave it there. She needed to talk, so she called Jess, but the answering machine came on. She didn't leave a message because she didn't want to take the chance of Brian getting it and hearing her cry. The fewer people who knew about what she'd done, the better. She hoped Jess would have save her from reading more.

She waited for Jess to come home, dialing her number what seemed like every five minutes. She held the journal tightly, pacing, trying to figure out what to do next. "Dammit, where is Jess when I need her? I can't call

Wanda in Guam. Lord, what am I going to do? I can't take
any more of this."

She walked into the hallway and just when she was
about to push redial, she heard James pull into the
garage. She ran into the bathroom in the hallway and hid
the journal in the linen closet under the towels. She knew
he wouldn't go in Kynosha's bathroom, and she wanted to
read more. She met him at the door. They went into the
kitchen and he watched her make turkey and cheese
sandwiches for dinner.

James noticed the sadness in her eyes. "Hey, is
everything all right?"

"Hm...hummmm. Everything is okay," she said.

"Why the sad look?"

"Oh, it's nothing. You know how I get whenever I
watch those tear-jerking movies."

"Yeah, you are a sucker for a sad movie," he said.

Inside she was fuming. Cutting the tomatoes, the
knife slipped out of her hand and fell on the floor, barely
missing her foot. James reacted quickly and bent over to
pick it up. It was obvious to him that something was
bothering her, but she assured him that she was fine. She
told him that she wanted him to fuck her, not make love to
her, but fuck her because she needed it. She told him that
she'd done something that she shouldn't have, and
needed to be fucked very hard for doing it. She told him
that what she did wasn't important, but what was
important was that she paid for her mistake.

James looked at her. "All right. Bring your ass with
me then."

She made Kynosha a sandwich. Without eating,
they went into the bedroom. Annette gave James what he
wanted, anal sex and he gave her what she wanted, a

good fuck. They had sex for an hour, and then she made their sandwiches.

Interrupting their dinner, the phone rang. It was Jess. Annette told her she'd call her back after dinner. She continued to eat, but James noticed she was rushing to finish and confronted her.

"Damn baby, y'all must have something juicy to talk about."

"What are you talking about?"

"Before the phone rang, you were taking your time." He laughed. "Now you're inhaling that sandwich."

"I am not, but we do have something we need to discuss."

"Y'all talk more than anybody I ever seen. Are you sure y'all ain't fucking behind my back?"

"Boy, please! If we were, you'd never know, now would you?"

"All right now, don't start no shit."

"I'll have you know, the shit has already started."

He looked up. "What's that supposed to mean?"

"What's with all the questions? Are you guilty about something?"

"No, I'm not," he said. By now, Annette was fuming. She got up from the table and went into the kitchen. James came in behind her.

"It's obvious something's on your mind, Annette. You know I'm not gonna pressure you to talk. If you need to talk to Jess, that's okay."

"You're right, James. I do have something on my mind and I need to talk to Jess about it."

"I hope everything's all right."

He left so she could call Jess back. As soon as he walked out the door, Annette called Jess.

"Hey Brian, is Jess there?"

Brian called Jess to the phone.

"Hello?" Jess said.

"Hey, it's me. Can you talk?"

"Yes."

Sniffling and almost out of control, she pulled herself together. "I know for a fact James is seeing someone else."

"Annette, how do you know that? Where is James?"

"He left so you and I could talk." Still crying, she said, "I read his journal and —"

"Now Annette, you know —"

"I know it was wrong. You don't have to say that, Jess. I know this already."

Annette talked to Jess because she knew Jess would tell her what she needed to hear; even though it wasn't what she wanted to hear.

There was a long silence. "Hummm. I'm sorry, Jess." Annette sniffled. "How could he do this, disregarding the sanctity of our marriage? We're swingers. He could have any woman he wanted."

"Annette, did he say he was seeing someone or are you reading into what he said?"

Annette went into the bathroom to get a tissue to wipe her nose. "No, I'm not reading into it. He talked about being afraid to tell me because I might leave him and how he was protecting me by not telling me."

"But did he actually say that he was having an affair?"

"No, not in the pages I read. I had to close it because I didn't want to know if he was. Jess, I don't know what I'd do if he's having an affair."

"Calm down. Maybe he's not having an affair. He's probably talking about something else. James loves you and Kynosha very much. You know that."

"I know he does and I love him too. What am I going to do Jess?"

Jess couldn't help Annette with her situation. She was certain that Annette would read more of the journal.

"Annette, there is no doubt in my mind that you're going to read more of James' journal. I know you realize the more you read the deeper you're getting. At what point will you stop?"

"Yes, I know that. But what am I suppose to do? Just go on pretending I don't know?"

"You have to either leave it alone or devoid his trust by telling him you've been reading his journal. You don't have too many choices."

"Jess, this is terrible timing. This couldn't have happened at a worse time, two days before New Year's Eve. What am I gonna do about New Years Eve?"

"What do you mean? What do you and James have planned?"

"We'll be at home spending a quiet evening with Kynosha."

"That should be easy to deal with."

"I guess you're right. What are you and Brian doing?"

"We're going to watch the fireworks, and then go dancing at the Embassy Suites."

"Sounds like fun."

"We're looking forward to it. We're meeting a few friends at the hotel."

"Have you finally talked Brian into swinging?"

"Hell no! He still doesn't know that I've resumed

exploring my bisexuality."

"You mean to tell me he doesn't —"

"No, he doesn't know. I haven't told him."

"What did James have to say about the weekend he and Kynosha went to Decatur?"

"Nothing. He doesn't know. I didn't feel a need to tell him." Annette stretched and leaned back on the sofa. "James wrote in his journal that sometimes, lying is necessary to keep from hurting the ones you love —"

"Annette, answer this question: Before you got married, did you and James ever talk about your past relationships and the people you had sex with before y'all got serious?"

"No, not really. Why?"

"I was just wondering. I've known y'all for a long time. I can't imagine James messing around on you. I really can't. He loves you, Annette."

"I know he does." She heard James' car pull into the garage. She told Jess she would talk to her later.

Annette went into Kynosha's bedroom to make sure she was getting dressed for bed. She looked in the mirror and saw that her eyes were puffy and red. She didn't want James to see her like that, so she took Kynosha into the hallway bathroom and locked the door. She heard James call out to her.

"We're in the bathroom!"

It was obvious to Kynosha that her mother had been crying. She asked, "Mommie, are you okay?" She hugged her and the tears fell; she was too choked up to respond. Kynosha leaned back. "Mommie, why are you crying?"

Annette knew she needed to say something to Kynosha before she told her father. She explained to her that she had a migraine headache and didn't feel well. Kynosha looked at her. "Mommie, why don't you let Daddy put me to bed and you go lay down?" Annette closed the lid on the toilet and sat down. She turned on the water and adjusted the temperature, then turned to Kynosha and placed her hands on her shoulders. "I'm okay, Baby. After I put you to bed, I'm gonna take an aspirin and go to bed. It'll go away." When Annette heard the door handle jiggle, she said, "We'll be out in a minute!"

"Unlock the door!"

"I can't get to it right now. We'll be out in a few minutes," Annette said.

Twenty minutes later, Annette and Kynosha emerged from the bathroom. They went into Kynosha's bedroom and she got into bed. Annette kissed her on the forehead. As she turned to walk away, Kynosha said, "I hope you feel better in the morning Mommie."

Annette walked over to the bed, lifted her, and said, "I'm sure I will, Baby. Good night."

"Good night, Mommie," Kynosha said.

She got up and left the room. She could feel the tears coming back. She saw James sitting on the sofa drinking a beer. To avoid having to look at him, instead of going into the living room, she spoke to him with his back facing her, went into the bathroom in their room, and locked the door behind her.

She had never locked the bathroom door before, so when James came into the bedroom, he thought it was unusual and asked why she had it locked. She made up a quick lie and told him that she was getting ready to shower and change into something sexy and didn't want him to see her. She turned on the water and filled both hands, then splattered it on her face. She spent at least twenty-five minutes in the shower, ten of which were spent crying.

James went into Kynosha's room to kiss her goodnight. She was still awake. When he leaned over to kiss her, she said, "Daddy, is Mommie doing better? When she got off the phone with Aunt Jess, she was crying. She told me she had a headache."

"Yes, Baby, Mommie is all right. She's in the shower getting ready for bed. Now you get some sleep. Goodnight, Baby."

"Goodnight, Daddy."

Disturbed by what Kynosha had said, he knocked on the bathroom door and asked how much longer she'd be. She ignored him. She didn't want to face him. She thought if she ignored him, he would leave her alone. However, the time came for her to come out of the bathroom and face him. She was wearing a sheer tee length black gown with black thong panties. She looked sexy, but inside she was dreading having to face James.

She'd made him believe that she was freshening up for him. She regretted having told him that she was putting on something sexy. He would expect sex. When she came out of the bathroom, he was sitting on the bed and she tensed. He called her over to him. She walked towards him and he reached for her hands. He lay back on the bed and pulled her on top of him. To her, it seemed to have taken him five minutes to lie back.

Her heart was pounding. She thought, *Oh God! I can't do this.* She rolled over and said, "James, I have a terrible headache. It feels like a migraine."

"But you don't have migraines!"

"That's what it feels like."

Still fully dressed, he laid down next to her. "I went

in to kiss Kynosha goodnight and she was still awake."

"She was?"

"Yes. She told me that you were crying when you got off the phone with Jess."

"What? What are you talking about? She was in her room when I was on the phone."

"Obviously, she came out of her room as you were getting off the phone."

"Maybe so," she said.

"Annette, would you like to tell me what's going on?"

"Look James, I do have a terrible headache. Can we talk about it tomorrow?"

"Sure. Did you take something?"

"I took two Tylenol when I was in the shower."

1997

Monday evening before New Year's Eve, Annette stood near the window staring into the night, struggling once again with reading James' journal. She'd encouraged him to go out with his friends since they were spending New Year's Eve at home with Kynosha. She knew he would be out at least two hours. That gave her an opportunity to read as much of his journal as she could stand.

She went into the bathroom, got the journal from under the towels, and locked the garage and front door. She put the inside security latch on the door. She looked in on Kynosha — she was watching television — then went into the kitchen to make a sandwich and pour a glass of Merlot. She went into their bedroom, dimmed the light and sat in the rust-colored chaise lounge in the study area. She turned on the lamp behind the chair and began to read. Simultaneously, she bit her sandwich and opened the journal to a different page and read.

One thing is certain: I know I would lose my family and career; there is no doubt in my mind. It would take reams of paper to illustrate my certainty of this fact. I know my wife. I know it won't be good for Kynosha if I'm not around. She needs me. I would give both my arms and legs if I could tell my wife about what I've done. I hate myself for keeping my terrible secret from her. We share everything, yet I can't tell her about what's killing me inside. I feel compelled to tell her and only her.

Annette finished her sandwich and glass of wine. She got up and put the journal face down on the chaise. She went into the kitchen to pour another glass of wine. She reached on top of the fridge and pulled down a bag of Doritos. She went back into the bedroom with the chips in one hand and the wine in the other. She sat the glass on the stand near the chaise and held the chips under her arm as she leaned down to pick up the journal. She sat down and began to read:

For the past three months or so, I've been a little down. I don't know why, I just know I have been. Everything at work is great. Hell, I'm up for major next year and I might get selected for CGSC. My professional life is outstanding. But my 'self' is in turmoil. I have such guilty feelings. Some days, I want to disappear and become a recluse. Hell, in essence, that's really what I am. In my mind and heart, I live alone.

How can I begin to understand the pain of disappointment and regret that she might feel? She could never understand or even imagine my feeling of loneliness, desperation and emotional shutdown that sometimes comes from denying her and me. We both can struggle through our situations, but what makes it harder is that we change as our lives change. I found in my adulthood that parts of me were left behind that I needed to integrate into my adult life. Day by day it gets harder to deal with because, just as I change, she changes too.

To me, my reluctance to share with her, that part of my life that I know will cause her to view me differently, seems very logical. Sometimes I ask myself, why am I reluctant? She's my best friend. Is it because of my circumstances and career? Or is it because I'm not comfortable with myself? Am I fighting for my own self-acceptance? A few years ago, Annette came home and told me about a therapeutic activity she gave her clients and suggested that I tried it. Of course, I told her she wasn't my therapist. Boy have I eaten those words over the years. She's the one who started me journaling. It's such a release to be able to write down my thoughts and later go back and read them and learn my mistakes and faults. She had her clients write about their past in detail, for their eyes only, and then read it. Next, they had to write the parts that were undeniably them, despite the fact they may have denied them for years. Then they had to identify the bad choices they'd made to avoid making them again. Then they were allowed to identify the good parts, the self-affirming experiences they wanted to share with others.

I believe my life is good in all respects, but sometimes it gets so lonely. The loneliness doesn't happen too often, but when it does, it hurts and I don't like that feeling. Damn, I'm so frustrated. I hate having to suppress my thoughts and lie to her. Doing this compels me to resent her. Sometimes I get so angry when we're together as a family. When I look at her and Kynosha, I see my guilt. They represent the lies that I've been keeping from her. I know it sounds crazy, but they force me to face my guilt.

Annette put the book on her lap and looked up at the ceiling. She was too numb to cry. She felt angry. She felt betrayed by the only man she'd ever loved, her soulmate. To her, what she was reading couldn't have been written by the man she'd married almost nine years ago. She was overwhelmed.

The phone rang. It was Thomas calling from L.A. He was spending New Year's Eve with Jenny and wanted to wish them a Happy New Year. She told him James was out with friends, but she would let him know that he called. Annette liked Thomas because he was *real.* He always made her laugh. She was closer to him than Jenny. Sometimes Jenny seemed too fickle and she didn't care to be around her. When Thomas and Jenny had come for New Year's last year, Annette had talked about her to Linda and Pamela. Pamela told her that she was jealous of Jenny because she was thin with big boobs. After doing a self-assessment, Annette admitted to herself that she was a bit jealous of Jenny because she was gorgeous.

After hanging up the phone, she went to the bathroom. After she came out, she picked up the wine glass and went into the kitchen for a refill. She was now on her third glass of wine. She heard the car pull into the garage. She left the glass on the counter and ran to remove the security lock. As she walked back into the kitchen, James opened the door.

"Hey, where are you going?"

Annette stopped in her tracks, turned around and said, "I'm getting my glass of wine I just poured. Can I get you something?"

"I'll take a kiss for walking in the door for starters."

Annette hadn't expected that request.

"What?"

"I said how about a kiss for walking in the door."

"Okay, let me get my glass. You sure you don't want a beer or something while I'm in here?"

"No, I'm gonna jump in the shower right quick."

"Wait a minute baby. Why don't you have a seat here on the sofa, and have a drink with me?" She brought him a beer and sat in his lap, kissing him passionately, but feeling nothing.

"Damn baby. If you're gonna kiss me like that whenever you want me to have a drink with you, you can offer me a drink everyday," he said.

"Just kiss me and shut up," she said.

They kissed for what seemed like twenty minutes. She felt a bulge in his pants and knew that sex was on the horizon. She still needed to go in the bedroom to get the journal. She'd have him undress there on the sofa. She told him not to go anywhere and that she would be right back; she needed to go to the bathroom. James sat there, naked on the sofa and waited for her to return. She went into the bedroom, put the journal behind the chaise on the floor, and then went back into the living room. She undressed as he watched. She kept on her panties and sat in his lap, moving around on his hard penis.

He tugged at her panties. "Take these off."

"I'm not ready yet. Let me just move around on it and massage my clit."

She moved her hips in a circular motion, massaging her clitoris. She knew if she was going to come, that was the only way it would happen that night because she wasn't into James at all. A melting pot of emotions was going on in her head and heart. Sex was the last thing on her mind.

"That feels good," he said.

She looked at the ceiling. "Yes, it does."

Still wearing her panties, she came by massaging her clitoris. James felt her crotch. "Damn baby, it feels like you're ready now. Why don't you take these off and sit on this hard dick?"

She had trepidation about him penetrating her. All she could think about was him and the woman he talked about in his journal. Did he wear condoms when he had sex with her? Did he kiss her as passionately as they kissed? Did he love her? What did she look like? Where did she live? Did she look better than her? Her eyes welled. She took a deep breath, pulled her panties to the side and sat on his erect penis. He never saw her agonize. James whispered he was coming, then released. She cringed. Afterwards, she stood up and ran into the bathroom. She told him she had to pee.

James was too weak to move, so he sat there for five minutes before going into the bedroom. He came into the bedroom dragging his clothes and by the time he reached the bathroom, she was already in the shower.

"Damn girl, you put something on me," he said.

She pulled the shower curtain back and said, "Aw, that was nothing, you know that. Oh, Thomas called and he's in L.A. visiting Jenny for New Years."

"Oh, okay. I'll give 'em a call tomorrow," he said.

Uninvited, he got in the shower. She told him she was finished and got out. She grabbed a towel from the rack and wrapped it around her. By the time he got out of the shower, she was in bed. He got in bed thirty minutes later. About 2:30 a.m., he went to the bathroom. Annette awoke. When he got back in bed, he rolled over to fondle her breasts and she pretended to be asleep. She turned on her stomach.

———————————————

Part 3

Her Demise

On New Year's Eve, Annette suggested they spend the celebration at church, and they did. They returned home around one o'clock. James carried Kynosha inside because she'd fallen asleep in the car. When he put her to bed, James went into the kitchen to get the bottle of champagne and two glasses. Upon his return to the bedroom, they made a toast to the New Year and their happiness. Annette didn't raise her glass very high to the toast, nor did she take a sip of the champagne. Annette made a resolution to lose weight. James made a resolution to be a better husband to her and a better soldier for his country.

Two days before New Year's, she'd noticed a slight roundness in her face and that her jeans were fitting a little snugly. She'd gained twenty pounds. She thought she might have been pregnant, but quickly dismissed that thought. She was ashamed of her weight gain. Their sex life had become occasional. Not only did she not want him to see her naked, but it was difficult for her to face him knowing that she'd read his journal and found out about his affair. Her calls to Jess were few. She withdrew into self-loathing. She'd not read James' journal since before the New Year and it was tearing her apart. She wanted to know more.

Annette began working late hours, so Kynosha had to go to the neighbors' house once she was out of school until her father came home. Kynosha told her father that she wanted to spend more time with her mommie. She told her father she missed her mommie helping her with homework. She didn't mind her friend's mommie helping her, but she'd much rather have her own. She also told him she missed her mommie putting her to bed.

Work became Annette's solace. She worked long hours to avoid going home and dealing with James. One day he confronted her about the long hours and how it had taken away from her time with Kynosha and him. James' journal and her weight gain had consumed her so much that she'd neglected everything around her. Kynosha went to bed several nights without even seeing her mother.

The same evening he confronted her, she told him that she would see about adjusting her schedule so she could spend more time with Kynosha. James didn't take too kindly to her resolve and said with a raised eyebrow, "What about time with me? I feel like I'm being neglected too."

"Right now, Kynosha is what's important. Stop being so damn selfish, James!"

James was livid. "What the hell you mean selfish! Here it is almost damn March, and we've had sex what, five times this year?"

She wasn't in the mood to fight that battle, so she went into the bedroom and closed the door. Kynosha heard her parents arguing, came out of her room, and stood in the hallway. James saw her and took her back into her room. He told her everything was fine and that he and her mommie were just having a disagreement. He went into the bedroom. Annette laid across the bed, pretending to read Terry McMillan's *How Stella Got Her Groove Back*. James walked in, slammed the door and said, "What the hell is going on with you, Annette? You've been acting strange every since before New Year's Eve. What's going on? I've been patient enough by not saying anything, but now it's affecting our daughter and I'm not gonna stand for it anymore. What the hell is going on with you?"

She slammed the book closed. "James, I don't want to talk about it right now."

"You don't want to talk about what?" he said.

She rolled over and sat on the foot of the bed. James remained near the door, holding the doorknob.

"Working these long hours has taken its toll on me. We're understaffed and they're taking forever to hire new social workers. I know I've neglected Kynosha, and it hurts." She began to cry. "I'm doing the best I can do right now," she said.

"I understand. I'm sorry. I didn't mean to add any pressure to your situation. I just needed to know what was going on with you. I'll give you some time alone."

Annette knew he'd leave her alone if she told him she was dealing with issues at work. They respected the others' need for space and time. That bought her time to write in her journal. She pulled it out and noticed that she hadn't written in it since December.

I can't believe I haven't written since December. Hell, that's probably why I'm so uptight. I've got all this shit inside me that needs to come out. He's got some nerve talking to me about neglecting him. He's the least of my concern. He should go and let whoever that bitch is he's sleeping with console his ass. Let her take care of his needs. As bad as I want him, I'm too angry to overlook what I've read. I know there's something in there where he admits to having an affair — I just have to keep reading until I find it. If I find out he really is having an affair, I'll take Kynosha and leave his ass faster than a New York minute. And he'll never see us again.

I understand the primitive rage that can be brought out in a person who is usually mature, loving, caring and understanding. James and I have been at some points cruel and verbally abusive to each other. He blamed me for him not making major last year, and I'm not even in the military. He blames me for his insecurities and faults. He even told me I'm the reason he drinks so much.

It's funny because at other times we've had deep love and compassion, as well as empathy for each other's pain. What's happened to us? I love and care for him so much. I want to be happy and I want him to be happy too, but I'm hurting so much right now and he is the source of my pain. I want to be with him, but I need to get away from him so I can feel better.

It's funny that I've become incapacitated, and I'm a social worker, someone who helps people. Damn, I can't even help myself. I need a therapist! One of the things I learned early on in my undergraduate classes was that I couldn't help other people if my life is not together. That makes me wonder about the quality of service I'm providing to my clients. Maybe I should take a leave of absence until I work through my issues...Hmmm. I wonder what James would think about me taking off for a few months. He's getting promoted to major this year, so he could sustain us for a while. Hell, I can afford to take off; we save for times like this. I'll talk to him about it tonight. The time off will also give me an opportunity to learn the truth about whether or not he is having an affair.

Lord, I know I said I wouldn't read It anymore, but I was wrong for making a promise like that to you and myself. I shouldn't have gone to the bargaining table with You. Being the woman I am just will not allow me to let it go. I need to know. Please forgive me, Lord.

That night, for the first time in their eight years of marriage, James and Annette slept in separate beds. She slept in their bedroom and he fell asleep the sofa.

It was Saturday morning and she got up feeling rested. James was still asleep on the sofa and Kynosha was sitting in the bed watching cartoons. Annette leaned over the sofa and asked James if he wanted breakfast. He told her he did, but wanted to go on a short run first. He got dressed and went outside. She held off cooking breakfast until he came back. When he returned she cooked and they had breakfast. Kynosha was the only one that had anything to say. She finished her breakfast and went back into her room to watch cartoons.

Annette broke the silence. Holding her fork loosely as it lay on her plate, she said, "James, I need to take a leave of absence from work. I'm tired and I feel over-worked."

"Damn. Do you think you should see a doctor? Do you feel sick?"

"Not physically, but I feel mentally drained. The time off will give me a chance to get back in shape too."

"I see. I know how much you love your job. Sure, I make enough to take care of the household. I'll make major in a few months, and we also have our savings if we need it."

They finished breakfast and James went into the office. Annette cleaned the kitchen. A few minutes later James came out of the office and asked Annette if she'd seen his journal. Startled by his question, she dropped the glass she was washing and it splattered over the floor. *Oh shit! I forgot to put it back!* "What did you say about your journal?" Kynosha heard the glass break and came into the kitchen.

"No. No, Baby, don't come in here. Glass is all over the floor." James came in and saw Annette sweeping the glass. He got the dustpan.

While holding the dustpan he said, "I want to write some thoughts, but I can't find it. I haven't written in it in a few months. That's one of my resolutions; I wanted to write more often."

"No I haven't seen it. Have you checked the shelves in the office?"

"Yes. It wasn't there."

After they finished sweeping the glass, he went out into the garage, looked around and came back in. Annette knew exactly where his journal was. She'd left it sitting behind the chaise lounge before New Year's Eve and forgot to put it back.

He walked into the kitchen. "Do we have anymore boxes of stuff we haven't unpacked?"

"I believe we have a couple of boxes with office stuff in them," she said. "They're in the closet in the office."

"I'll look later on this morning," he said. He left the kitchen, went into the bedroom, and got in the shower. She went into the bedroom and looked to make sure he was in the shower, then got the journal and put it in one of the boxes. She sat at the computer to check her email. James walked in the office with a towel around his waist. He looked in the box and found his journal.

"Found it!" he said.

"You did? Good. I lost mine in one of those boxes too, but I found it."

James went into the bedroom, and Annette went into the kitchen to get a glass of water. She leaned over the sink. *Damn! Now I'll never know who this woman is he's having an affair with! I've got to find out where he's gonna put his journal.*

She followed him into the bedroom and sat on the chaise. She began talking to James while keeping her eyes on the journal sitting on the dresser. Trying to distract him, she asked him about his run. She told him Pamela and Russ wanted to know if they were coming to visit them in Washington, D.C..

James walked out of the bathroom. "I'm going into the office today."

"But it's Saturday! Why do you have to go in?" Annette didn't care. In fact, that was perfect for her.

"As a commander, you have to do that sometimes," he said.

Annette saluted him and laughed. "All right, Sir. I hear you, Sir."

"That salute will get you put out of the military. What was that?"

"How long will you be gone? Later this afternoon I

wanted to take Kynosha and her friend to the mall."

"I should be home by noon." James picked up his journal and went into the bathroom. He hid the journal somewhere in the bathroom and Annette had plans to find it. She sat on the chaise. She fidgeted like someone with hemorrhoids. James noticed and said, "You seem fidgety, Annette. You okay?"

"Must be the coffee," she said.

She couldn't wait for him to leave. She searched the bathroom high and low. After twenty-five minutes of searching, she found his journal. He had hidden it in a secret compartment in his toiletry travel bag. She went into the living room with the journal and sat on the sofa. She wanted to make sure she heard James' car when he pulled into the garage.

Before she began, she went in Kynosha's room to check on her. "Are you doing okay in here, Baby?"

She nodded. Kynosha spent a lot of time in her room. When she wasn't at her friends' house, she was in her room watching cartoons. Annette went back into the living room. She sat on the sofa then adjusted her position, lying on her back. She opened the journal and thumbed through the pages, choosing one at random.

I've shared some of my most intimate secrets with Annette because I love her so much. I knew I had a past and I wanted to share it with her. Now, there is no doubt in my mind about what I mean to her or who I am. I know it's important to tell her the truth, but damn, the consequences scare the hell out of me. I want to give her the option to be in this marriage. I want to take her blinders off for her. I'm the only one who can.

Annette sat up, eyebrows almost touching from her frowning. "What is he talking about? Blinders? What damn blinders? I know you're cheating on me, Motherfucker! That's probably where you are right now!" She didn't notice the tone in her voice had heightened.

Kynosha came into the living room. "Mommie, who are you talking to?

Annette laughed. "I'm just read something funny, Baby, that's all. This is a funny book I'm reading."

"Can I have a sandwich, Mommie?"

"Sure you can, Baby. I'll get up right now and make you one."

They went into the kitchen. Annette reached into the cupboard and pulled out a jar of Jif peanut butter. She got strawberry jam and milk out of the fridge. Kynosha stood watching her mother as she was about to make her sandwich. "Mommie, can I have a grilled cheese?"

"Of course you can. I guess I should've asked you what kind of sandwich you wanted, uh?"

Kynosha nodded.

Annette kept watching the clock. It was 11:15 a.m. She rushed to make the grilled cheese so she could get back to the journal. She flipped the sandwich a few times in the hot skillet, took it out and put it on a plate, then told Kynosha to sit at the table. As she walked back to the sofa, Kynosha opened the slices of bread and saw that the cheese wasn't melted. "Mommie, the cheese is still hard on my sandwich."

"What?"

"The cheese is still hard on my sandwich."

"What do you mean it's still hard? It was in there long enough to melt."

"But it didn't melt."

"Eat it anyway; it ain't gonna hurt you."

Reluctant to eat the sandwich, she played with it, eating the edges of the bread. She eventually ate the sandwich.

After Kynosha finished her sandwich, Annette called Jess.

"Hello?" Jess said.

"Hey girl."

"Well, well. Where have you been? Haven't heard from you in what, almost two months?"

"Has it been that long, Jess?"

"Yes it has. I called you a few times, but I got your machine. You know I don't like leaving messages."

"How have you been? How is Brian?"

"I'm doing all right. Brian — well he's another story. A better question is how are you and James doing?

"Not so good. I mean, he's doing great, but I'm getting to the point where I can't stand the sight of him."

"Damn, Annette. What happened?"

"You know I told you I thought he was having —"

"You read his journal again, didn't you?"

"I'm holding it in my hand right now. Listen to this." Annette began reading aloud the part she'd just read from James' journal.

She laid the journal face down on the sofa. There was a death of silence. "Jess, are you there?" Annette said.

"Annette, I'm so sorry. That does sound like he's having or had an affair. I can't believe James would do that to you. You two are such a lovely couple."

"Jess, I'm so damn mad right now. Answer this: What's the point of staying married if your spouse is seeing someone else?"

"There is no reason to stay married if they are," Jess said.

"I mean, I'm not talking about the standard answers like for love or financial security. I mean, tell me Jess!"

"Annette, you need to calm down —"

"No! Don't tell me to calm down! Brian isn't having an affair!"

"Okay, I hear you. Where are James and Kynosha?"

"He went to his office — at least that's where he said he went — and Kynosha's in her room."

Jess was silent. She let Annette vent.

"This is the kind of shit that makes me question my own values and beliefs that I've held close to my heart for almost nine years. I don't know, Jess. I mean, what keeps a marriage sacred and special, and *worth* maintaining and keeping intact, when there's no longer anything within it that you couldn't find on the outside?

"Damn Annette, that's a deep question. I hope it's rhetorical," Jess said.

Annette stood up and began to pace. She walked around in the living room, and then went into the bedroom. She walked back into the living room and looked out the window. "No, I'm serious Jess. What's the point?"

"Girl, that question requires deep thought and I ain't

got that kind of time right now. It's a good question though. Hell, you've given me something to think about."

"Jess, I thought I was his *only* love. I told him years ago that it was necessary for our marriage to survive in that, outside of our swinging lifestyle, I was the only woman in his life. I don't think I can even consider staying with him if he loves someone else. A life loving me and somebody else ...mmm, no, I couldn't do it," she said.

"I don't think I could either," Jess said.

"It seems that just destroys the basis of the relationship," Annette said.

"I agree."

Once again, there was silence. "Jess, are you there?"

"Yeah, I'm here. I'm thinking about what you said about keeping a marriage in tact. I would think that what keeps a marriage special is having something in it that you don't have with anyone else. Brian and I don't have that either. Hmm...that's interesting," Jess said.

"So could that be the reason some people cheat, because they don't share a special bond?" Annette said.

"I don't know if I would say that's why they cheat. But I think having a special bond is why some people stay together," Jess said.

"Maybe you're right. Guess it's like Kynosha, she's got this stuffed Goofy doll that she got from Disneyworld when we were in Tampa. She loves that thing; it's special to her. And I guess if we got her another one and she had two, they wouldn't be special in the same way," Annette said.

"Yeah, that sounds right."

"But the fact remains, there are still two women involved," Annette said.

"Well damn, I didn't say that makes it right, Annette!" Jess said.

"Jess, I'm gonna say this, and then I'm hanging up. James is the love of my life. I have only one place in my heart for a man in my life and that's for him. If I put another man in that place, even if only for one night — and I've done that before — I would be displacing James. And that would make him not special to me in the same way. Now, I'm getting —"

"No you're not Annette. You cannot say something that deep when you're ending a conversation. What in the hell is wrong with you? You're spitting out all this deep shit from your soul and you want to just leave it be? I can't let you do that," Jess said.

"Jess, you have no other choice because I don't want to talk about it anymore."

"Damn you, Annette. I'll call you later."

"Okay. 'Bye. Oh, tell Brian I said 'hello.'

"Okay. 'Bye Annette."

Annette hung up and continued to read the journal; then the phone rang. It was James. He called to let her know that he would be home in about thirty minutes. He was running late, and it was now 12:05 p.m. That gave her time to read a little further into the pages. She perused the pages, looking for a confession or something saying that he was in fact, having an affair, and with whom. But she came across something even more interesting. As she looked through the pages she saw where he talked about Thomas and Jenny.

I like hanging with Thomas and Jenny. Too bad she couldn't stop through here with him during the New Year's Eve holiday. It was good seeing him even though he was here for only a few hours on his layover.

Annette slammed the book down on the sofa. "He didn't tell me Thomas was in town." She continued to read.

I'm glad we got a chance to hang out. I needed that break. Annette and I haven't been intimate, so it was good having a friend to talk to. He told me that he was getting out of the military and planning to start his own business, a partnership with an old friend. He'd always talked about opening a communications consulting firm that would provide information for the appropriate kind of equipment for military intelligence. He brought the subject up again about him and Jenny getting married one day. I know Thomas hate that he and Jenny can't get married. Being married is the ultimate commitment two people can make. It supersedes all of a person's prior relationships and goes beyond a friendship. But like we talked about before, one day they will have it where people of the same sex can get married.

"What! Naw, I don't *believe* this!" she said. "You mean to tell me Jenny is *a man?* Bullshit! I don't believe that!" she said. "I gotta call Jess."

Annette hit the redial to call Jess. Jess answered.

"Jess, remember the couple I told you we met in Watertown? His girlfriend lives in L.A. and she visited him periodically for a month or two at a time?"

"Hello. Who would you like to speak to?" Jess said.

"Jess stop playing. I'm serious," Annette said.

"Yes, I remember them. He was the one you said looked like a young Rock Hudson, a ladies' man," Jess said.

"Yeah, that's him. Guess what?

"What Annette?" Jess said.

"I'm sitting here reading James' journal and listen to this. Now I'm reading this straight from his journal," Annette said.

"Okay."

She read to her the part she'd just read to herself. Stuttering, Jess said, "Wa—wa—wait a minute! Are you telling me she's really a *he*? *Jenny* is really a *Johnny?*"

"That's exactly what I'm telling you. Jenny is a damn man. He's a transvestite, and a cute one at that," Annette said.

"Oh my God! James never told you about this?"

"No! I don't know, maybe they kept it a secret because Thomas is in the military. But I had a strange feeling about Jenny once before. I just couldn't put my finger on it," Annette said.

"What do you mean?" Jess said.

"We had gone out to dinner, the four of us, when we were in New York and I noticed her, I mean him, flirting with James. I didn't think too much about it because that's what people do. They flirt."

"You don't think James —"

"Girl please! James is not that way. As much as he loves pussy, I'd be hard-pressed to believe that James of all people would fuck a transvestite."

"Okay, calm down. I didn't mean to insinuate anything," Jess said.

"Now, you know I have to ask him about this, Jess. I don't know how, but I wanna know the details."

"That's gonna be a hard one. Maybe you can ask him about the last time he heard from them," Jess said.

"Yeah, that's another thing. Thomas had a layover here the day before New Year's Eve and James saw him at the airport. He didn't tell me Thomas had a layover here. Yeah, I'll ask him when was the last time he saw them and see what he says," Annette said.

"Annette, whatever you do, be careful. I have to go. Brian and I are meeting some friends at the Underground. Call me later and let me know how it went," Jess said.

"All right. I know I don't always tell you, but I'm so glad you're my friend. If you weren't there for me, I don't know what I would do."

"You're a good friend too, Annette. You're always there for me when Brian gets on my last nerve. I love you, Girl. I'll talk to you later," Jess said.

"Okay. 'Bye."

Annette looked at the clock and saw it was 12:45 p.m. James could walk through the door at any minute. She put the journal back in the bag. Just as she walked out of the bedroom, James came through the door.

"Honey, I'm home!" he said.

"And?" she said. "Shall I sound the horns?"

He closed the door and smiled. "I don't see any reason why you shouldn't."

"I can give you several reasons why I shouldn't," she said. Before saying something she might regret, she walked towards Kynosha's room. James came up behind her and pinched her on her right butt cheek. Reacting to reflex, she slapped his hand.

"Mommie, why you hitting daddy?"

"Yeah Mommie, why you hitting Daddy?"

"He deserved it, Baby. He pinched me," she said.

James pinched her again. This time she slapped him on the shoulder. Kynosha laughed. They looked at each other and laughed.

That afternoon, as a family they went to the movies and had dinner. It was late when they returned home. They put Kynosha to bed, but Annette wasn't ready to go to bed. She showered and sat in bed to read. After James got out of the shower, he joined her. He touched her arm and smiled. He said, "Hey, are you in the mood for some of me?"

"My period is on James."

"Oh, okay," he said, as he slid back over on his side.

Annette smiled, but didn't let him see it. She was tired of playing the charade she'd been playing all afternoon. She went through the channels and came across *The Pelican Brief*, then changed the channel again and *The BirD.C.age* was on. She kept the channel there, thinking *The BirD.C.age* would give her the chance to probe and find out what James knew about Thomas and Jenny.

"Why are you watching that? Why you didn't leave it on the *Pelican Brief*?"

"That's too serious. I want to watch something funny. I need to laugh. I love Nathan Lane and Robin Williams in this movie. Nathan Lane plays the hell out of his part."

"Yeah, I must admit, the first time we saw it back in '96, it was funny as hell."

She snapped her fingers. "*That's* who he reminds me of!"

"Who? What are you talking about?"

"Albert, Nathan Lane's character. He reminds me of Jenny!"

"How in the hell does he remind you of Jenny?

They don't look anything alike. Besides, he's a helluva lot older than she is, not to mention Nathan Lane is a man." James said.

"They have a similar mannerism, that's all. I've noticed Jenny's hand movements. They're very feminine. Guess they should be, since she is a woman."

"Well, I'm going to sleep. You enjoy your movie."

"How are they doing anyway? You heard from them since he called right before New Year's Eve?"

"Yes, I have. In fact, before New Year's when you told me that he called, he wanted to let me know that he was going to visit Jenny the next day, and had a six hour layover. He wanted me to come to the airport and have a beer with him. He also told me that he was getting out of the military this year."

Annette was mystified and confused. She didn't know what to think. He was telling her the truth.

"Oh, he did?"

"What? You sound surprised."

"No, not really. Just wondering why you didn't mentioned that to me. Why is he getting out?"

"It wasn't important. I forgot about it. He and some man are starting their own military intelligence consulting business."

"Oh, I see."

"You see what Annette?"

"Nothing. Just a figure of speech. That's good. James, what ever happened to your dream of owning your own business? Remember you shared that with me a long time ago?"

"Yeah, I remember. Well, I don't wanna own a construction business anymore, that's for sure."

"Why not?"

"Back then, I thought that was all I'd be doing, until I joined the military. Now, my outlook is different. I haven't really thought about owning my own business lately."

"I have."

"What do you mean? How are you going to start your own business when you're getting ready to take two or three months off because you're stressed at work? You know, owning your own business is hard work. You just think you're over-worked now."

"I hope you're not trying to discourage me from doing this."

"Of course I'm not. I'm proud of you for wanting to do it."

"Besides, I don't think owning my own practice will be that strenuous. I can set my hours to my convenience and when I need a break, I can take one. I just need to decide when I want to do it."

"When do you want to stop work?"

"I was thinking just before Kynosha's tenth birthday."

"That's next month, Annette!"

"That way, I'll be home when she gets out of school. You know she's been complaining about that. In addition, I'll be with her during the summer. When she goes back to school in the fall, I'll look into the state requirements for independent practice."

"That sounds okay to me. You know I'm here for you."

"I know you are, James. Now go to sleep."

"But remember, I'm being pinned with my major leaves this summer, and next year, we move to Ft. Leavensworth, Kansas, so you might want to think about that."

"Shit, I forgot about your school. How long will we be in 'Dorothy land'?"

"What?"

"You know, Kansas, Dorothy from the *Wizard of Oz*?" She laughed.

"You're crazy, Girl. We'll be there for ten months."

James leaned over to kiss her goodnight and she gave him a light peck on the lips.

"What's with the air kiss?"

"What?"

"Surely you can do better than that."

She kissed him on the lips.

"That's better. Goodnight."

"Goodnight. I'm gonna watch this movie."

Five days passed, and Annette had not read his journal. One evening she locked herself in the bathroom while James was in the living room watching television. She pulled his travel bag from the linen closet and unzipped the secret pocket only to find that the journal wasn't there.

Oh shit! Damn, he took it out! Where did he put it? She searched through the bathroom. *I wonder why he moved it. Maybe he found out that I've been reading it. But there's no way he could know that.* She tapped her forehead. *Damn, that's it! Last week, watching the movie and asking him questions about Thomas and Jenny. He knows I've been reading it! I'm slipping. I gotta be careful.* She went back into the living room. Lo and behold, he was writing in his journal. The volume on the television was low. She went into the kitchen to pour a glass of wine. He had a beer sitting on the coffee table.

Maybe he doesn't realize I've been reading it. Hmmm...Later on tonight I'll check to see if he puts it back.

She went back into the bedroom and turned on the television. James walked in carrying his journal. She got up and went into the kitchen, giving him enough time to put the journal back in his bag. When she returned, he was laid across the bed watching television. She looked around for the journal, but didn't see it. Later that night she found it. He had, indeed, put it back in his bag. She was relieved. She knew now, that he didn't know she'd been reading it.

Two days before their ninth anniversary, and in an effort to rekindle Annette's energy, James researched the Internet for a single Black man for Annette to play with. Annette didn't mind, she was already mad as hell because she thought he was having an affair. When she first learned of James suspected affair, she had thoughts of paying him back by sleeping with a man she worked with at the hospital. He told her that he'd been looking for a month, trying to find someone he thought she'd like.

In the past, she was reluctant to play with other men. She would say James was enough man for her. However, because she suspected him of having an affair, she saw it as an opportunity to sleep with another man. Besides their group activities, this was the first time they'd ever invited another man to a threesome. Their threesomes were normally with women, most often with Annette's playtoy Wanda. James knew the kind of man she liked. He told her he'd been looking for someone to play with who lived closer to them.

That same evening, he called her into their office and showed her a photograph a man had emailed them. One of things they agreed upon was that she must know about anyone he wanted them play with. Annette found the young man attractive. He was tall and dark, just like she liked them. In addition, he had a pretty smile with nice teeth. She was excited. He was thirty-eight and lived in Houston.

_____

The next morning when James went to work, she removed his journal from the bag and took it to work with her. She spent her lunch break sitting in the hospital parking lot in her car, reading.

The week before New Year's Eve, I had a lot of extra time at work to think. Sometimes when I engage in thought, it can cause problems for me. This particular day, I was thinking about my situation, and the more I thought about it, the more depressed I became. In fact, I was glad I didn't have a gun. If I'd had one, I probably wouldn't have made it home that evening. Carrying a lie I've hidden from her for all these years feels like a ton of bricks. The pressure I feel from keeping my secret is enormous. Facing the possible consequences seems less toxic and more appealing to me. Holding my secret has created an overwhelming sense of isolation. It's a very lonely place.

She held the journal with one hand and put her other hand over her mouth. "Oh my God! What is he talking about? What is he going through that makes him want to kill himself? Is he unhappy with me? With our marriage?"

I'm so glad I got a chance to go to Houston and see Daphne. While I was there we had a very long talk. I was so afraid of what she would think of me. A few weeks had passed since we talked and…I just didn't know. I ended up telling her what happened to me growing up. She told me that our father molested her when she was ten years old. When I asked her if she'd told mother, she said "No! She wouldn't have believed it anyway." She told me that's why she has never been married…she doesn't trust men. I told her she should get counseling, and she told me she might if she can ever build up the nerve. We held each other and cried. It felt so good to be held by my sister. I needed to feel that she still loved me. She told me she'd never told anyone about what happened to her. I gave her my word that I wouldn't tell anyone.

I told her about an encounter I had back in Watertown. Thomas and I became close friends. She'd spoken to him on the phone a couple of times. I gave him her number as a person to contact if he ever needed to find Annette and me. We met at the gym on post and worked in the same building.

Annette was sobbing openly. She pulled herself together and laid the journal on the car seat, then reached into her purse to get her cell phone. She called her office from the parking lot and told them she wasn't feeling well and was going home. It was warm, so she turned the air conditioner on. She was unaware that she was thirty minutes late. She didn't care. She reached in the glove box and took out some tissues. "Oh-my-God! No, no, no, no, please Lord, No! Oh-my-God!" She knew what was coming next. She continued to read.

Over the months we became bosom buddies, hanging out at the bar on post. One night on the way home, because I was too drunk to drive, he drove me home. He stopped the car on a dark, quiet street. I flashed back to my childhood experience when Darryl took me into that dark alley. I wasn't nervous. Thomas pulled out his penis and stroked it. I pulled mine out and did the same thing…

Annette looked at her watch and it said 4:30. Oblivious to any responsibilities she had, she continued to read.

I told her there are so many men who are doing this. They are best friends who get together and sometimes have sex. I can't talk to Annette about this. I love her so much it hurts! Who can I tell? I took a chance by telling Daphne; I didn't know what she would think. Fortunately, she took the news well, as only a sister could. She told me no matter what, I was still her brother and she loved me unconditionally.

Annette turned the page. The next page was titled, "Here's My Story, Annette." She frowned. "What? What does he mean by his story? Why did he put my name in the title? There's no need to tell a story about it!" She was extremely angry. She looked at her watch through the transparent shield of water in her eyes. It was 5:00 p.m. She laid the journal on the seat, started the car and drove off. On her way home, she detoured, went to a local hotel, and got a room. After parking the car, she called James and told him that she was working late, and might not be home until tomorrow. She turned her cell phone off, grabbed the journal and went up to her room. She kicked off her shoes, flopped down on the bed, and began to read his story.

Although my bisexuality surfaced in my early thirties, I recognized the tendencies as an adolescent. I was surprised by my feelings and fought the attraction to my fantasy. The fear of contracting HIV and AIDS made it easy for me to hold off and not pursue my interest. When I first acknowledged my bisexuality, I had come to terms with myself as a person; I needed to move beyond my limited existence. I needed to self-actualize. I was fulfilled. My sexual orientation is just one part of who I am. It's not the whole me. Sometimes Annette tells me that she only has one place in her heart for a man, and that man is me. I have two places in mine. One for her, the love of my life, and one for the 'need' to be with a man. At the core, they are very different. Annette fills one place; and since acknowledging my bisexuality, Thomas has sometimes filled the other. Neither could fill both.

Sometimes I have feelings of a human need, a need to be close to another man, not necessarily in a sexual way. My desire to be with a man is different from Annette's desires to be with a man. It's also different from a straight man who wants to be with a woman. I can't explain the feeling, but I do know that sometimes, not too frequently though, it [the need] raises its head to be sated. I don't know, take air and water for example. Which do we need more? We definitely need to breathe, but we'll perish without either. If we have air, but are dying of thirst, then all we can think about is water. Annette is my air and Thomas is my water. Like air, I couldn't live without

Annette but when my need for water emerged, Thomas was there to quench my thirst. My need had nothing to do with being unhappy in my marriage. I'm very happy with my family life. Although I've compared the two, there is no real comparison. Annette's never had to compete. It was nothing she did or didn't do. In fact, the need has nothing to do with her.

I want to be comfortable, able to spend time together talking openly, without fear; with understanding of the needs and desires we experience. That's what Thomas provided for me...that kind of closeness. Physical sex with a man is okay, but it's a much lower priority than the friendship, companionship, and honesty. For me, it's a basic human need, not a want.

Incidentally, I'm attracted to the whole woman, as well as her body, especially Annette. I experience great passion with her, more than with a man. I sometimes fantasize about other women. When the need arises, I fantasize about Thomas. In conversation with Thomas one day, we were discussing sexuality and labels, his in particular and how he knew he was gay and not bisexual. He told me that when he was married, he fantasized about men. Although he was in love with and attracted to his wife, he still lusted after men. He told me he fantasized about sex with men in porn, and was attracted to muscles and penises. He told me the only reason he was sexually attracted to his wife, was that he was in love with her. He said he didn't particularly care for looking at naked women and definitely didn't like giving her oral sex. It would be a travesty to label myself as gay and leave out my love and long-lasting sexual relationship with Annette. Yes, I've participated in a homosexual act, but that doesn't make me gay. If labels are required for people to understand, it's important for them to understand that homosexual is same sex, and bisexual can be both sexes. Whichever way the pendulum swings more often, is probably the way you are.

We decided that labels cause more confusion than anything does. I don't believe that one's sexuality can be placed inside a tiny box to be one particular way. I've accepted myself as a bisexual, if I have to label myself. I'm in a passionate and fulfilling relationship with my wife, but sometimes, my need can become an imposition, and when that happens I can't ignore it. I was lucky that Thomas was around sometimes when it emerged.

I found sex with Annette is far more satisfying than it is with a man, and an orgasm from foreplay is equally satisfying with a man. What I love about sex with Annette is that she gets pleasure from just looking at me and touching me, whereas with a man, I only get the sense that he's getting just as much pleasure out of giving me pleasure as in receiving it from me.

Acknowledging this helped me become more relaxed and understanding towards other people. Although I've hidden it from Annette, I was able to integrate it into my life. At first, I didn't feel the self-loathing, fear and denial that so many men like me feel. But as the secret got older, the fear and anger set in. As time went on, it became more prevalent. Not because of my sexual orientation, but because I couldn't tell Annette, I couldn't share it with her. I didn't know how she would look at me. I don't want her to think that I'm any less of a man because I'm not! I've projected my life without her and Kynosha many times, and it's very distressing. I don't want to lose them.

Annette is supportive of me and I'm supportive of

her as well. She's never complained about a lack of sex. We are best friends and our lives are intertwined. We do almost everything outside of work together. There has never been a lack of romance or affection. She showers me with gifts and flowers, just because. And I do the same for her. My secret has somehow diminished me as a person, disabling me to live up to and realize my full potential as a husband and a father. I long for the day that I can wake up free to speak openly; to live to my full capacity without looking over my shoulder and covering my tracks, without worrying about Annette finding out about my secret. I pray for that day.

My professional life went untouched. I base all of my decisions on my comfort level and family situation. But when I become so uncomfortable in a situation that it effects my being, I have to find a way out of it. Suicide wasn't an option for me, although I have contemplated it before.

God knows I didn't intend to deceive Annette this way, but I had nowhere to turn. It's not an excuse, it's the truth. Unfortunately, for me, and others like me, we're born into a world where bisexuality in men is not accepted. It's not accepted in women, but society seems to tolerate it more easily. For me, that's a good reason to hide. We live in a world where years ago, Blacks were not allowed to read. They hid; they went where no one would find them. We live in a world where years ago, Blacks and Whites were not allowed to like each other, let alone love each other; they had to keep their affairs secret. And lastly, we live in a world where men aren't allowed to be sexually involved with other men. Some marry women and have children, suppressing the need to be with another man or seeing the man secretly.

That's what I've done with Thomas. I know deception is wrong, and I'll be the first to say that I'm wrong, but I cannot blame anyone else for what I've done…not even myself. It's a tragedy! It isn't right for me to deceive her, nor is it right for me to have to hide that part of me without suffering enormous social and personal consequences. It's a domestic disaster. We're caught up in this tragedy that was created by our culture, and because of it, we're experiencing our own private pain. I hate that Annette has to suffer; I know she will. A few weeks ago, I saw the emptiness in her eyes. My heart aches when I look at her. I wonder if she noticed the hollowness in my eyes, the pain I suffer from living out my bisexuality in such a distorted and secret way. I'm not saying that I don't have to make moral decisions, because I do, and I realize that.

I've never had a desire to be in a relationship with a man. I love my wife. I'll lay down my life for her. I feel authentic as a husband, father, and soldier.

Our swinging lifestyle meant Annette and I being able to trust one another and that we would stick to the agreement we made of having no outside affairs. I've broken that trust by having sex with Thomas. I'm supposed to make her feel safe, but now she has to worry about whether I'm hiding something from her. I've betrayed her trust. I'm so, so sorry.

At 7:00 p.m. she let out a loud sigh and closed the journal, holding it close to her heart and lying across the bed in the fetal position. With all the lights on, she cried herself to sleep. She awoke about 2:00 a.m., barely able to open her eyes. She was still lying in the fetal position, holding the journal and a ball of tear-drenched tissues close to her heart. She turned on the television and put it on mute. Tracks of tears and mascara ran down her cheeks. She pretended to watch television.

"My husband had sex with a man!" She sobbed. "No, no, no. Lord, please tell me it isn't true! Tell me this is just a dream! How could I have been so stupid! So blind! I want his ass *out!* Why didn't I see it! How did this happen! Why didn't he tell me this shit before we got married! Damn you, James! Damn you! Damn you!, Damn you! Oh God! Did he use condoms? What if he didn't and I have AIDS! Oh! That motherfucker!" She threw the journal across the room, then rose to look at the clock; it was 3:45 a.m. "I need to go home so I can get Kynosha ready for school. I don't wanna see that motherfucker. I don't know what I'll do if I see him." She went into the bathroom, washed her face, and left.

When Annette got home, she laid her keys in the bowl by the door. The living room night light was on. She went straight into the bedroom bath and turned on the shower. James awoke. He went into the bathroom, pulled back the shower curtain, and said, "Hey, Baby." She ignored him, letting the water beat against her face as if she was getting a face massage.

"Annette!"

"What!"

"How you doing, Baby?"

"I'm fine. Please close the curtain, James. I feel a draft."

He closed the shower curtain, used the toilet and got back in the bed. She came out about thrity minutes later. She looked at the small clock on the vanity. It was 5:01 a.m. She went into the kitchen to make some coffee. James followed her.

"Aren't you tired, Baby? Your eyes are red."

"Yeah I am, but I'll be all right," she said. "I gotta get Kynosha ready for school, so I need to stay awake."

"I can get her ready. You know I'm off today."

"You are? Why are you off?"

"I took off to be with you. It's our anniversary, remember?"

"I forgot about that. I'm not in a celebratory mood right now."

"That's because you worked all night. Maybe after you get some sleep, you'll feel better."

"Yeah."

James went to Kynosha's room to make sure they hadn't woke her. Annette poured a cup of coffee. She made enough just for her. He sat at the table with her. She couldn't face him. She poured the coffee down the drain and told him it was too weak. He offered to make some more, but she told him she was going to lie down and asked him to leave her alone so she could get some rest.

When she finally went to sleep, it was 6:15 a.m. She slept for eight hours and laid in the bed for another two. She heard James in the living room, and pretended to be asleep. James went into the bedroom to wake her.

"Annette, are you asleep?" he said.

She repositioned herself. James thought she was getting up. He went over and nudged her.

"Hey, Annette. You gonna get up? It's four o'clock.

You know we're meeting Reginald at six."

"Who? What are you talking about? Who the fuck is that? I don't know no damn Reginald."

"The man from Houston. He's here. We're meeting for drinks at the bar."

"James, I –am *not* in the mood for that."

"But Annette, he's already here. We planned this together for our anniversary."

"So! I said I don't feel like it. I'm not in the mood, James! Can't you understand that? I was up all night."

"But you just slept for ten —"

"And? I can sleep for as long as I want to."

"What's wrong with you?"

"Ain't nothing wrong with me. What's wrong with you? Don't be trying to make me do something if I say I'm not in the mood for it!"

"Lower you voice. Why are you talking so nasty to me?"

"Oh, you haven't *heard* me talk nasty to you James. You know what? I think you need to leave me alone right now. Let me get myself together."

"Yeah, okay. Are you going to the bar or not?"

"No, I'm not going. You go ahead."

The door slammed. Annette was glad James had already sent Kynosha to the neighbor's house for the weekend. She planned to confront him when he returned. She wasn't concerned about what he was going to think about her reading his journal. All she knew was that she needed to talk to him about it. She was so anxious and hyped that she went jogging. She ran for thirty-five minutes. When she returned, James was sitting in the living room with Reginald.

"Annette, this is Reginald. This is my wife,

Annette."

"Nice to meet you, Annette."

She was still breathing heavily from her run. "It's nice to meet you too. I'd shake your hand but I'm sweaty," she said. "Please excuse me. I have to shower."

She was livid. She hurried into the bedroom, closed the door and got into the shower.

"I guess he's in there sucking that motherfucker's dick or getting a quick fuck before I get out the shower. Faggot sonofabitch! I wish he *would* fuck that motherfucker in *this* house! I got something for his ass. I'm gonna play this little game tonight and see if he fucks him or gets fucked. I wanna know what I'm dealing with here."

She was in the shower for ten minutes. She put on her sheer black teddie with black thongs and a pair of three-inch black high-heeled sandals, then walked into the living room. James and Reginald were sitting across from each other, both drinking beer. She went into the kitchen to pour a glass of wine. They turned to watch her as she passed by. When she returned, she had the bottle with her. She sat on the sofa next to Reginald. They talked and within twenty minutes, she'd had two glasses of wine and was working on her third.

"Hey James, why don't you put on some Anita Baker?" she said.

"Okay, what you want to hear baby, *Rapture*?"

"Yeah, that's fine. You know any song by Anita is good for me."

"I know. She's one of your favorites."

James turned on the stereo, then searched the CD rack for *Rapture*.

"Baby, I don't see that CD."

"Well, you'd better find it because it was there two days ago."

They had over 250 cd's, stored on four racks. He looked on all four racks and found it. After he put it in the cd player, he turned. "Are there any objections to me videotaping our activities tonight?"

"No," Annette said. "What about you, Reginald?"

He seemed hesitant. He looked at James and Annette. "Naw, I don't mind.

James went into the bedroom. He returned with a silver tripod in one hand and a video camera in a blue carrying case in the other.

"You want me to give you a hand with that?" Reginald said.

"Yeah. Stand the tripod up and I'll get the camera ready," James said.

Annette slumped down on the sofa, sipping from her third glass of wine. Her legs spread open, giving both James and Reginald full view of her crotch. She noticed James fumbling with the camera, trying to get it to record and asked, "Are y'all having a little difficulty boys?"

"No. Just trying to get it to sit right on this damn tripod," James said.

"Got it!" Reginald said.

Annette gave them a round of applause. They tried to find the *on* switch. Annette suggested they use the remote control to turn it on since they obviously were too drunk to find the switch. James took her suggestion and turned the camera on using the remote.

"I see the power light on the lens," she said.

Reginald tried to focus the camera on Annette lying on the sofa. James watched.

"So whatcha see?" she asked. "Is it recording?"

"Yeah, it's recording. I can see your legs. You have some pretty legs, Annette."

"Thank you, Reginald."

James told Annette to remove her panties.

"Yeah, come on, Baby, take 'em off," Reginald said.

Annette took a sip of wine. "Fuck both of y'all!"

After five minutes of trying to decide who would undress first, they decided to undress on the count of three. They disrobed and Annette sat on the sofa. Reginald walked over, got on his knees in front of her and spread her knees. He buried his face between her legs. James stood watching as he massaged his semi-erect penis. She moaned. She put her hand on Reginald's head, pulling it closer. James stood in front of her, then climbed up on the sofa and straddled her, putting his now erect penis in her mouth. She grabbed it to help guide it in. After about fifteen minutes, she wrapped her legs around Reginald's head and whispered, "I'm coming!"

James stepped down off the sofa and sat on the love seat. He began to massage his erect penis. Annette repositioned herself to face James on the love seat.

"That feels good," she said.

"What was that, baby?" James said.

"I said his tongue feels good. Shit!"

She grabbed his head with both hands. James moaned. He got up and sat next to Annette, still massaging his erect penis.

"Here, let me do that for you," she said.

James moved his hands, putting them both behind his head as he extended his legs.

"Oh yeah, eat that pussy Reginald. Does it feel good to you, Baby?"

"Yes it does."

James went to adjust the camera. Fumbling, he managed to zoom in on Reginald licking Annette's exposed clitoris and resume videotaping.

After what seemed like an hour of oral sex, Reginald started humming on her clitoris. She moaned.

"What was that, Baby?" James said. "Have you come yet?"

"Yes, I have."

"You've come already?" James said.

She'd had enough and her clitoris was tender. Annette raised her head, looked down at Reginald, and told him to stop.

"Are you ready to suck that dick yet, Annette?" James said.

"Say what?"

"You ready to suck that dick yet?"

She rolled her eyes and said, "I'm ready to get fucked!"

"What was that, Baby?" James said.

"I'm ready to get fucked!"

"Shit! That's enough; I can't take this anymore! I'm ready to get fucked!"

James and Reginald ignored her.

"Open that pussy. Let me see it, Reginald."

James zoomed in on her clitoris as Reginald massaged it with his fingers.

"Spread it open, Reginald."

Reginald exposed her pinkness.

"There you go." James lost control of the camera and it fell off the tripod. Reginald gave her clitoris a break and began suckling her breasts. James put the camera back on the tripod and repositioned it. He moved the camera and zoomed in on Reginald's semi-erect penis.

"Why don't you put the camera down and come over here," she said. He ignored her and walked away.

"James!" she said.

He turned around. "I'll be right back"

He walked over to the camera bag, pulled out another 35mm tape, and put it on the coffee table, then he went into the hallway bathroom. When he returned, Annette pushed Reginald's head away, sat up, and took a long sip from her glass. "Okay, that's enough! Y'all got me dehydrated."

James stood in front of her as she sat on the sofa. Reginald got up to operate the camera. She slid to her knees and took James' erect penis into her mouth as she looked up at him.

"That's it, suck it, Baby," Reginald said.

"Ah shit!" James said.

"Sounds like you can really suck that dick, Baby," Reginald said.

"Ah yes she can," James said.

James looked down at Annette and asked her if she was ready to be fucked. She ignored him. James repeat the question two more times, and she ignored him both times. James moaned. Reginald continued egging Annette to suck James' penis.

James turned to look at Reginald. "You want to fuck Annette? You ready to get this pussy?"

"I want that ass!" Reginald said. "I wanna fuck her in the ass."

"No. That's way down the road. That's way down the road," James said.

Annette stopped sucking James' penis and looked up at him and then Reginald. "Yoo who, I'm down here.

Y'all cannot make decisions about who I'm going to suck, fuck or let fuck me in the ass. What the hell is wrong with y'all?"

James pulled away from Annette and looked at Reginald. "You ready for her to suck your dick?" James said.

"Oh yeah," Reginald said.

"What if I don't want to suck his dick? Who the fuck you think you are? *I* decide if I want to suck his dick, not you! You decide if *you* wanna suck it," she said.

Reginald went and stood in front of Annette. She looked at his limp penis then took it in her mouth. James operated the camera. He lost control of the camera, videotaping the empty beer cans and wine bottles sitting on the coffee table. After regaining control, he zoomed in on her.

"Suck it Annette, suck it. Make it hard," James said.

Anita Baker's *Fairytales* played in the background. Annette stopped. She bobbed her head, snapped her fingers and began to sing:

"I found the poison apple, my destiny to die. No royal kiss could save me. No magic spell to spin. My fantasy is over. My life must now begin."

She held Reginald's penis in her hand. He reached down to put it in her mouth and she pushed his hand.

"Put your arm down, your left arm, Reginald," James said, as he focused the camera on Reginald's buttocks. Annette stood up and said, "Okay, I'm ready to get fucked!"

"Go get a blanket then," James said. She went into the guest bedroom and pulled a quilt from the shelf in the closet. She walked back into the living room and stopped short of the threshold, her eyes wide open. She didn't say a word. She just stood and watched as James, who was on his knees, performed oral sex on Reginald. She looked at the camera to see if it was recording.

Reginald threw his head back and closed his eyes. They didn't notice she'd returned. James was suckling his penis as if he was in love with it. He swirled it around in his mouth as he moved his head in a circular motion. She couldn't believe what she was witnessing. James looked up at Reginald, his tongue taunting the head of his penis. She broke the silence and said, "Looks like you've done that before, James." He didn't comment. She took a sip of her wine. The camera was loose on the tripod and she fumbled with it, trying to make sure it was recording. She took another sip of wine, this time emptying the glass. Reginald put one foot on the sofa so Annette could have a better view. With his other hand, James massaged his own penis. He leaned back and looked up at Reginald.

Annette fumbled with the camera, knocking it off the tripod. James and Reginald moved to the center of the sofa.

"Damn! At least y'all can stop and help me with this damn camera!" she said.

They looked at her but didn't stop.

"Open it up," James, said. "Open it."

Reginald spread his legs. Annette fumbled with the camera. James continued suckling Reginald's penis, while stroking his own. They were oblivious to her presence. She heard them laughing, but couldn't hear what they said. Then she heard James say, "You want me to get in your ass?"

"No," Reginald said.

"Go ahead, say yes," James, said.

Annette heard James and said, "How can you make him say 'yes' when it's not what he wants to do?"

James looked at Annette. "Say what, Baby?"

"You can't make him say 'yes' when it's not what he wants. That's what *you* want."

Annette looked towards the front door. *It's true, he is bisexual.* She felt the tears building up as she turned to watch the life she once knew die a slow, painful death. "Our life together will never be the same," she said.

"Did you say something, Annette?" James said.

"No, just thinking out loud."

"You wanna fuck me in the ass?" James said.

"What!" Annette said.

"I'm asking him if he wants to fuck me in the ass," James said.

"Oh! You been fucked in the ass before James?" Annette said.

"No. It's virgin, but I don't mind trying it to see what it's like," he said.

"No," Reginald said.

Annette became more and more frustrated. She poured another glass of wine, took a sip, and said, "You're not tired of doing that James?"

He didn't respond. He pointed to his penis for her to come over and sit on it. She laughed and said, "I'm having fun doing what I'm doing. If I sit on your dick, you might come. You know that. Let it go! Give it a break! Damn! Hey! Hey! Hey!" He didn't respond. Reginald moved away from James. James looked at Annette. "Come sit on it, Baby."

"I thought you were about to get fucked in the ass, James," she said.

"He's afraid of my dick, Baby," James said.

"Okay, but still, I thought you were about to get fucked," she said.

"He's scared," James said.

"You must be scared too," she said, as she and James looked at Reginald. James lay back on the sofa massaging his penis and pinching his nipples. Reginald sat on the sofa massaging his limp penis. Annette operated the camera.

"I wanna see him fuck you," Reginald said.

"Why you wanna see him fuck me?" she said.

"I like watching."

"You do?" she said. "You don't like participating?"

"Yes!"

"I had a finger all up his ass, Baby," James said.

Annette rolled her eyes at him. "Did you now? Did you enjoy that?"

James continued massaging his penis as Reginald watched.

"He's afraid of this big dick," James said.

"You're back on that. Give it a rest James," she said. "He's not afraid, he just don't want it."

Reginald looked at James. "She want, it." He pointed to the floor. "Go on down there and give it to her."

"I'll get it in due time. I might not even get it tonight," she said.

"Why not? You don't want it?" Reginald said.

"That's not it. Because it's my choice," she said.

"Oh is it?" Reginald said. "Why is that *your* choice?"

"It's my pussy, *That's* why! If I don't want it, I don't have to get it."

Feeling left out and still massaging his erect penis, James joined the conversation. He looked at Reginald.

"You wanna fuck my ass?"

Annette walked away from the camera and into the kitchen to get another bottle of wine. She returned and gave the bottle and corkscrew to James. He opened it and filled her glass. She took a big sip. "You ready for that, James?"

He looked at her, but didn't respond. He turned and looked at Reginald. "Do you want to fuck my ass?"

"It sounds like you just told me to shut the fuck up!" Annette said.

James looked at Annette and said, "He's afraid."

"How do you know he's afraid? You didn't give him time to answer."

"I gave him plenty of time to answer."

"Yeah, give me a chance, all right?" Reginald said.

Annette couldn't believe her eyes. The man she once knew had become a stranger in a matter of two hours. She noticed how calm he was. His demeanor had changed from what she knew. He was relaxed. She turned the camera to face Reginald. "Do you wanna fuck him in the ass?"

He smiled and scratched his head. "Do I wanna fuck him in the ass?"

"You heard me. It's okay. If you do, go ahead and fuck him in the ass and shut him the fuck up!"

Reginald continued to massage his semi-erect penis as he fondled his nipples. Annette turned her wine glass up and emptied it. "I'm glad I'm getting drunk, cause I couldn't witness this shit sober!"

She turned the camera on James, still massaging his penis. He looked at Reginald. "Don't you wanna open this ass up? It's a virgin ass. I've never been fucked in the ass before."

Annette put her glass on the table. "James, you've never been fucked in the ass?"

"No, Baby, I haven't. Have I ever fucked anyone else in the ass? That's a different story."

"What do you mean?" she said.

James looked at Reginald. "It's a virgin ass. Don't you want to open it up?"

"No, no!" Reginald said.

Annette laughed. "Go ahead, try it. If you don't like it, stop!"

"He's scared, Baby," James said.

"Ah, don't try that psychology bullshit, James," she said.

"I'm afraid," Reginald said.

"He doesn't want me to put this all up in his ass," James said.

"Well you ain't gonna put that up his ass. He is gonna fuck you!" she said.

Reginald laughed. "Oh yeah? 'Cause I'm not there yet."

"I think you're afraid," James said.

"Yeah, I ain't gonna lie, I'm afraid," Reginald, said.

"What are you afraid of?" she said.

"My finger slid—"James said.

"I've never done that before. I don't do that."

"But Baby, my finger—"

"Oh, okay. So you've never done it before." she said.

"But Baby my finger —"

"Who knows what the future holds," she said.

"That's true. That's true," Reginald said.

"But right now, I think James wants you to fuck him in the ass, so y'all need to stop all this bullshit."

They all laughed.

Reginald began massaging his limp penis. "It ain't ready."

"If it's supposed to happen, it'll happen. You ain't ready to fuck James in the ass," she said.

"Nope, I'm not."

"He ain't ready, James," she said.

"Let me fuck you, Baby," James said.

Annette looked at Reginald. "How about you? You wanna fuck me?"

"Down the road, you never know," Reginald said.

"This is true," she said.

"You can't get out of here tonight without putting your dick up my ass!" James said.

"Well, I guess y'all will be in here fighting," Annette said. She and Reginald laughed. "I'm going in the bedroom and go to sleep."

James sat massaging his penis as he watched Annette and Reginald laugh.

"You're being Ms. Conservative behind the camera," Reginald said.

"Naw, he said you weren't leaving without —"

James slid to the center of the sofa. "Come sit on this hard dick, Annette."

"So y'all are gonna be in here fighting," she said.

"Baby," James said.

She turned. "Yes?"

"Come sit on this dick."

"Why you want *me* to sit on your dick?"

"Cause he want you too," Reginald said.

"That didn't answer my question," she said.

"You know that pussy is good, Annette," James said.

"I know that."

"Let me feel it then."

"Can I get on the floor?" she said.

"You can get it anywhere you want it, Baby," James said.

"Okay. Can I turn the camera off?" she said.

"No. I wanna watch this shit," James said.

"Yeah, I wanna tape it," Reginald said.

"Can I get on the floor?" she said.

"Anywhere you want it, Baby," James said.

"Okay. You gonna spread the blanket on the floor?" she said.

"Yes."

"Then get your ass up and do it!" she said.

"Did you see me suck his dick Annette?" James said.

"I got it on tape," she said.

James got on the floor on his knees. Annette walked towards the blanket with her back to James and Reginald. She turned and reached for James' hand. He had detoured towards the love seat where Reginald was sitting and was sucking his penis.

"Damn! I thought you were getting ready to fuck me! You changed your mind?"

James shook his head.

"I'm feeling hurt," she said.

"You shouldn't," Reginald said.

"I shouldn't! Hell, he is supposed to be fucking me!"

"It's nice to share," Reginald said.

"No, wait a minute. I thought he was getting up to come fuck me."

"Well, he is gonna fuck you," Reginald said.

"He's ready now baby," James said, as he held

Reginald's erect penis.

"Is he?" she said.

Reginald laughed.

James knelt. While holding his penis, he moved closer to the sofa. Reginald pushed James back. "No, no."

James stopped. "Okay, okay, hold tight."

Reginald laughed.

"James, stop forcing yourself on the man! That's not what he wants! Stop trying to force yourself on him! Don't do that!"

James got up and moved over on the blanket. Annette stood watching him as he lay down, waiting for her to join him.

She shook her head. "What are you doing?" she said.

"I'm on the floor baby," James said.

"But you're not on the blanket James," she said. "You need to get a condom."

James got up, walked over to the coffee table, and got a condom. Reginald repositioned the camera, pointing it at the floor. Annette laid on her back and watched James put on the condom. They got in the missionary position; her legs wrapped around his waist, feet clasped. Reginald had a clear shot of James buttocks. James rose to his knees and put Annette's legs on his shoulders. After about a minute, he let them own and stretched them as wide as he could get them, then reached back, grabbed his buttocks, and spread it open for the camera. Reginald continued to operate the camera and coached James along. After about ten minutes, Reginald joined them on the floor. He positioned the camera to record them.

James asked Annette if she wanted to change positions. She told him yes and got on her knees with him behind her. Reginald went back to the camera. Now in the doggie-style position, James said, "Tell him to get on that clit baby." He repeated himself three times before she responded. Reginald came over to join them. He positioned himself underneath her in a '69' position. After about three minutes James said, "Ah yeah, lick that dick."

Annette stopped, turned and looked back at James. His head was tilted back. She told him to fuck her. He came but his dick stayed hard. Annette's body went limp. She was just going through the motions. She faked an orgasm to get it over with. She moved forward and James slipped out and onto Reginald's face, hitting him on the forehead with his dick.

James removed the condom and laid it on the floor. Annette slid over and watched James as he let Reginald suck his penis. She got up and went into the bathroom. Just as she was coming back into the living room, James said, "Shit! I'm coming!" Afterwards, she told Reginald to leave, saying nothing about what had just happened. James fell asleep on the blanket and she went into the bedroom, took a shower, and got in the bed.

The next morning, she got up and made breakfast. James was still asleep on the floor. She took the journal from her purse and placed it on the table. James got up. Fully extended on the floor, he stretched and yawned.

"Damn, what went on in here last night?" he said. He looked at the beer cans, wine bottles and the condom on the floor. "Look like somebody had a party in here."

Annette went into the kitchen. She didn't respond. She put on a pot of coffee, then mixed the pancake batter.

James came into the kitchen. "Good morning, Baby."

"James, we need to talk."

He dropped his head, turned to walk out of the kitchen, and said, "I know we do, Annette. I wanna get rid of my dragon breath and take a shower. I'll be out in a few minutes." As he left the kitchen, he noticed a journal sitting on the table. He didn't realize it was his. He went into the bedroom, showered, and shaved.

Annette stood with her back against the counter next to the stove, drinking orange juice. "God dammit!" She smelled the bacon burning and removed the skillet from the fire. "Fuck it! I ain't cooking no breakfast. I'm not hungry anyway." She turned the burner off under the grits, put the eggs and bacon back in the fridge, and then sat at the table with the journal in front of her. She got up and poured a cup of coffee, then put her hand on her forehead. "Damn, I have a headache! I must be hungover."

She put her coffee on the table and walked into the living room to pick up the beer cans and bottles. She left the condom for James to pick up. She rolled the quilt and put it in the laundry room. When she returned, James was standing in the kitchen wearing his brown terry cloth robe. He poured a cup of coffee. She went into the kitchen. "I thought I smelled breakfast cooking," he said.

"You did, but I changed my mind. I'm not hungry right now. Let's sit at the table James." They left the kitchen and sat at the table.

"Did you enjoy yourself last night, James?"

"Damn, what's with the evil eye? Yeah, it was all right. Did you?"

"That's what I want to talk about this morning. I always enjoy it when you and I have sex, James. So, yes, that part of the night I enjoyed. But watching you suck another man's dick came as a shock to me."

Annette I wanted----"

"No, don't say shit to me right now. Just listen. I don't give a damn what you are going to say after I say what I have to say. Whatever you think or feel is moot, as far as I'm concerned."

She picked up the journal. "This is your journal, James!"

"What are you doing with —"

"It would behoove you to shut the fuck up and listen to what I have to say." She held the journal up in front of his face. "I've read most of this journal. My heart ached as I read it and found out that you had had sex with another man."

"But Ann---

"No, shut up James! I could go off on your ass and start yelling and cussing and screaming and throwing shit, but that wouldn't solve anything. Besides, I'm not going to tear up my own shit. I never would have thought my husband, my friend, the father of my child, would do this to me — deceive me; deceive *us*, Kynosha and me, this way." She started sobbing. "As I lay in the bed this morning, reflecting, trying to figure out where I —"

"This has nothing to —"

"Shut up James! Please don't interrupt me anymore!"

"Okay, I'm sorry."

"As I tried to figure out where I went wrong in this marriage, I couldn't see where I did. I gave you everything you wanted from me as a wife. I even let you fuck other women, fucked you in the ass with my strap-on, fucked another man so you could watch from the closet, went out to clubs, came back, and told you about the dicks I'd felt because you liked hearing about them. I was open with you! And this is how you repay me, by fucking Thomas? I guess all those things I was doing for you should have told me something was up! James, you brought him into our home knowing you'd fucked him. You brought his transvestite partner into our home, knowing he was a man. How could you do this us? How could you tear our marriage, this family, apart like this? How could you ruin my life? You have ruined my life, and I hate you for that!"

Annette dropped her head on the table and cried. She had the journal under her head. James sat there confused. He touched her on the shoulder.

"Get your goddam hand off me! You are a no good sonofabitch! Do *not* fucking touch me, you faggot bastard! I can't believe you told your motherfucking sister before you told me! *I'm* the one you sleep with every motherfucking night! *I'm* the one who gave you a daughter! *I'm* the one who has been by your goddam side since fucking high school! You should have come to me! We talk about *everything* James — *everything!*"

"Anne—"

"I don't wanna hear it James. I don't want to hear shit you have to say!" She pushed back from the table and ran into the bedroom crying.

"Annette!"

"Fuck you, James!"

He ran behind her. She slammed the door and lay on the bed, her face pressed into the mattress, as she screamed at the top of her lungs. James leaned his head against the door. He opened it and stood there crying as he watched her. He felt helpless.

"Annette, I'm so so sorry. I didn't know how to tell you, how to explain it to you. I didn't know what you would think of me."

She turned her head to the side. "You're fucking trifling! That's what I think about your ass!"

"After you questioned me about Thomas and Jenny that night you were watching *The BirD.C.age*, I sensed that you had read my journal, so I had to find a way to tell you the truth. I put it back in my bag so you could find it again. That's why I wrote what I wrote and put your name in the title. That was my way of telling you who I really was. I didn't know how to come to you. I was so afraid. I didn't want to lose you."

"You *should* be afraid, motherfucker!" She sat up on the bed. "You're telling me that you did this shit on purpose? You hurt me on purpose? What kind of sick motherfucker are you? Get the hell outta this house! I don't want to see you right now! I can't stand the *sight* of you, James! Get the fuck out, *now!*"

She got up and pushed him out of the bedroom into the living room, then slammed the door. He was still wearing his robe. He sat on the sofa and cried. "Lord, what have I done? I've torn my family apart. I've ruined my life. What have I done? If I could change who I am, I would."

At 10:45 a.m. after about thirty minutes, Annette came out of the bedroom wearing a pair of sweat pants and a t-shirt.

"I'm going out; I want you gone when I get back."

She went for a forty-five minute jog. When she returned James was gone. She went into the bathroom to see if he'd taken his overnight bag. He had.

She got in the shower. After she got out, she laid across the bed for twenty minutes before picking up her journal. There was no way she could tell anyone about what had happened that night, and she definitely couldn't tell anyone about what she'd read in his journal. Now that he was out to her, she was in the closet. His secret had forced her into a cocoon, a place she found very uncomfortable.

Annette called her mother. She needed to talk to her, hear her voice.

"Hi Mom, it's me. How are you doing?"

"I'm doing fine. I was just thinking about you yesterday, wondering how you were doing since I hadn't heard from you in a couple of weeks."

There was silence. Annette was almost in tears.

"Annette? Baby, are you there?"

"Yes Momma, I'm here. I felt like I had to sneeze, so I was trying to fight it off."

"You coming down with something? How's the weather out there?"

"The weather is good. It's warm, but not too bad. How are Cora and Dennis? You heard from them lately? I haven't talked to them in a while."

"Yeah, both of them came home last week. How's James doing?"

Annette tried desperately to fight back the tears.

"Momma, can you hold on a minute? I hear somebody at the door."

"Okay."

Annette went into the bathroom, threw water on her face, dried it and came back to the phone.

"It was nothing. Nobody was there. James, he's doing all right. He makes major next month, and he got selected to attend school in Ft. Leavensworth, Kansas. He goes next year."

"Kansas? What's in Kansas besides Dorothy and Toto?"

They both laughed.

"That's the same thing I said."

"Well, tell him I said congratulations."

"I'll Momma. I love you, Momma."

"I love you too, Baby. 'Bye."

"'Bye Momma."

She lay across the bed, holding the phone on her stomach. *I should call Jess. I need to talk to somebody. But I can't tell anybody about this. Damn you, James!*

She went into the office and got her journal. She wanted to write, but couldn't. She got up and went next door to get Kynosha. She wasn't ready to come home because she was playing with her friend and knew she was supposed to stay until Sunday. Annette saw her unhappiness and let her stay. Annette didn't want to be alone.

She kept watching the clock and looking at the phone. She wanted to hear from James, but at the same time, she didn't. She missed him. She loved him.

I'm angrier at his deception rather than about him being with Thomas. He gave me no options in this whole thing. How could he control my decision like that? I can never forgive him for that. I was a good wife to him. Now, I'm captive, held in a blanket of deceptive secrets. How could I have been so blind? I'm glad to know he used condoms. That's the only good thing that's come out of this whole experience.

The day was long and the night was even longer. Annette went over to get Kynosha about 9:30am. When she got home, she wanted to see her daddy. She went into the office, but he wasn't there.

"Mommie, where's Daddy?"

Annette choked. She hadn't thought about what

she would tell Kynosha.

"He had to go into the office early this morning. He should be home this evening."

"Did you eat breakfast, Baby?"

"Yes, we had cereal."

"Okay. Go and unpack your bag. Come here." She gave Kynosha and big hug. "I love you so much, Baby."

"I love you too, Mommie."

The last thing Annette wanted was to have James come back home, but she had no other choice. Kynosha wanted to see him. She hadn't come up with a thought plan of how to deal with him seeing her. She went into the bedroom and called his cell phone.

"Hello?"

"Hi James, how are you?"

"Hey, Baby. How are you doing? I was lying her thinking about you and Kynosha. How is she?"

"That's why I'm calling you. She asked about you just now. I told her you were at work and would be home this evening. When you get here, we need to come up with some kind of plan on how we're going to deal with this."

"Okay. I'll be there around three o'clock."

"Okay. 'Bye."

"'Bye Baby."

After she hung up, she sat on the side of the bed. *How can we do this without her finding out that he's not living here anymore? I know! He can stay here until she goes to bed, then he can leave. I'll see what he has to say about that when he gets here.*

James arrived home at 3:00 p.m., just as he said he would. Kynosha ran to the door and gave him a big hug. Annette, almost in tears, stood there watching. He walked over to kiss her and she turned her head. He kissed her on the cheek. He threw his gym bag on the floor, picked Kynosha up, and sat her on the sofa.

"Would you like some dinner, James?"

"Yes, thank you."

She turned and went into the kitchen to feed Kynosha and James. She cooked baked chicken, mashed potatoes, and peas. She'd bought a cheesecake for dessert.

After dinner, Kynosha went outside to play. Annette went into the bedroom. James came in behind her.

"Annette, please, can we talk?"

"Yeah, we can talk. We need to figure out a way for you to see Kynosha without her knowing that you're not living with us."

"How are we going to do that?"

"Well, I thought maybe you could come over after you get off work and stay until she goes to bed, then leave."

James looked out the window and sighed.

"Annette, please don't do this to me. There has to be a better way to deal with this. What will they think at work?

"If you don't tell anybody, nobody will know."

"I can't — I don't want to do that."

"Well, you have no other choice. This is part of the consequences for your actions, your deception, so deal with it."

"So you're punishing me for withholding the truth to protect you, my family, and my career!"

"Lower your voice, James. You weren't thinking about those things when you were playing your game of charades!"

"I thought you said you read my journal. That's *all* I thought about Annette...not being able to tell you. That's where all of my guilt and sadness came from. I knew I was hiding something from you. You don't know what I went through. I even thought about killing myself, because I knew if you found out about what I had done, you'd be devastated, and that caused me more pain than anything did. Please believe that, Annette."

She got up and went outside to see where Kynosha was. She was next door playing with her friend, so Annette came back into the house.

"James, all I know is, right now, this is the way it has to be until we can come up with another alternative. I don't want you staying here."

"We have a guest bedroom, why can't I sleep in there?"

"Because you'll still be in the house and I don't want you here!"

He stormed out the door and got in his car without saying goodbye to Kynosha. She ran in the house.

"Mommie, where is Daddy going? Did he have to go back to work?"

"He'll be back later Baby. Go on back outside and play."

She skipped to the front door and went back outside.

Annette got James' journal and sat on the sofa. She opened it at random and began to read.

As I look back now, I'm convinced that the love I have for Annette is real. I loved her through college and I love her now. I believe I even loved her my last two years in high school. I just wasn't sure what love was. We have too many years together for me to abandon her, but my secret has forced me to. I should have come forward about my thoughts prior to our marriage. Nevertheless, I hoped they would have disappeared. She did and I admire her for having the courage to do so. She is a great woman. I struggle with this every day.

For years, I successfully suppressed that side of me that society deemed unacceptable. In any event, if it were not for Thomas I probably would have died never knowing that I wasn't alone. I was able to search the Internet anonymously for other married men who were dealing with the same issues. But that was short lived after receiving so many emails from men looking to have sex. That wasn't what I was looking for. Being able to discuss my feelings with Thomas helped me deal with the guilt and other related issues that I could have never resolved by myself.

The worst part about my situation was the inability to ask for help and advice or finding anything to read that could tell me how to deal with my feelings without exposing myself. The guilt I have carried all these years has been my biggest hurdle. I have done a lot of thinking and rationalizing, trying to justify my desire to act upon these forbidden feelings, especially since I have been faithful to her since the day we were married. On the other hand, I have rationalized that what I'm doing in seeking the company of another man is not cheating on her, because I was looking for something that she couldn't provide. I felt that it was something I needed to do for my own peace of mind.

My life became better the day I fulfilled my desire with Thomas. My feelings for Annette are unchanged. For the first time in my life, I'm a complete person without any unanswered questions in my mind or empty places in my heart that I'm longing to fill. It would be impossible for me to explain my position and for her to understand my feelings, no matter how hard I try. For a few months, I didn't think I was living a double life, because society forced me to hide my true feelings, and in this case, the truth would only cause Annette pain and deep hurt.

Although Thomas and I have not spent a vast amount of time together, we talked regularly on the phone. We developed a friendship, a bond. He experiences some of the same feelings I experience. Although he considers himself gay, he understands my feelings. He used to be married to a lovely woman. What Thomas and I had complemented the love I have for Annette, making me feel more like a complete person by filling voids that were never filled until now.

Annette got up and went to the bathroom. She was surprised that she wasn't crying. She returned and continued reading.

I must say, the concept of having different kinds of love without one being exclusive of the other came as a surprise due to my upbringing. Religion and society has conditioned us to believe that it's unnatural and wrong to feel for another member of the same gender, emotionally and physically. Other married men in the same boat would understand. They have the same goals and priorities in life. They have similar demands. If you are involved with a single gay man, he will inevitably force you to make a decision. There will be times when he is alone at home, while the bisexual man is at home with his family. Moreover, as time passes, the jealousy and pressure

*starts setting in and both of you start to feel it. This may
cause a reaction that neither of you expected. That's why
to me, it's better to be involved with another married man.
They considered themselves married, so that's how we
deal with each other.*

*I don't believe gay men can understand these
feelings. Thomas told me he had a friend who was
married, got divorced, and got in relationship with another
woman, but all of his homosexual experiences were with
gay men. He said they would tell him that he was either
gay or straight, but couldn't be both. Obviously, to a gay
man who is not attracted to women, that possibility
doesn't exist.*

Annette laid the journal on the bed and went
outside to get Kynosha. James still had not returned, nor
had he called. Annette told Kynosha to take a bath and
she called James on his cell phone. He didn't answer, so
she left a message asking if he had plans to come back
that evening. He returned the call within a matter of
minutes. He told her that he would be back in an hour.

_____

After three weeks of living in the house without
James, isolating herself from everyone, eating, drinking
and lying to Kynosha about his whereabouts, she decided
to let him move back in and sleep in the guest bedroom.
The atmosphere was strained and neither of them
mentioned the incident. It was a week before Kynosha's

tenth birthday, and they needed to plan for her party. They hid it from her by keeping all of his things as they were. She never saw him sleep in the guest bedroom. They took Kynosha shopping and to the movies. Any activities they did as a family was for Kynosha. When she went to be at night, Annette went into her room and closed the door and James went into the guest room.

Annette stopped working a week before Kynosha's birthday. Wanda flew in the same weekend. She transferred to Arlington, Virginia. Annette and James now, had to sleep in the same bed. Annette told him if they were going to sleep in the same bed, she didn't want him touching her. She prepared the guest bedroom for herself.

When Wanda got there, they spent a lot of time together since Annette was no longer working. They had sex everyday. Annette used the strap-on that James had bought for her. Wanda also had brought some of her toys. She had a pink double end dildo that she and Annette played with for hours. James was there when they played at night, but he was unaware of the sex they had during the daytime. Neither told him. They bonded on a different level. She never told Wanda about the journal, nor did she tell her about the night of their anniversary.

One afternoon while James was at work and Wanda was stuffing envelopes with invitations, Annette went into the bedroom to read the journal, but didn't get a chance too because Wanda knocked on the door.

"Hey, are you all right in there?"

"Yeah, I'm fine. Be out in a minute."

"Okay. Just checking on ya. You've been in there for a while."

Damn, I just came in here. She put the journal

away and went into the living room. She began touching and kissing Wanda.

"Would you like a glass of wine, my dear?" Annette asked.

"No, you go ahead Annette. I don't want any right now."

"When I come back, be undressed."

Annette's dominance was uncharacteristic. She returned to the living room. "Why aren't you undressed my dear?"

Wanda stroked her face. "Hey, what's going on with you? I can see that something's on your mind."

"Nothing's wrong Wanda. I just wanna make love to you. Right here, right now. I've missed you."

Wanda gave in and they had sex. They stopped ten minutes before Kynosha walked in the door.

They were a few days from Kynosha's birthday and hadn't bought the decorations for the party. James was responsible for picking up decorations. The next-door neighbor was baking the cake. They hand-carried the invitations to all of Kynosha's friends at school.

Kynosha's party was a big success. She was happy her Aunt Wanda was there. She was even happier when her mommie told her that she was off for the rest of the summer. Wanda flew out the day after the party. That same night, James went back into the guest bedroom.

Over the next weeks and months, they kept the pretense of a happy couple and things slowly returned to a resemblance of normality, the only difference being the absence of sex.

———————————

In the fall, Annette decided against going back to work. Their situation hadn't changed much, and she knew she couldn't give 100% performance dealing with the issues she had. She spent her days eating, sleeping and drinking. She went into her cocoon and stayed. Her weight ballooned to 187 pounds. She ignored phone calls, letting the answering machine pick up. She didn't answer emails either. She was afraid to talk to anyone because she knew her emotions would overwhelm her. She did speak briefly with Jess and Wanda, though, so they wouldn't worry about her too much.

James was promoted to major and doing well. He was due to leave for Kansas next year. Annette decided she and Kynosha were not going with him; instead, she planned to move back to Atlanta. She contacted her old employer and they told her she could come back. Jess told her she could stay with her and Brian until she found a place to live.

By Christmas, she'd gained 41 pounds. Sex with James was non-existent. They talked about the possibility of them ever having sex again, but Annette couldn't fathom the idea. The holidays were quiet. Kynosha got everything she wanted. James and Annette didn't exchange gifts, but it went unnoticed by Kynosha because of all the gifts and toys she had. New Year's Eve was just another day. They were in bed before midnight.

Annette explained to Kynosha that her father had to go to school and it required him to maintain focus and that's why they were moving back to Atlanta and not going with him. She was okay with the idea. Annette told her that she would take her to visit him. They moved back to Atlanta after Kynosha got out of school in May. James left for Kansas shortly after the New Year. They talked on the phone and via email everyday. Annette's weight gain was a big surprise to Jess. She knew something was eating at her core. She attempted to get her to talk, but she wouldn't. She suggested they start working out together as they had in the past, but Annette wasn't interested.

In June, two weeks after Kynosha's eleventh birthday, Annette received a call from Cora, her younger sibling. She told her their mother was in the hospital. Her cancer had come out of remission and had spread. She was now terminal. Annette was furious because no one had told her that her mother had been sick and back in the hospital for the last week. Cora told her their mother didn't want them to worry too much and that's why she didn't tell anyone except her sister Josie.

Annette explained to Jess and the staff that she had to go to Decatur to be with her mother. Jess held her close. She knew in the past that Annette's mother had been sick. Her supervisor put her on an extended leave of absence.

She left for Decatur that afternoon and called James on her way. She could hear him cry. She asked him if he could come home and he told her he'd be there, no matter what. Even if it meant him never making lieutenant colonel or them putting him out of the Army, he would be there by the weekend. He kept his word.

He arrived at the hospital on Friday evening. Kynosha ran to him and he lifted her in the air. He told her she was getting too big for him to lift her like that. He saw Cora and Dennis standing in the waiting area and asked them where Annette was. They pointed to their mother's room, and he went in. Annette was sitting by her mother's side, her head resting face-down on her mother's arm. When she looked up and saw James, she felt relieved.

They held each other with Kynosha between them. James pulled back and walked to her mother's bedside, then leaned down and kissed her forehead.

"How are you doing, Momma?"

Her voice was weak. She turn her head to see who was talking to her "Obviously not too good. I'm in this hospital bed." She tried to laugh.

"Well, I guess that's true."

She smiled at him. "How are you doing, Baby? Annette told me you were in Kansas playing with Dorothy and Toto."

Laughing he said, "Yeah, that's where I am, but I ain't there for fun and games."

"Where's Annette?"

She moved in front of James. "Here I am Momma. I'm right here."

"Girl, you better keep this man. Any man who will leave Dorothy and Toto to come and be by his mother-in-law's side is a good man." She gasped for a breath of air.

Annette turned to face James. "Yes, I know Momma. I will. He is a good man."

"Don't let no other woman take your man. Nowadays, don't let no other man take him either."

"You can believe me, Momma, ain't nobody taking him from us."

Annette couldn't believe what her mother had said to her. It was as if she knew what was going on between them. Shortly afterwards, she died.

They all stood in the room around her bed crying. All Annette could think about was what her mother had said. She turned to James and said, "That was an angel talking to me. Momma had already died and her soul went to Heaven, but that angel kept her functioning to tell me what she told me. It was as if she knew, James. God is omnipotent, omnipresent. He sent that angel here. You are a God send, and I love you so much."

"I love you too, Baby."

They held each other tight and Annette broke down crying. James had to carry her into the waiting area to comfort her. Kynosha stayed in the room with Cora, Dennis, Aunt Josie and Uncle Joe. She wanted to give her grandmother a kiss. Dennis picked her up, she kissed her on the forehead, and a tear fell on her grandmother's cheek.

After leaving the hospital, they all went back to their mother's house to make arrangements for the funeral. They chose a plot next to their father, who'd passed away five years earlier.

After they buried their mother, Annette, Cora and Dennis went back to Atlanta. James stayed in Atlanta for two days before going back to Kansas. Annette struggled with not talking about what happened. She was out of character and didn't like who she'd become. She told James they needed to discuss the situation so they could come to some kind of closure.

On Sunday evening, he invited her to dinner at the hotel where he was staying. They had a civil conversation and were able to address the situation. Over the last four months, they'd talked and talked, cried and agonized over their situation. Annette tried to come to grips with the most overwhelming thing she'd ever experienced, but found it extremely difficult. James told her he felt a sense of relief, guilt, and helplessness over seeing what he'd put her through with his deception. He felt relieved because he no longer had to hide anything from her; he could be completely honest with her because he was now a complete man. She told him that she would consider reconciliation, but for that moment, she needed more time. James respected her need for space. He flew back to Kansas on Monday morning.

Annette spent the next year rebuilding her self-image and repairing her spirit. She resumed working out and eating right. She limited her drinking to social occasions. While running on the treadmill she thought about what her mother had said about holding on to James. That motivated her to give everything she had in her workouts. She wanted to keep her promise to her mother, and to herself. Kynosha was doing great in school. She was an honor roll student and loved math. She told her mother, and she wanted a job working with numbers.

James transferred to the Washington, D.C. metropolitan area after completing CGSC in Ft. Leavensworth, Kansas. In the winter of 1999, Annette and James spent the holidays together in Maryland. On New Year's Eve, the three of them watched the ball drop in Times Square. For the first time in two years, they made a toast and kissed. On Sunday, January 2, 2000, Annette and Kynosha flew back to Atlanta. She had to return to work on Monday and Kynosha had to go back to school. She and James talked three times a day. Their distant relationship grew closer. By March, they were discussing reuniting. James told her he wanted her and that when they were together in the past, he was sexually satisfied. He told her he was tired of the mistrust. Annette didn't want to hear anymore; she understood what he was going through. She told him that she would rather focus her attention on resolving the issue. She also told him that she'd deceived him by having sex with Phillip, the man from the club that he'd watched her have sex with from the closet. In addition, she told him about the weekend he and Kynosha had gone to Decatur and she'd had girl sex with her four friends. James wasn't upset at all; because what she'd done couldn't compare with the torment he'd put her through over the last almost four years.

On Friday, April 14, 2000, James flew to Atlanta for their anniversary weekend. Annette made plans for Kynosha to stay with her Aunt Cora for the weekend so she and James could talk. On Saturday, they had a long talk at his hotel, and another one on Sunday evening before he flew back to D.C.. Annette asked James about Thomas and the last time he'd spoken with him or saw him, and he told her he hadn't seen or spoken with him since 1997. At dinner, he told her that during their separation, he was satisfied with porn and fantasy. As a turning point, she offered to help with his fantasies to make them more sexually fulfilling. James was ecstatic. He saw the light at the end of the dark tunnel he had lived in without his wife and daughter, his family. He asked her how she filled her sexual desires, needs, and she told him that she masturbated a lot and that Wanda had come to visit her a few times. She told him that she didn't think about sex too much because she didn't feel she deserved it because of the way she looked. She'd since lost 42 pounds and was back to her normal self. She told James that she wanted to try being married again, as well as continue the lifestyle they once lived, but in a different fashion. She told him that she was willing to help satiate his 'need' whenever it emerged by finding couples who were bi like them.

After ordering dessert she said, "James, let me ask you this. How often...I mean, is there a certain number of times this need emerges in you? I mean, should I expect to hear about it everyday, once a week, or what?"

"No, Annette. It seems to emerge maybe once every two or three months and sometimes more or less frequently. Whenever it comes knocking, I'll let you know."

"Do you think swinging with other bisexual couples will help?"

"It might, but at the same time, if I'm not feeling that need, there's no reason to be with another bi couple."

"I see. Guess I'm trying to do prevention work here. I just don't want this to happen again, James. I couldn't take it anymore. One more question. I need to ask this. Which do you prefer? Are you a top or bottom?"

"Annette my love, it won't happen again. You have given me what I've needed for a very long time, the ability to talk openly to the woman of my dreams about my need to be with another man. As for me being a top or bottom, I'm a top. I don't have any desire to be in a relationship, hold anyone's hand, or kiss another man."

"I want you to promise me that you will never allow another man to penetrate you. You can save that for my fantasies and me."

"I promise. I don't have that desire and should I get it, I'll share it with you."

"Shhh, don't get too loud now. Everybody isn't as accepting as I am. I want us to be able to talk about everything. The one thing I hated you for three and a half years ago was that you didn't give me an option. You didn't let me determine the course I wanted to take in this marriage. You guided me through it the way you wanted me to go, which was deeper in love with you."

"Again, I know I was wrong for that, and I'm so sorry Annette."

"I believe you. You know, after reading through your journal, it became clear to me that we're different. Our psychologies are different and that's where I went wrong. I understand now what you mean about having two places in your heart and how one has nothing to do with the other. It's like the love we have for our daughter, sisters, brother, and aunts. I understand that now. I know how you can feel incomplete if there is another part of you that's unfulfilled. When you and I were apart, that place in my heart for you was empty. I once thought that you being with another man were like me being with another man, or a straight man being with another woman. It just isn't true. I would have never believed it had I not experienced it and allowed myself to understand it. I thought about filling it with meaningless sex from another man, but I needed more. My emotional connection is with you and that's what I needed. Sex with someone else would have only been physical.

I don't believe I would be having this conversation had it been a woman because to me, that would violate your commitment to me as the person you chose to fill that place in your heart. Hell, it bothers me more when you look at other women than it does when you look at another man. It seems strange to say that, I know."

"God knows I've longed to hear those words Annette."

A tear fell from the corner of his right eye as he got

down on one knee. Everyone in the restaurant turned to look as he reached in his front pocket and pulled out Annette's wedding ring. Annette began to cry.

"Annette, will you do the honor and remarry me, making me the happiest man in the world?"

She got down on both knees crying. "Yes. Yes, I will James." Everyone who saw them and clapped as she accepted.

James stood up and helped Annette back to her chair. They gazed in each other's eyes from across the table. She also told him that she wanted to have sex with him, but under one condition and that being, he had to wear a condom until she felt better about their relationship. There was still an issue with trust. He agreed and swore to be honest with her in the future now that she'd opened the door for that kind of communication. That night they made love. The sex was most satisfying.

On Labor Day, Annette and Kynosha flew to D.C. to be with James. It was like the old days. They toured the monuments and with Kynosha now thirteen, she understood their meaning better.

Gradually, over the next few years, they recovered and worked on strategies for making their marriage strong while enabling James to be himself. There wasn't a problem with Annette expressing her bisexuality. Society made that easy for her. They'd both sought counseling in the private sector while living apart. After the terrorist attack on September 11, 2001, Annette relocated to be with James. He also received a promotion to Lieutenant colonel. They went to counseling together. James was reluctant to use a military counselor, due to the nature of his issue. Bisexuality is an unlawful act in the military and is punishable under the Uniformed Code of Military Justice.

In 2003, they decided to tell Kynosha about James. To their surprise, she was very accepting. "That doesn't matter to me, you're still my daddy and I admire you for telling me." That made all the difference in the world to him and Annette.

Kynosha is now seventeen and a senior in high school. She will graduate in June 2005, and plans to attend Howard University. Annette has a private practice in the D.C. metropolitan area where she provides counseling to married couples dealing with bisexuality. James plans to retire in 2006. James is very secure within himself. He has read every book E. Lynn Harris has written. He is not afraid to watch *Queer as Folk;* in fact, he and Annette watch it together along with *The L Word.*

Throughout my turmoil of separation from my husband, I was able to reassess our situation, even my own demons. Being a bisexual woman, I must admit, is a helluva lot easier than being a man and bisexual. After witnessing James' homosexual act, I was ready for divorce. I wanted to call a lawyer the next day. Even after he went to Kansas, I picked up the phone several times, only to put it back down. I was lost and confused. How could I, a bisexual woman, call the kettle black? He was just like me. I was hurting deep inside. He was a mirror image of me. I began to feel his pain because it was easy for me to put myself in his shoes. I wore them everyday. Nevertheless, what he'd done was unforgivable, or so I thought until I looked in the mirror. One day listening to the radio, "Because You Loved Me" sang by Celine Dion, came on and it made me realize even more how much I loved my husband. Here are the lyrics:

For all those times you stood by me
For all those truths that you made me see
For all the joy you brought to my life
For all the wrong that you made me right
For every dream you made come true
For all the love I found in you
I'll be forever thankful baby
You're the one who held me up, never let me fall
You're the one that saw me through it all
You were my strength when I was weak
You were my voice when I could not speak
You were my eyes when I could not see
You saw the best there was in me
Lifted me when I could not reach
You gave me faith cause you believed
I'm everything I am
Because you loved me
You gave me wings and made me fly
You touch my hand I could touch the sky
I lost my faith you gave it back to me
You said no star was out of reach
You stood by me and I stood tall

I had your love I had it all
I am grateful for each day you gave me
Maybe I don't know that much but I know this much
is true
I was blessed because I was loved by you
You were my strength when I was weak
You were my voice when I could not speak
You were my eyes when I could not see
You saw the best there was in me
Lifted me up when I could not reach
You gave me faith cause you believed
I am everything I am
Because you loved me
You were always there for me
The tender wind that carried me
A light in the dark shinning your love into my life
You've been my inspiration
Through the lies you were the truth
My world is a better place because of you
You were my strength when I was weak
You were my voice when I could not speak
You were my eyes when I could not see
You saw the best there was in me
Lifted me up when I could not reach
You gave me faith cause you believed
I'm everything I am
Because you loved me

I thank God for letting me hear that song during my time of strife. It gave me a different perspective of betrayal.

If we never fulfill our needs and desires, we go into deep depressions that are unexplainable to those who see us hurting, and not knowing why. When we act on our desires to be with another like ourselves, we must deal with overwhelming guilt. It's a double-edged sword. I'm able to see the pain my husband bore while trying to nurture my hurt and pain. He was afraid that if he told me, I would trample on the love he had for me because I knew what he was hiding from the rest of the world. He went to every extreme to protect me from the pain. The bisexual man or woman betrays himself or herself when they are unable to share all of who they are with their mate. I never really saw James' inner pain because he did an excellent job of protecting me. I realize that bisexuality is a part of what makes him and I, and he is what I needed. I love everything about him and if I could change anything, I would change nothing. Now I have the opportunity to help take away some of his inner pain and assure him love in its purest, unconditional form. We now enjoy a love that only a few people have the privilege of knowing. We look forward to each day. We are forever grateful for what we have found in each other. He gives me all I need, and I feel compelled to do the same.

Questions to Ponder

Check your views on sexuality

1.   If I were a woman in a relationship with a man, but have sex with other women, would you consider me a bisexual?

2.   If I were a man in a relationship with a woman, but have sex with other men, would you consider me gay?

3.   If I were a man in a relationship with a man, but had sex with women, would you consider me bisexual?

4.   If I were a woman in a relationship with a woman, but had sex with men, would you consider me bisexual?

5.   If I were a man who sleeps with both men and women, would you consider me bisexual?

6.   If I were a woman who sleeps with men and women, would you consider me bisexual?

The Handkerchief Code

I learned about this code purely by accident while searching our files on the home computer. I called my husband and asked him what it was. He explained to me that it's an old code once used in the homosexual community to signal to other men what their preference was. He told me that its use is not as prevalent as it was in years past. I thought it might be useful information. When I asked him what he was doing with it, he told me his friend Thomas had emailed it to him. He told me Thomas educated him on the homosexual community, as he knew it. I believed him.

"It pays to advertise," as the saying goes. Why should advertising sex be any different? A number of ingenious ways have been created to advertise one's sexual preference in the homosexual community — sometimes subtle, sometimes bold. One of the best-known methods of advertising is the Handkerchief Code. It rose to prominence in the early post-Stonewall days. It aspired to encode the gamut of sexual kinks by means of the color and position of pocket-handkerchiefs.

In the 1970s, the handkerchief code was a way for men to recognize each other when they meet on the streets or in bars, clubs, movies, and parks. The handkerchief code used location and color as a sign of the sexual interests of the potential sex partners. Some trace it back to the Gold Rush days, when dancers in all-male mining town saloons would divvy up into "men" and "women." The pretend women would wear identifying handkerchiefs wrapped around their arms.

Much of the code is for entertainment only; however, a few symbols are in more or less widespread use. In general, the guiding principle is that a handkerchief in the left rear pocket indicates a "top"; one in the right pocket indicates a preference for being on the bottom. Therefore, someone with a navy blue handkerchief in his left pocket likes to hump, while one in the right pocket shows a desire to be the humpee. Or it could mean they have a runny nose. Therein lies the problem; many of the most-used handkerchief colors are very common ones. For someone who has been around the scene, the handkerchief code may be useful for them in bars and at parties, where knowing who's into what can speed things along. It's quite risky, though, to assume that some stranger on the street is using his red handkerchief to show he might be into fisting. Actually, the red handkerchief seems to be one of the most widely used of the codes, because fisting requires experience and knowledge on the participants' part. Navy blue seems popular as well. Light blue indicates, depending on position, liking to give or receive oral sex.

Left Side	Color	Right Side
Anal sex, top	Dark Blue	Anal sex bottom
Anything goes top	Orange	Anything goes bottom
Fister	Red	Fistee
Food fetish top	Mustard	Food fetish bottom
Gives golden showers	Yellow	Wants golden showers
Hustler, selling	Green	Hustler, buying
Light S/M top	Robin's egg blue	Light S/M bottom
Oral sex, top	Light blue	Oral sex bottom
Uniforms/military, top	Olive drab	Uniforms/military, bottom
Bondage, top	Gray	Bondage, bottom
Recruiting a virgin	White	Is a virgin
Gothic romance, top	White lace	Gothic romance, bottom
Heavy S and M, top	Black	Heavy S and M, bottom
Scat, top	Brown	Scat, bottom

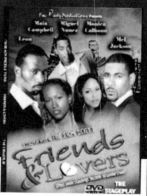